Friday night at the Hellfire Lounge ...

Purgatory? Nice place to visit, but ... well, actually it's a pretty *lousy* place. The upshot is your final destination, assuming you're on the fast track to Heaven. Even then, there's a good chance they'll lose your luggage.

For those bound for the *other place* ... well, these stories may or may not forcibly demonstrate that crime does not pay ... but you can't say you weren't warned.

Name your poison!

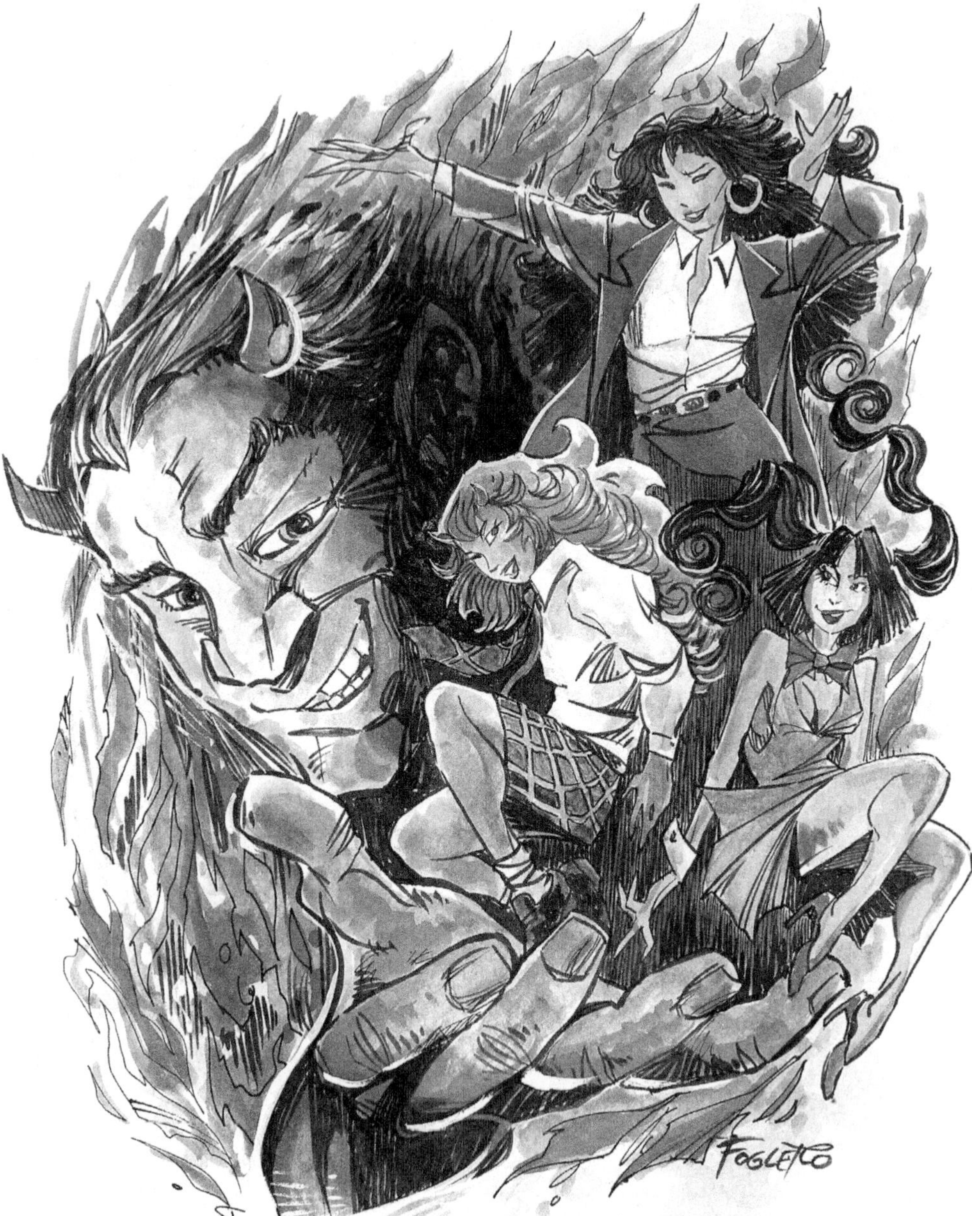

R. Allen Leider's

Hellfire Lounge

#5 Purgatory Potpourri

KT Pinto, John L. French,
CJ Henderson, R. Allen Leider,
J. Brad Staal, Patrick Thomas,
Patrick Loveland, Jean Marie Ward,
Danielle Ackley-McPhail,
April Grey, Robert Waters

BOLD VENTURE

BOLD VENTURE

Book Design: Rich Harvey
Cover art: Ben Fogletto
Interior art: Ed Coutts

Copyright © 2016 R. Allen Leider, Black Cat Media. All Rights Reserved.

"The Hellfire Lounge" and "Wicca Girl" are Trademark TM 2016 R. Allen Leider, Black Cat Media. All Rights Reserved.

The stories contained within are copyright © 2016 by their respective authors. All rights reserved.

Retail cover price $16.00: ISBN-13: 978-1534770027

All rights reserved. No part of this book may be reproduced or transmitted in any form or by any means without express permission of the publisher and author.

All persons, places and events in this book are fictitious, except Satan. Any resemblance to any actual persons, places or events is purely coincidental.

Bold Venture Press: www.boldventurepress.com

Contents

Macbeth: The Untold Prelude   R. Allen Leider 6

The Judgment of Dennis   KT Pinto 13

Impossible Love   CJ Henderson 25

The Knight's Watch   J. Brad Staal 46

B9 Fate   Patrick Thomas 63

Iris and Kayyali: Beyond Trolltown Patrick Loveland .. 73

Personal Demons   Jean Marie Ward 93

And the Cat Came Back   Danielle Ackley McPhail ... 115

Willow Pond   April Grey 132

Pure and Clean   John L. French 140

Conception Monkeys   KT Pinto 152

Circus Act   Robert Waters 164

Love is in the Air   R. Allen Leider 186

Author Profiles 196

Illustrator Profiles 201

MacBeth:
The Untold Prelude

"The Truth Be Known"

R. Allen Leider

The Scene: *A clearing in a rocky gorge in the Scottish mountains It is dark and stormy. Thunder and lightning boom in the distance Three witches attired in gray robes stand around a bonfire on top of which is a large, boiling cast iron cauldron.*

All: Fair is foul and foul is fair, hover through fog and filthy air.

First Witch: I love the smell of haggis in the morning.

Third Witch: Where hast thou been, sister?

Second Witch: Killing swine.

Third Witch: And Sister, where thou?

First Witch: A sailor's wife had macadamias in her lap, And munch'd, and munch'd, 'Give me,' quoth I: 'Aroint thee, witch!' the rump-fed ronyon cries. Her husband's to Aleppo gone, master o' the Tiger: But in a sieve I'll thither sail, And, like a rat without a tail, I'll do, I'll do, and I'll do.

Second Witch: I'll give thee a wind.

First Witch: Thou'rt kind.

Third Witch: Please, no wind. You've had broccoli for breakfast again. Enough with the wind.

First Witch: I myself have all the other, And the very ports they blow, All the quarters that they know I' the shipman's card. I will drain him dry as hay: Sleep shall neither night nor day, Hang upon his pent-house lid; He shall live a man forbid: Weary se'n nights nine times nine Shall he dwindle, peak and pine: Though his bark cannot be lost, Yet it shall be tempest-tost.

Second Witch: What are you blathering on and on about?

First Witch: I'm gonna cause a nasty storm and sink the friggin ship. Jeez, I was taking poetic license. (*pause*) Oh! Look what I have.

Second Witch: Show me, show me.

Third Witch: And me.

First Witch: Here I have a pilot's thumb, Wreck'd as homeward he did come.

Second Witch: Thumb you say. Nay! Nay! Thumbs do not have foreskins.

First Witch: What pray? Oh, crap! So I see.

Third Witch: How come by you this 'memento', sister?

First Witch: It was the wreck of the good ship 'Barry Fitzgerald' out of Aberdeen. Loaded with whiskey he was …

Second Witch: It was …

First Witch: Yes, it was … the ship was loaded with whiskey and so was he. The storm came up and he … .er … it came down fast. Bobbed and weaved he … it did. Broke in two and sank like a stone. The pilot lashed to the wheel was at my mercy. I took my snee and sliced off the thumb …

Second Witch: Not a thumb …

First Witch: It was dark. There was mayhem left and right, thunder and lightning I' night. I'm composing a ballad, "The Wreck of the Barry Fitzgerald."

Third Witch: This is all cock'd up. What to do with that thingy?

First Witch: Sing it, of course at the Samhain next year.

Third Witch: The naughty bit I mean. What do we do with the naughty bit? It points the way to destiny of the day. I have the spell. This is an entirely different situation.

First Witch: Forget about it! The deed is done. The pilot's done and I have prick'd his destiny. That's a joke, sisters! (*Tosses the "item" in the cauldron*) (*Drum beats within*)

Third Witch: A drum, a drum! Hold your wind, Macbeth doth come.

First Witch: It's about time. We've been here since cockcrow. It's cold and I have to pee. All The weird sisters, hand in hand, Posters of the sea and land, Thus do go about, about: Thrice to thine and thrice to mine And thrice again, to make up nine. Peace! the charm's wound up.

First Witch: All hail, Macbeth! hail to thee, Thane of Glamis!

Second Witch: All hail, Macbeth, hail to thee, Thane of Cawdor!

Third Witch: All hail, Macbeth, thou shalt be King hereafter!

First Witch: Cool it, sisters. It's not Macbeth who cometh this way. Tis a lassie in a red leather dress.

Second Witch: Who goes there?

Druscilla Marie d'Lambert (Wicca Girl): Druscilla Marie d'Lambert.

First Witch: Why is that name familiar?

Second Witch: Tis her, the Queen of Witches, chosen by the Dark Lord himself.

Third Witch: Successor to Hecate — The Cannibal Witch of Blackbridge. What brings Your Majesty to these rocky mounts in times less favorable to travelers? Dammit, there's a war going on!

Druscilla: I come on a mission from the Dark Lord himself. I'm taking a census, counting all the heads of every witch and sorceress in the land. And who might you be that are cooking in the mountains at seven in the morning. Arte you witches and Iron Chefs as well?

First Witch: I am called LaVerne by day.

Second Witch: And I Maxine they say.

Third Witch: And I am Patty if you may.

Druscilla (*Refers to a leather-bound book she carries*): The MacTavish sisters?

All: McAndrews!

Druscilla: (*Makes notes in the book*) And what's in the pot?

All: Shrimps and rice. Very nice … .Dah-da, Dah-da, Dah-da, Dah-da, Da-da.

Druscilla: I thought Scots ate porridge or oatmeal for breakfast.

First Witch: This is for dinner later. It has to simmer as doth the battle yon. We await a hero of great note with prophesies for his future.

Second Witch: He's claimed victory and now seeks his destiny.
Third Witch: We bide our time until our brave warriors return victorious.
All (*Singing*): "Don't sit under the hanging tree with anyone else but me … if you know what's good for Ye. Dah-da, Dah-da, Dah-da, Dah-da, Da-da."
Druscilla: Ok, Ok. I get the idea. I can see where this bit is going. Excuse me a moment. (*Druscilla ducks behind a bush and rubs her Pentagram Ring*)
First Witch: Where'd she go?
Third Witch: (*stirring the cauldron*) Behind that bush is she is sorting out the mystery.
Second Witch: Well, we all have to go behind a bush now and then, don't we?
(*there is a clap of thunder and a bright flash of light*)
First Witch: She's gone!
Third Witch: I thought she'd stay for supper with Macbeth
First Witch: That's the trouble with royalty nowadays … no time for the little people.
Macbeth: (*Enters left*) Excuse me, ladies, but I seem to be lost. Mmm-mmm, something smells good.

And so history was made.

Meanwhile, May 25th, 2016 at midnight in London's Hellfire Lounge, there is a blinding flash of blue light in the ladies' room as Druscilla arrives in the present from her journey. In the main room, the joint is jumping with lecherous Elvis and his mischievous elves in the casino, Mongo the man-eating plant trying to consume anyone foolish enough to pet it or feed it a morsel off their appetizer plate, and Celeste, the Vampyress, trolling the bar for a new boyfriend while avoiding Elvis.

Of course, the usual gang of celebrities, supernaturals and politicos have gathered to let their hair down and party all night, all 'Hell-bent' on having a good time while owner and entrepreneur Nick Nussbaum looks on with that big Devilish smile.

MacBeth: The Untold Prelude 11

*Miller time at the Hellfire Lounge ... Although Druscilla and Cher opt for martinis. Shaken **and** stirred ...*   Art: Paul London

"I wonder where Druscilla is?" remarked Cher to her horned daddy as she sipped her apple martini at the bar.

"Probably fighting traffic in Piccadilly," Ray the reptilian bartender replied with a big yawn. "I hear there's some sort of demonstration going on, students picketing or something."

Just then Druscilla entered the room, motioned to Cher and the two quickly occupied their favorite banquet.

"I'm here. I'm here," Druscilla announced in a low voice so Nick would not hear. "I just had to make a short trip back to Scotland in the 11th Century to finish that census your father wanted back then. I never got to it, so I pop back there now and then and do it on the iPad I hide in this hollow book. I guess one day it will be finished and I will go back to 1099 again and drop it off. Heh, heh, I love this technology. Oh, and I met those three witches from Macbeth's time. Lousy cooks, fairly good singers. The MacAndrews Sisters. Really!"

"Seriously!" Cher replied.

Ray the bartender came over to the table and delivered refreshing beverage for Druscilla and inquired. "Have you seen who's here tonight?" as he indicated a guest on the opposite side of the room in a banquette.

"It's that supernatural investigator, Piers Knight!"

"Everyone at the bar thinks he's poking around here on a case," Ray whispered. "He knows that supernatural beings hang out here, witches included. I think he was involved with one at one time."

"Well, things can get dicey when your girlfriend is a witch" said Druscilla. "I heard of a guy who had a really complicated romance with one."

"How is that?" asked Ray.

"You haven't heard the story? Just listen to this … "

The Judgment of Dennis

KT Pinto

I**T'S TOUGH** being popular.

That was the thought that went through Denny's mind over and over again throughout his first three years at Tottenville High School and now, as a senior, it had become pretty much his mantra. It wasn't something he said out loud very often though, because it was a gripe that usually elicited very little sympathy.

This was especially true of his girlfriend Cynthia, known to her friends as Bangles. Having been an outcast most of her scholastic life — both for her taste in clothes and her knowledge of what people considered 'witchcraft' — she never understood why people made such a big deal and tried so hard to be a part of the popular world. Denny, as a member of the football team, had no choice but to be immersed in the 'in' crowd, along with the parties, gossip and scandals that went with it.

The worst part of being popular in Denny's mind was Homecoming season. In most schools, Homecoming was just another event during the school year. But at Tottenville, the only public school on the south shore of Staten Island, Homecoming was treated like a week-long festival, and Homecoming Day, which included the game and dance, had been made an actual school holiday. The school was closed except for Homecoming activities, alumni took off from work and traveled from all over to participate, and local junior highs and even non-participating high schools planned school trips to watch the game.

But none of this concerned Denny; what bothered him about Homecoming season was how it completely disrupted his life. Not only was there extra football practice before and after school, but there was also the organizing, planning and executing of the Homecoming Party. Normally he wasn't involved in the party, but he was told that, since this was his last year, and since he had been a member of the Homecoming Court twice, he had been selected to be a member of the Homecoming Committee. This hassle he could complain to Bangles about, because his committee duties affected her life as well as his.

He had found his girlfriend in front of her locker and tried very hard not to look inside. Although she was a 'white' practitioner (although she insisted she was 'grey') she made a point of making her locker look like that of a black magic witch, just to freak those non-witches who shunned her because of her Faith. He knew inside she had bones hanging from leather straps, a huge tarantula (that she insisted was not real) crawling around the locker and a couple of vials of liquid dragon's blood. He knew the "blood" was just a resin, but in those vials …

He watched her face as he explained why she wouldn't be seeing a lot of him in the upcoming weeks. She was keeping her face neutral, and he couldn't see her eyes behind her rose-tinted glasses.

"I tried to get out of it," he said, shifting from one foot to the other. "Really, I did! But even the coach got on my case about showing team spirit by participating. But between that and football and schoolwork … you just gotta bear with me on this, OK?"

Bangles tilted her head slightly. "I'm sorry, was I supposed to be listening?"

He made a face. "Cyn … "

"Look, am I complaining? You put up with me and marching band and the newspaper and yearbook and everything else I get suckered into. Why would I gripe?"

He shrugged. "I dunno. I hoped you'd try to talk me out of it."

"Why? It's not like you can back out."

He leaned against the lockers next to hers. "I sure wish I could though."

"What's the big deal?" she asked, leaning against him. "You pick a theme, throw up some balloons and streamers and bam! You're done."

"It's not that simple," he replied, watching the underclassmen rushing past. "I mean the theme, yeah, I could care less and would just vote with the majority."

"Ah yes, spoken like a true leader of men!"

He ignored her. "But we gotta choose the Homecoming King and Queen. That is not something I am looking forward to."

Bangles looked up at him with curiosity on her face. "Can't you just vote with the majority on that too?"

"Oh, sure. The voting's not the problem. We take the top three after the school has voted and then pick the one we'd like to represent the senior class." He paused as the late bell rang, then grabbed his and her books and started down the hall. "It's the campaigning that's going to kill me."

"Why?" she asked as they walked into automotives class. "It's not like they're campaigning directly to you or anything."

He chuckled. "Just you watch," he answered as they put on their coveralls. "You think I'm popular now?" He rolled his eyes. "Just wait until the nominees are announced."

***

There were five nominees for both the king and the queen of the Homecoming Ball. Of the ten, six of them were pretty much moot. Everyone knew that Keith was going to be the king. Even the stoners who hung out in the woods more than they were in class knew and liked Keith. He was one of the few people in the popular crowd who wasn't part of any sports team. He was an actor who played the lead in Sing, the spring musicals, and even the holiday extravaganzas four years running. He volunteered often, got good grades, and always had a smile or nice word for people. The other male nominees already knew they were going to be part of the homecoming court, not king, and they had no problems with that.

Among the girls, two of them had no hope of being queen. Both were underclassmen — one a junior, the other a sophomore — and were chosen more for their potential than anything else. That left three: Jeanie, Natalie, and Angela, and that was where the drama was going to happen.

The three girls were rivals: captain of the twirlers, cheerleaders, and track team, respectively, the three competed over everything, from fashion to grades to boyfriends. They demanded the best clothes, the best cars, the best position in the spotlight; in this case, that meant being the Homecoming Queen. Another thing that they had in common was their complete and total ruthlessness; their desire to get what they wanted at any cost. And that came out loud and clear the day the nominations were announced.

It was then that Bangles understood why Denny had been dreading his role on the committee. As much as the three nominees accosted everyone in the school to win their votes, when they saw a committee member, they put it on full force.

They were aggressive, yet simpering. They praised the mundane and pouted when they thought it would help. They invited the female committee members to manicure appointments and out for coffee, while the men they asked to dinner or the movies. They brought in baskets of chocolate and cupcakes to hand out to students throughout the day, and the halls were plastered with their posters, each one bigger than the last, with their larger than life heads smiling down at the masses.

Denny did his best to ignore it all. He walked through the halls with his head down, trying very hard not to make eye contact with anyone. He started making a habit of going through rarely used side hallways, the basement and the auto bays just to avoid the nominees as much as possible.

He had just come out of the boiler room on the way to physics class to find Bangles standing in the hallway waiting for him.

"Are you going to dig a tunnel out next?" she asked.

He smiled ruefully. "I may have to."

"When is the vote taking place again?"

"Next week," he answered. "You know, that date that's plastered on every one of those posters on the walls?"

"I thought that's when we vote."

"It is, but then we have the final vote later that day." He gave her a look. "This is the fourth year you've been through this holiday, you know."

"Not me," she answered. "I could care less who's Homecoming Queen." She rolled her eyes. "And this is not a holiday. Yule is a holiday; Beltane is a holiday; Arbor Day is a holiday. This is not a holiday; this is something made up by local football fanatics."

He sighed; he'd heard this rant before.

She heard the sigh and got back to her point. "But this time around I need to know when voting is so I know how much more of this crap I have to endure."

He took her books from her hands. "If this is about me having to sneak through the back corridors … "

"That's part of it." She stopped walking and turned to him. "Look, you know how much I enjoy being unpopular, right?"

He knew she was being serious. "Yes, I do."

"People leave me alone; I don't get involved with any drama outside of my small group of friends; I don't get invited to any parties … it's a life I like, you know?"

He nodded, wondering where she was going with this.

"And I know that you have to be popular in order to play ball, or vice versa. I get that too."

He started walking again before they were late to class. "Yes, you're one of the most understanding girlfriends ever."

"Yes, I am. But these days … It's very difficult for me to not punch the Homecoming Queen nominees in their respective mouths. They won't leave me alone. They keep chatting with me like we're old friends, calling me by my nickname and trying to involve me in small talk. Natalie actually asked me if my religion still approves of human sacrifice!" She gave him a small smile. "I told her that I had someone of the cheerleading persuasion in mind for this upcoming Samhain. As much fun as seeing her expression was, the sudden attention is still aggravating."

"In all fairness," Denny said, smiling at her spunk, "You have known Jeanie for over a decade. There's really nothing wrong with her talking to you, is there?"

"Oh, she won't talk to me. She says it should be a given that I vote for her and that's when I told her I wasn't voting for anyone, and she got pissed."

"You know if you had just said that you were voting for her, the other two would've left you alone."

She stopped at the door of her English class and took her books back. "You know as well as I do that that's not true."

"Yeah, you're right. I'm sorry."

"It's not your fault," she answered with a smile. "I just needed to vent. I'll see you at lunch."

He turned and walked towards physics, hoping that things didn't get any more aggravating …

***

"Hi Denny," Angela said as he walked out of class. "How weird, bumping into you!"

He didn't answer her as he walked down the hall towards the stairs. She had to walk double-time to keep up with his purposefully long strides.

"I just … " She paused to catch her breath. "I was just wondering if you had decided who you were voting for Homecoming Queen."

"Nope," he answered, taking the stairs two at a time.

"Well, I thought you may want to take this into consideration … can you stop for a minute?"

He stopped and leaned against the wall, out of the way of the crowd. "I have to get to lunch."

"I'll make it fast," she said, catching for breath. "If you vote for me for queen, you will be going to the dance with the hottest girl in school."

Denny raised his eyebrows. "I already am."

Angela looked genuinely confused. "I thought you were going with that witchy chick."

His eyes narrowed. "Her name is Cynthia," he replied, "and yes, I am."

"Well then, I don't understand … "

"Look, you can't buy my vote, so please stop trying."

"But to be on the arm of the queen … "

"First of all, just because I vote for you doesn't mean you'd win. Secondly, if this is the only thing you're offering, does that mean all the male judges are going to be your date if you win? And, thirdly, I'm going to the dance with Cynthia."

"But, your reputation … to be seen at the dance with her … "

"My reputation was held up for the past three and a half years just fine."

"But, now with her eyes glowing all red … "

He let her sentence hang in the air for a moment. "Her what now?"

"Her eyes! Certainly you know that the reason why she was those ridiculous glasses is because it keeps people from noticing her glowing red eyes … "

He turned and glared at her. "Keep talking, and I'll be certain not to vote for you."

He then left her on the landing, looking angry and completely confused.

Denny pushed through the throng, his mantra running through his head. It's tough being popular … it's tough being popular … it's tough being popular …

***

Denny heard the footsteps before seeing the heeled feet stop beside the car he was working on.

"Denny?"

He closed his eyes and sighed. He had really thought the auto bays would be a safe place to hide out during his free period. "Yeah?"

"It's Natalie, if you can't tell. Can we talk?"

He sighed again and rolled himself out from under the car, wiping his hands on the rag on his lap. "Yeah?"

She was dressed in a tight, white dress and spiked heels; not exactly the best attire for a garage. She took a step away from him as if the grease on his hands was going to jump onto her. "I wanted to know if I had your vote for Homecoming Queen."

"No one has my vote just yet," he answered, not bothering to sit up.

"I'll make my decision after you give your speeches on Monday."

She balanced herself with her hand on the car's bumper as she knelt next to him. "Well, I was hoping that a little … incentive … may help you with your decision."

Denny closed his eyes and took a deep, calming breath. "What incentive?"

"Well, you know that my dad owns the car dealership by the expressway, right?"

Who didn't know that? "Yeah … ?"

"If you vote for me, I can get you a great deal on a new beamer."

Denny sat up and turned to her. "A new beamer?"

Natalie nodded, thinking she had hooked him. "Yes. My dad gets a deal with the manufacturer which he extends to friends and family, and he would definitely consider you a friend if you voted for me."

He chuckled softly and patted the car he had been working on. "You do know I have a car, right?"

"But this one's old! Wouldn't you rather have something new?"

Denny's eyes narrowed. "This is a '78 firebird. There's a difference between an old car and a classic one. Besides," He stood and walked over to his tool chest. "I'd rather have something I rebuilt myself than a leftover from the showroom that no one wanted."

She stood as well, and he could see anger flash in her eyes. "I understand. You take the weekend to think it over."

He slammed the tool drawer shut. "I will think it over after I hear your speeches on Monday."

Natalie tossed her head. "Fine, but don't complain when this hunk of junk dies on you."

Denny's lip curled as she stormed away. He tried very hard not to hope she would slip on one of the oil slicks and land hard on her very white backside …

***

Denny helped the lanky freshman on the weight bench guide the barbell back into its holder before turning to Jeanie. "Not you too," he said by way of a greeting.

"Not me too what?"

"Look, your speeches are this afternoon. After I hear them, I will make a decision."

"I know; that's what Bangles told me."

He was about to correct her, but remembered that the captain of the twirlers had known Cynthia long enough to use her nickname. "So then what do you need?"

"Well, I was wondering if you knew if Bangles was mad at me. I mean, she told me about the speeches, but she seemed so cold and distant when she spoke to me."

"She's been putting up with a lot this past week," he explained as he reached for his bottle of water. "Don't take it personally."

"But I do!" Jeanie replied, stamping her foot. "She's destroying a really long friendship because she's having a bad week."

"And you're going to end a friendship over that? Because she's not having a good week?"

"Well, it's also because I'm not having a good week either." She smiled slyly. "Now, if my week got better ... "

Denny choked on his water. "Are you telling me that if I don't vote for you, you'll end your friendship with Bangles?"

Jeanie feigned innocence. "Denny! You're making it sound like I'm threatening you!"

"Now why would I think that?" He rolled his eyes. "Look, what do you with your social life is your own business. I'm not going to be blamed for your actions."

"You might want to run that past your girlfriend before making a decision, because if you think she's unpopular with me as a friend ... "

"Jeanie, I think you should leave before something heavy falls on you, like a barbell or something."

She looked like she was going to answer, but changed her mind and stormed out of the weight room.

Denny sighed and went back to helping the frosh lift his fifty pound barbell ...

***

"Why in the world would I care what Jeanie does?" Bangles asked, slowly moving the lit sage back and forth. "Be my friend, don't be my friend. My life goes on."

"But I feel bad that you're getting this grief because of me."

Bangles smiled and waved the sage at him as they sat on the bleachers. "No, I'm getting grief because Jeanie's a shallow, self-centered bully. But I've known that for years." She put the sage on the bench next to her and zipped up her purple band jacket. "The bigger her desire, the nastier she gets."

"Well, if I vote for her ... "

"Don't you dare!" Bangles exclaimed, her eyes flashing behind her glasses. "You vote for who you think should be Homecoming Queen, for whatever reasons you have."

"But she pretty much threatened to blackball you."

"How can you blackball someone who's already unpopular?" She opened her thermos and took a swig of hot chocolate. "What is she going to do? Make me wear something worse than my marching band uniform?"

He chuckled. "That's true."

"Look, put it out of your head. Worry about what they said both during their speeches and elsewhere after the game." She raised the sage towards him again; he didn't like it the smell much, but she felt is cleansed his aura and protected his body from harm. Who was he to argue? "For now, worry about tackling people and stuff."

He shook his head and kissed her. "One day, I am going to get you to understand football."

"Yeah, whatever. Go play."

Denny ran down the bleachers, glancing back once to see Bangles being joined by a few of her close - also outcasted – friends, most like her dressed in their band outfits. That's when he realized that losing Jeanie's friendship would be no great hardship to his girlfriend.

By the time he arrived on the field, he had come up with a solution to his Homecoming Queen problem ...

***

Denny sat at a table next to Bangles and a group of her friends, watching the teens on the dance floor moving to one of those annoying party songs that is played at every catered event ever created. He glanced across the room to where the homecoming hopefuls were sitting, and wondered how much damage they would make once the queen was announced.

"You have a weird expression on your face," Bangles said as the DJ asked people to take their seats.

"Just a little tense," he replied, rolling his head from shoulder to shoulder.

"You want to leave?"

"After the weeks I've been having? No way! I'm going to see this through to the end."

The DJ then asked the judges to come up to the stage to announce the new Homecoming King and Queen.

There were no surprises when it came to the king. The audience said Keith's name along with the announcer. The guys who he beat out were already standing there with his crown and scepter ready.

Next came the queen. Bangles noticed Denny take a step away from his fellow judges as they announced the winner of the crown.

"For the first time ever," the announcer said, "we have a tie!"

The two underclassman girls took a step back, leaving Natalie, Angela and Jeanie standing in the spotlight, all obviously tense and determined to be wearing that crown.

"Our new queens are … Jeanie, Natalie and Angela! Can you believe it? Three queens! Keith, that's a winning hand!"

"How is that possible?" Natalie asked angrily. "There's an odd number of judges! There shouldn't be a tie!"

The judges turned to look at Denny. "I abstained from voting."

"What!" Angela yelled. "Why?"

"Because the queen should be a senior, and I don't think any of you are worthy enough to represent our class, or be Keith's queen." He shrugged. "I had wanted to vote for Cynthia, but I was overruled."

The three new queens started arguing, trying to out-yell the others in order to be heard. Denny ignored them and walked back to his table, where Bangles was waiting. She had taken off her glasses, and that's when he noticed that her eyes were a deep blood red. He wondered when she had time to go to Goth-in-a-Box to buy those costume contacts.

"Wanna dance?" he asked.

She smiled at his lack of reaction. "Sure."

He walked her to the dance floor, and the DJ was smart enough to start playing a slow, romantic song. Couples began to join them, the drama of the queens already forgotten.

Bangles leaned her head on his shoulder. "Very smooth Den. I liked that last bit, even though it's a bold-faced lie."

"What? I would like to have made you queen." He smiled at her. "You would've hated every minute of it, but that crown would have looked really good on you."

She chuckled. "Sorry, that crown only fits on popular heads. I'm not ready for that kinda pressure. I'll leave all that tough being popular nonsense to you."

"Gee, thanks." He grinned and pulled her close, and over the music heard his mantra repeating in his head. It's tough being popular … it's tough being popular … it's tough being popular … He smiled as he heard Bangles sigh against him. But sometimes, he thought, being me isn't half bad, …

And so the evening begins …

"I guess that's where *Wicked* gets that 'popular' song from," Cher commented.

"Yeah, maybe," Ray mused. "I still can't get over the fact that Piers Knight is in our club. I wonder what or who he's investigating? Maybe it's someone here?"

"Does Daddy know he's here?"

"Yeah, I pointed it out. He's still getting over the reports of Knight's last case."

"Which is what?" Druscilla inquired.

"Oh, you were time hopping, you missed it." Ray continued. "It was a big conversation topic last night. I'll fill you in. Now, get this … ."

Impossible Love

A Piers Knight Adventure

C.J. Henderson

"Whoso loves believes the impossible."
— *Elizabeth Barrett Browning*

"Piers, what a surprise."

Professor Piers Knight's unannounced visit at the home of his acquaintance, Albert Harper, was somewhat of an unusual thing for the professor. Knight was not normally the kind to risk wasting time dropping in on people who might not be where he presumed they should be. He liked things confirmed. He liked them neat.

The professor worked as a curate at the rightly famous Brooklyn Museum. As such he had access to religious and blasphemous articles of historical significance from throughout human history. On occasion, he had found it practical to borrow certain items for the purpose of self-sponsored experiments and investigations. In his time Knight had seen horrors and wonders. And, every time he survived the things he found, the professor found he wished to spend more and more time with the Harpers.

After a while, his former student thought he knew why; he had become for Knight a case study. Or, if not himself, his family.

The Harper clan was an entity consisting of but two souls — Albert Harper and his daughter Debbie. Both were victims. Debbie of the ravages of Down Syndrome. Albert of the monstrous appetite known as divorce. When Debbie had been born, it had only been a matter of days before her condition was diagnosed. She was afflicted not only with the Downs, but with its severest strand.

"Yes, well," answered the professor, "I could say something inane about just being in the neighborhood, here with someone you've never met, but that would be what we in the business call, 'a lie.' Mind if we come in?"

Many children with the same handicap lead nearly normal lives. The training was grueling for the parents and teachers, but it happened every day. It was possible. Working harder than regular students, they could learn to communicate with their parents, after a fashion, of course. They could go to school, ride bikes, play with others, watch and understand television programs. In adulthood they could move about town on their own, hold down simple jobs, even marry and grow old with someone.

For a while the media adored them, a new minority to fawn over after women and blacks and gays had all been properly exploited. The world learned of them, was taught how to cherish them in the politically correct manner, and then they were shuffled off back to obscurity. But, even as abruptly as the Hollywood romance ended, in some ways the attention made things easier for many parents of Down children.

Parents of high end performance children, that is. Not children like Debbie.

Debbie was not high end. Debbie Harper would never be able to communicate with her parents, in any fashion. She would never go to school, ride a bike, or play with others. She did watch television programs, but she did so without understanding. Her eyes were simply drawn to the colors and the movement. In adulthood she would not go anywhere on her own, hold down any kind of job, or marry anyone. It was not even certain she would grow old.

"So," asked the former student as the two men came into his home, "what's the reason I'm unexpectedly playing host to a man who never drops in out of the blue and someone I don't know?"

Albert had raised Debbie for the last seven years on his own. Her mother, Linda, had stayed with her and her father for almost eight months, after which she could not take it anymore.

It.

"It" was her word for what their lives — her life — had become. She wanted a daughter that gurgled and cooed, one that had eyes which shone with recognition of shapes and faces, one that delighted at new sounds, that turned her head with interest and excitement when new experiences were in the offering. She wanted a normal, regular, healthy baby, one she could dress in pink, one she could take inordinate pride in as she learned all the simple things babies learn with time.

Once it had become obvious that she was never going to have her long-dreamed-of perfect, bright-eyed child, that her baby would not be an accessory of her life, but that she would be one of her baby's — a constant care giver, the rest of her days devoted to a child who could barely respond to the simplest stimuli — she had begun talking with Albert about placing their daughter in a home. Such was not an option as far as he was concerned. And so it was after a year and five months of marriage, and twenty-two weeks of parenthood, Albert was left alone with his speechless daughter to stare at the numbing future ahead of them.

"This is a friend of mine," answered Knight. Giving his companion a moment, he allowed the ancient black woman time to summon her strength for an introduction. It had been a long walk, up the front walk from the curb to the car, and she was old.

It was obvious she had been beautiful in her time, a lush and handsome force whose footsteps had known three centuries. Her eyes told Albert nothing about her, except that the way the woman before her viewed the universe differed from his the way his did from his daughter's.

"Her name is Madame Sarna la Rainellea." Pointing toward the child sitting motionless in the living room beyond, he added;

"She's going to sit with Debbie for a few minutes while we take a walk outside." Before Albert could say anything, the professor turned to the old woman. Responding to the question she could feel within him, she said;

"As we discussed, I shall talk to her, Piers. Constantly. I will keep her engaged."

"Good," answered Knight. "As long as she doesn't answer, everything should be fine."

Without a further word La Rainellea entered the living room and began an endless stream of conversation. She spoke with the girl about cartoons she remembered, the snack cakes her mother baked her before love came from a factory wearing a bar code, how fascinating it was that leaves changed colors in the fall — apparently anything that came to mind. Albert noticed that his eyes seemed extremely focused on Debbie.

On her eyes, he thought. She's watching her eyes.

And then he finally responded to the gentle pressure on his arm and allowed the professor to maneuver him out onto his front porch. As the two men headed for the sidewalk, Albert asked;

"Going to tell me what this is all about now?"

"Yes, I am. And I'm not certain how you're going to react. I have something very ... well, not to me, but to you ... "

The older man stopped speaking, obviously at a complete loss as to how to proceed. It was clear something of great importance was clawing at him, demanding release. But, it was equally evident the professor thought how that thing was released of extreme importance as well. Suddenly struck by inspiration, Knight said;

"Albert, you once told me the story of the first time you held Debbie. Tell it again, won't you."

The father looked at his friend through hard eyes. His lips drawn thin, he started to protest, but the professor cut him off gently, saying;

"I understand your reluctance, my boy. More than you can know. But I promise you, I have a purpose. I do."

Albert turned his head away, his shoulders shaking slightly. The young man remained silent for a moment, then closing his eyes, he began to speak.

"It was in the delivery room. Debbie'd just been born. I was standing there a little stunned. They'd cut Linda; I wasn't expecting, no one had warned me ... blood had just flown through the air. 'Normal,' they said — chuckled it, really — but I wish someone had prepared me for

... anyway, let's just say I was in a state, you know."

Knight nodded, listening patiently.

"So, while I'm still reeling from it all, out of nowhere the nurse brings Debbie over to me." Albert's face softened, the approaching memory so gladdening his heart the air seemed to freshen about him.

"She was so tiny, so fragile, I took her from the nurse, and I was staring at her. Of course, her eyes weren't open, but I could feel this, this need, you know, spilling out of her, looking for something to grab onto, and before I knew it, I raised her up to where I could press my forehead against hers, and when I did that, I swear I felt her inside my mind. I ... "

Knight waited, but Albert stopped his thought, choking it back, suddenly tired. Spent. Feeling foolish, he muttered;

"Anyway, you know all that."

"Yes, but I wanted to hear you tell it again. I wanted to see if you still believed it."

"Why wouldn't I believe it? I was there; I know it happened."

"Yes," agreed the professor, "but after all these years, with Debbie's reversal, with no further contact with that mind you swear you felt, it is possible you might start to believe you imagined the whole thing." Knight let the fall breeze blow about them for a moment, then interrupted its soft whisper by asking;

"Have you, Albert? Have you ever been tempted to think you were wrong about that day?"

Albert Harper's eyes narrowed. Puzzlement fixing his gaze on the professor, anger coiling about his spine, his voice came out low and growling, bitter with sarcasm;

"Sure, all the time. That's why I let my wife walk out; that's why I still won't put Debbie in a home; that's why I'm working double shifts, driving my mother and aunts to distraction baby sitting — how can you ask me that? How — Goddamnit? You know what Debbie means to me!"

"I do, Albert — "

"I'm telling you ... " The young man paused, his voice choking, eyes threatening to betray him, "I know — I know she's in there somewhere. I felt it. I goddamn well felt it, do you understand? You're not taking that away from me. Nobody's taking that away from me!"

"I'm not trying to," the professor told him softly. "And I apologize for exciting you. But, well, it had to be done." Knight tilted his head down for a moment, running a hand through his hair and then down the back of his neck. Keeping his attention on his friend, though, he explained;

"You see, I'm going to tell you something incredible. Something you may not be able to understand. But you must trust me about one thing. I believe what you just said. I don't just believe that you believe it, I think it happened just as you said.

"And after that," Knight added, his voice going dark and stiff, "I think something monstrous happened. Something I don't quite know if I will be able to explain or prove to you."

The younger man turned to stare at his one-time instructor. The two had reached the end of his neighborhood, come to a stop on the edge of the local business district. Moving them a few feet further, in between two storefronts with a great deal of electricity pulsing through their front displays, the professor said;

"Albert, I'm going to simply say this as bluntly as possible — I do not believe your daughter has Down Syndrome. I believe she is possessed." Debbie's father merely stared, his mind racing through scores of responses. Rather than wait for him to pick one, Knight told him;

"You must understand, I came across the idea the first time years ago. It's an ancient notion, and in older times people were more prone to recognize the signs. But, simply put, often times what we think of today as Alzheimers, or Parkinsons or DS, even some cancers, all manner of ailments, they're really cases of demonic possession."

"You're not one to make sick jokes, professor — " Albert struggled to say. His voice a whisper, he said, "I know it. So, I'll ask you, what am I supposed to say to this? What do you want me to do? Call the church? Get a witch doctor — what? What?!"

"Calm yourself, Albert." As the younger man began to move, his friend put up a hand and gently stopped his progress. "And, please trust me when I say you shouldn't yet want to leave this position." As his former student stared, Knight told him;

"My research lead me to a number of cross-culture references to priests and shamans throughout history waiting for rainstorms so they could prepare their defenses against such creatures." Pointing to all the pulsing lights behind them, the professor said;

"Apparently these things have trouble hearing through electricity. If there is a demon involved here, and it is trying to listen to us, it shouldn't be able to make anything out through all the interference these signs should provide."

"You're serious, you're really serious. Aren't you?"

Albert Harper concentrated his vision on the professor as if seeing him for the first time. He studied the man carefully, intently, searching his face through eyes ready to brim over with tears or hatred. Quietly, sternly, Knight answered him;

"Yes, Albert, I am. And if after all the years you've devoted to your daughter, if you're ready to risk throwing what time you have left on this Earth away in a desperate gamble of freeing her from this thing's clutches, I may be able to help you."

The father stopped simply responding at that point and worked on actually considering what his old instructor had told him so far. Part of his mind, of course, instantly rejected what he was hearing out of hand. It was, obviously, insanity.

New age grasping at straws. Superstition.

Nonsense.

On the other hand, a different section of his mind added, knee-jerk reactions were often born from fear. Applying only a tiny bit of rationality to the subject, Albert had to admit the professor had travelled the world to seek out the supernatural and the occult in each and every of its dark and terrible places. The older man had told him incredible stories over the years, swearing they were true.

Oddly enough, if anyone else had told Albert such tales he would have laughed them away. It was not that Knight was a particularly riveting storyteller as much as he was an indifferent one. The things he talked of, as incredible as they were to his students, they appeared merely to be lecture points to Knight.

He seemed like a father explaining pennies to his babies, thinking it harmless in a world of million dollar bank notes. And that is why Albert believed him.

His old instructor, the younger man knew — could feel deep within his soul — that Knight would not have come to him that day if they were not friends. Looking into the professor's eyes, he understood it was time for him to make a decision. He admitted he was not certain what he believed, but he could not think of any reason why Knight would lie about such a thing. And, so deciding, he glanced left and then right, looking first at the electrical signs supposedly protecting his thoughts, and then at the man who told him such was the case, and said;

"All right, let's not waste all this fine electricity. Tell me what you know."

***

What Knight had to tell his friend did not take a great deal of time. Demons, in these deceptive cases of possession, were not torturing the souls they possessed. Their purpose was far more devious. They tortured the care-givers; crippling their lives, disrupting possible futures by diminishing those it was deemed good to distract. Reshaping fate, the monsters terrorized with guilt and duty, forcing those they feared to bleed rather than build.

"Holy men in every century have been attacked thus, their families set upon by afflictions brought, we have been told, by minions of Satan."

Knight was careful to look about from time to time. He felt safe from supernatural spies between the glaring neon displays, but drawing unwanted attention from the plain folk of the world was not so easily discouraged. The professor did not relish the notion of what might happen if the night ahead of them were invaded by various annoyances and their video cameras.

"It's not anything as mundane as the standard Christian Hell that's sending out things like these, using them to feed off our world, manipulate it — but it's real, and it's terrible. Then again, so are scorpions. So's carpet bombing of civilians. We can get used to anything we can comprehend. And moreover, my friend, we can stand up to it, as well."

Once Knight had gotten Albert to the point where he was willing to accept the possibility of Debbie's possession, he then told him what he might be able to do about it. The professor had explained a technique through which Albert might be able to actually enter his daughter's mind. When his former student had simply stared at him, struggling to keep believing, Knight focused all his attention upon him, then whispered;

"That day in the hospital, when you placed your head to hers, when you felt her mind, new and fresh and searching, touching yours, melding with yours — don't think it can't be done. You've already done it. All you need to do this time is go further. Go all the way inside ... "

Knight paused for a moment, taking a deep breath. His eyes still locked with his friend's, he dropped the tone of his voice to a growl, then finished, saying;

"And once you're there, you'll have to find this thing, and drag it out of Debbie — kick its Goddamned ass until it leaves her for good."

"I just go into her mind and stop this thing, just like that?" Albert's tone was not so much disbelieving as incredulous. "I mean, saying this is all real, this demon I'm going to go after, it's been doing this kind of thing for thousands of years. How am I supposed to, I mean ... shouldn't I ... I – I don't know, get some kind of training — what? I ... "

The professor made to speak, but Albert cut him off, racing forward with his thoughts.

"I'm not afraid, not of dying — that's not it. It's Debbie. If something did go wrong, if I screw this up, from what you said before, I could get destroyed in there, wind up brain dead, or completely dead — right?" When Knight confirmed his evaluation, Albert added;

"Okay, say it happens. I'm not good enough. I go down. I'm dead. All right, what happens to Debbie then? Who takes care of her?"

"You're taking it straight," answered Knight, "so I'll give it to you that way. The way Debbie is now, it really doesn't matter who cares for her — does it? If you die, she becomes a ward of the state. She lives out her vegetable existence and then follows you into oblivion. End of the Harpers."

Albert swallowed hard. The professor darted his head from side to side, checking the traffic flow around them one last time, then added, "La Rainelle has travelled the dreamplane before. She'll take you in and help as best she can. There might be something she and I can do, but the thing you have to concentrate on is that if you can catch this thing by surprise you could give Debbie the rest of her life. If you can't, then really … " Knight paused for a moment, then in a voice filled with nothing but cold practicality, he asked;

"Is it actually going to matter to her how much time she has left … or if you're there or not?"

The inside of Albert's head fizzled with anger. Knight was correct, of course. He hated to admit it, had to admit it. There was no connection between himself and his daughter. She was a lump of breathing meat that he cleaned and fed and dressed and put to bed. She could not button buttons, take herself to the bathroom, brush her teeth — not reliably. None of it. She did not know who he was. If he was dead, she would not care.

She did not know how.

A tear trying to break free from his left eye, the young father steeled his will, sucked the moisture back into himself, then growled;

"I'd call you a bastard, but you'd still be right. So, all right then, since you've got me in the mood where I'd like to kill something, let's go see if I can."

***

Twenty minutes later it had begun. Upon returning to his home, Albert had taken La Rainelle into the master bedroom on a pretext while the professor had remained with Debbie. Knight had started in with the same kind of distracting chatter the balding man had thrown at her, keeping her attention while the assault to come was prepared.

Quickly Madame La Rainelle gave Albert an open bottle, instructing him to breath deeply of its fumes. The pungent vapors relaxed him completely. Then, while the father stretched out on his bed, the old woman had taken up a position in the chair next to the bed. Beginning her own deep breathing exercises, she cautioned Albert to not wander off into his dreams.

"You must try to keep focused. Wait for me to arrive. Once we find each other, we will then search for your problem." Albert nodded. Then, just as he was drowsing, the old woman added;

"And remember, dear boy, this is the dream plane where we go. If you can imagine something, you can will it to be as real as anything around you."

"Meaning?" Allowing herself the energy to paint a crafty smile across her face, La Rainelle told him;

"Whatever this thing throws at you, just throw it back ... "

Everything worked as Knight had said it would. In only a handful of seconds, Albert was asleep. Remembering what he was supposed to do, he concentrated on finding the black woman. He searched his memory, bringing the image of La Rainelle clearly into his mind. The drawn face, silvered hair, delicate hands, stiff, slender body —

And then, suddenly the two were together, the scenery within Albert's mind taking on a disturbingly real substance. The two stood on a vast and open plane, a red and purple expanse that stretched in all directions. As vague bits of crimson dust began to swirl about them, La Rainelle said;

"Concentrate, Albert. Return yourself to that first moment you saw your daughter, back in the delivery room — remember it, take yourself back to it — be there ... "

Time shattered into millionths of a second. In each passing fraction Albert saw pieces of his most cherished memory reconstructed. Bit by bit, it all fell into place — the unexpected cut, the gushing blood, his shock, the assurances, and then the nurse, walking forward, only moments later —

"Would you like to hold your daughter, Mr. Harper?"

He took the bundle without hesitation. Held her for the briefest of instants, then raised the tiny, fragile body upward, and touched his head to hers once more —

—*flash*—

Albert Harper fell to his knees — screaming. Bolts of pain shattered his chest, ricocheted off his nerves, blasting his senses, spinning him around and slamming him to his back —

"Look at the maggot come to love his little freak."

Albert tried to drag himself away from the assault. Molten metal poured over him, searing flesh from bone, evaporating his skin, boiling his blood, dissolving him —

"I just knew I was going to meet you in here some day."

The taunting voice did not issue from a mouth of any kind. It rode the electric jolts pummeling Albert, crawling into his organs and ripping them open one after another. It had a female lilt to it, but it was not Debbie's. Was not even meant to be Debbie's.

"I wish I could say it was good to see you again."

But it was one he knew. Recognized notes it struck here and there, began to identify its pattern. Despite the numbing pain lashing throughout every fiber of his essence, still he was beginning to pull a face together within his mind.

"Linda?"

"That's very good." The sneering voice chuckled. "Now I suppose you're going to pull yourself together and, now, how did he put it … kick my Goddamned ass until I leave for good. Is that next, Albert, dear?"

Harper strained to open his eyes. La Rainelle was nowhere to be seen. The scenery had changed. He was no longer in the delivery room. He was further back in the past, sitting in a movie theater, the voice of the creature hissing behind him.

"This is where we met, isn't it, darling? This is where you fell in love with me — right, baby?"

Everything was prefect — exactly as he remembered it.

Of course it's the way you remember it, the back of his mind growled at him, it's your memory. You've got this thing in your head now.

"Is it all coming back to you, sweetheart? Is it?"

Albert remembered it all, being in a bad mood, going to a movie alone, not caring what he saw. He remembered throwing himself into the middle of the emptiest section of the theater. Remembered two women coming in and sitting directly behind him. The two talked throughout the film, but having his theater-going experience interrupted by the pair did not bother Albert. He was too busy falling in love with one of them.

"It never did dawn on you, did it, Al? A beautiful woman, with an interest in mystery novels, and gaming, and comics ... a beautiful woman who voted the same way you did, who couldn't wait to leave the theater and go to the new Vietnamese restaurant ... how vain are you?"

Albert turned in his seat.

"What are you saying? Do you think I'm going to believe anything you tell me?"

"Baby," the form of his wife said sweetly, gently lifting her arm into the air, "do you think I care?"

An arc of blue-white flame fell from her hand, cascading over Albert, roasting the skin from him, boiling his eyes. Remembering himself whole, inside his shower, he drenched himself, regenerating his body as he screamed;

"I don't give a rat's ass what you care about, what you think, or what you have to say. Just get out of my daughter's head!"

"Al, sweetie," the familiar thing smiled. "What makes you think I'm in her head anymore?"

The Linda-like thing waved its hand and boils flooded forth from every pore of Albert's body. Hundreds, thousands of them, they burst open, pus and blood bubbling up from each of them. Albert endured the torment for a moment, then rejected the plague, throwing it off as he had those before them. As he did, the ever-changing landscape settled once more into the red and purple wasteland in which he had first found himself. As Albert steadied himself, the Linda thing strode purposely into his field of vision.

"Very slow, sweetheart," it told him. Hands on its knees, body bent to show all its parts off to their best advantage, the thing told him, "too slow, really. I mean, seriously, what do you think can really come of all this?"

Before Albert could answer, the ground opened and swallowed him. He tried to leap away, but he could not compensate for the slam of crushing gravity sent to shovel him into the latest torment. As he fell below the surface of the dreamplane, the ground rushed in, sand and gravel and choking dust not just piling atop him, but grinding against him, digging its way into his skin — tearing it from his body, shredding it. First one layer, then the second, hair torn away, scalp bloody, nails being etched, eye brows and lashes ripped out by the roots —

"No!"

Albert clawed his way to the surface, breaking the ground open with his back and shoulders. His head felt cracked; blood sluiced over his ears, down his forehead. His hands ached from clawing his way free. The Linda thing cackled as he gasped for air.

"You can't do it, you know."

"Do what?" Albert's voice was a ragged, panting thing, weak and feeble.

"Beat me. It can't be done."

"Bullshit," spat Albert weakly. "Human beings been … kicking the ass of your, your type for centuries."

"True, true," admitted the Linda thing. Sitting on a large violet rock seemingly carved to resemble a great, rolling tongue, the torturer added, "but that takes real faith."

With a snap of its fingers, the thing unleashed a ravenous horde of insects to devour Albert. As quickly as the young father could shield himself, regenerate his flesh, the overwhelming waves of chittering creatures would find their way to him once more, begin chewing again, ripping again, tearing, slicing, stinging, gnawing —

"You've got no chance there," the thing snickered. "When Linda first sat down behind you, you had no faith in your chances with her."

Albert cleared his mind enough to summon a great wind to carry the horde away from him. He had nearly a full second's respite before the Linda thing turned his body to glass and began tossing shards of rock at him.

"When she started to talk," the thing laughed, shattering Albert's left arm at the elbow, "you wanted her so badly. But you never believed you could. You never really believed you could have her."

Concentrating, Albert was able to reform his body, but only for as long as his opponent allowed it. While he wiped at the sweat running down his forehead, half of it water, half of it tiny glass beads, the Linda thing took the moment to finish its thought.

"You don't have the belief in you to get rid of me, sweetheart, and that's what's going to make this so much fun."

"Fun?" asked Albert, confused. "What fun? What's going to be so much fun?"

"Why, us — darling."

Before the gasping father could react, the thing was behind him, its all-too familiar arms encircling his chest. The touch jarred too many memories, splitting him, rending him — making him ache for his ex-wife the way a man's back aches after waking from having slept on a rock; dully. Throbbingly; wounded by pain and not really knowing why.

The feel of her was fire; crisping skin, sweat that tasted like bacon — alluring, forbidden, salty and delicious. Her breasts came against his back in exactly the way he remembered; the heat of her breath curled across his neck, into his ear. He had been so long without female contact — any female contact — let alone hers, that his body surrendered to the touch involuntarily. Craving it; luxuriating against it — simply, pitifully, longing for it to never end.

"You're my dog, Albert," the thing whispered. "You may fight against me, but I've got you."

The young man struggled against the all-too-pleasant hold binding him. The arms held him securely while their owner whispered;

"Poor boy — you just don't understand yet, do you? You can't resist me. No matter how many pains you endure, how many trials you turn back, I can always think up more. You don't have any way to resist me. You don't have any faith in anything, sweetheart. And, without faith, I can't be driven away."

Chuckling, it's voice a mad titter swirling the dust about his head in never-ending spirals, the creature shifted its grip on Albert and suddenly drove its hands into his sides. Pulling organs free from his body, it tossed them casually over its shoulder as it said;

"And, even if you could ever drive me out of your head, what would it gain you? You sad, stupid man ... "

Albert sagged, tiring from the pain, the endlessness of it — the futility of it hurt too much, so terribly, terribly much, that he simply had to rest. As he gasped, struggling desperately to marshall his thoughts, the red-handed thing above him sighed, dribbling spittle into Albert's face

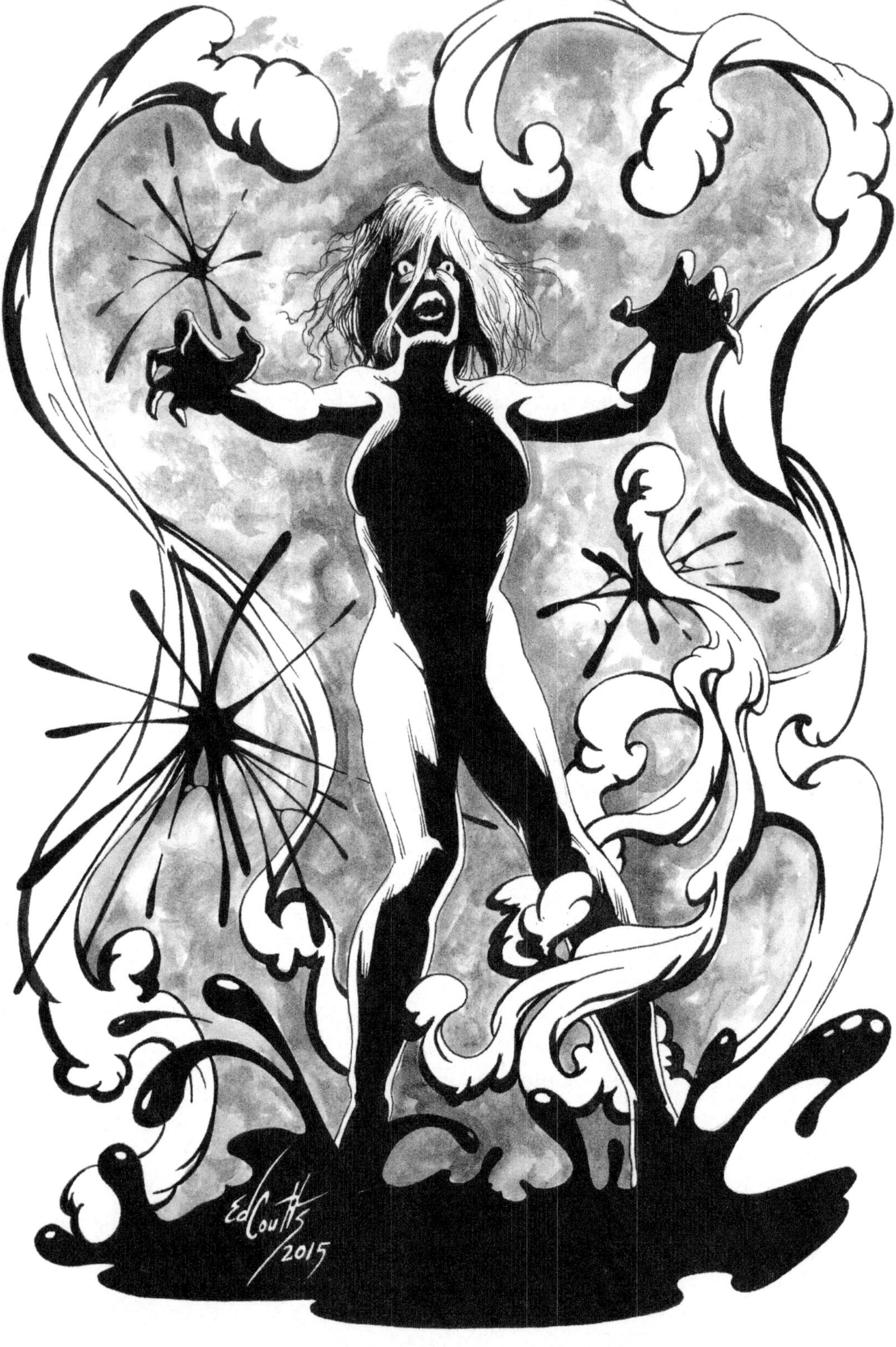
Ed Coutts
2015

as it said;

"After all, if you ever get me to run from you, where do you think I'll go?" The demon did a little dance, spinning itself madly as it screeched;

"I'll just go back into Debbie."

The taunting voice grew louder as Albert pushed himself toward his scattered bits. Beside itself with laughter, the Linda thing watched with amusement as its victim labored to pull himself back together. Stretching its body out to its fullest, the creature cooed;

"Face it, sweetie, you've got no chance. Not you or your little bitch."

Albert glowered, summoning every bit of resentment he had ever felt toward his ex-wife. Every hurt, every scorn, every bit of meanness that festered within him. If his enemy wanted to play those rules, he told himself — okay, fine — he could accommodate it.

"You bitch ... "

He muttered the words, staring for a moment, taking in once more the face that haunted him. Then, the young father spun away and used the image to focus, shielding himself in familiar armor. Without warning, Albert threw himself upward, flashing backward across the dusty plane at the Linda thing. The creature dodged his efforts, but he turned in mid-air and followed its path. His life over, shattered by one thing or another, he approached the monster's taunts with all he had.

Wrapping all the hurt he had within him around his fists, Albert burst with a dark brilliance which collapsed its way through all barriers and knocked the demon onto its back. His eyes wild with the flash of a thousand moments in time racing forward to a single instance, he slammed the laughing thing across the jaw repeatedly; he split open its mouth, broke its nose — closed one eye. The creature tittered as it wagered;

"I bet you've wanted to do this for a long time."

"Not as much as I do ... "

Both Albert and the Linda thing turned toward the new voice. Hands made of lightning and fire grabbed up the creature, squeezing its insides into jelly.

"You made my mommy leave me!"

The shape of Linda Harper disappeared, replaced by a noxious form, a repulsive thing comprised of a squat, flaccid body animated by long, angular hind legs. Its eyes were a frightened yellow hue, bulbous things filled with a red liquid which sloshed freely inside them. As the monstrous creature bellowed, its gray voice echoing raggedly across the dreamplane, the terrible hands tore it into smaller and smaller shreds, finally incinerating the bits when they were too tiny to grasp.

Albert Harper watched as his daughter dispatched the last scraps of their foe. Smiling, he attempted to rise to his feet. Finding he could not, he tried to speak. No words came forth, however, and he collapsed in a broken heap, all the fight gone from him. Silent, but content.

**

"Hey, look who's awake."

Albert blinked. The room was only dimly lit, but even the single, shaded bulb was more than he could take. Feebly placing a hand over his eyes, he croaked;

"Wha — what, what happened?"

"Shhhhhhhhh," answered Knight. "Don't try to talk. You rest. I'll explain." Albert nodded weakly. He could just make out the figure of La Rainelle somewhere in the background behind the professor. His body hurt so fiercely, he felt that the only thing keeping him from screaming was the simple fact his voice could barely work.

"If you're thinking you were sent into all that without all the facts, it's true," Knight admitted. "I knew the demon would enter your mind. Indeed, I was counting on it. It had all the advantages. Because of your connection with Debbie, the one you created when she was born by bonding with her, it's always known what was going on within your mind. There was no way you could hide anything from it."

"So ... "

"So, Madame La Rainelle lead you to it, then abandoned you. And, while you held it off, we repeated the same procedure with Debbie."

"I, I don't ... "

"Albert," Knight admonished, "please, don't try to talk. You'll only injure yourself further. Anyway, the rest is simple. Remember, with the demon no longer blocking Debbie's higher functions, she could think as clearly as anyone else."

"She is a quite remarkable child," said La Rainelle. "One of the things adults, in their arrogance, tend to forget, is the quite simple fact that children are not stupid. They simply do not possess as much information, as their elders." The old woman paused to catch her breath, then added;

"Your Debbie, once that horror had fled her mind, could think as clearly as anyone. It took me but a few minutes to inform her as to what was happening. She knows who you are, Albert Harper, and all that you have done for her."

"You have to understand, Albert," Knight said softly. "She's always known what you were doing for her, or at least, one half of her mind has. The demon sat at the juncture between those sections of the mind where knowledge was stored and where it was utilized. With it no longer there, she could suddenly make sense of all she's learned over the years."

Albert blinked, the pain from the effort nearly unbearable. Although his encounter had left him with no actual physical damage, his nerve endings were afire, all his muscles bruised. As he pieced together what Knight had told him, he whispered harshly;

"You mean … "

"I mean, there's someone here who wants to say 'hello.'"

And then, the professor and his companion stepped away from each other to allow Debbie access to the room. Heading for her father's bed at a run, she threw herself through the air, arms outstretched, hair flying wildly, eyes ablaze with happiness as she screamed;

"Daddy!"

Both Knight and La Rainelle winced as the thirty-eight pounds of joy slammed against Albert Harper's pain-drenched body. Lifting his arms, agony traveling through every inch of him as he did so, Albert wrapped them around his daughter and pulled her closer — wanting the pain of his movements, needing it — laughing as he did so.

"Oh, baby girl," he sputtered, his broken voice drowning in tears, "it's, it's … impossible."

"Silly daddy," the girl answered, her innocence trumping his belief, "nothing's impossible."

La Rainelle and Knight backed slowly out of the room. Not only were they were no longer needed, their continued presence would only have been a distraction. Father and daughter had much to discuss. Staring into Albert's eyes, Debbie smiled at her father with a warmth only a child can bestow. Then, gently lowering her forehead back to his, she eased his pain with her love.

To Wash or Not to Wash ...

"I hope he makes a habit of coming in here," Nick commented as he perused something one of the patrons had scribbled on a napkin..a linen napkin!

"Now I have to find out who did this and decide if I want to keep it, "Nick said. "Many years ago Picasso doodled on a linen napkin at the Paris Hellfire Lounge and some idiot put it in the laundry. Fortunately. someone plucked it out. Do any of you know what this napkin is worth today?"

'A few million bucks," Cher replied as she looked around at the crowd milling around the bar.

"Five million francs at least," Lucia D'Amore, the head waitress and sometime hostess interjected as she delivered a pitcher of frosty pina coladas to the table. "Ray just whipped this up for you. It's a new recipe, which means it'll knock your hats off and make you see weird things."

"He's always experimenting on my guests," grumped Nick. "One of the elves freaked out on an absinthe Shirley Temple last week and chased imaginary gargoyles around the dining room with a baseball bat."

"But gargoyles aren't imaginary," Lucia replied. "They've been around for ages."

"I know," Nick said. "Cher picked up that little one in Kolchis when she was in Greece. She rescued him from a monster of some sort."

"A basilisk, Daddy," Cher commented.

"Yeah, whatever, she keeps the little green runt as a companion. What's his name again?"

"Poe," Cher replied. "He's a rascal. I'd bring him in here, but he gets hysterical when the elves act up so I leave him at home with mother."

"Yeah, I know. She told me. Ha Ha Ha, Ruby thinks he's a rare breed of Chihuahua!" Nick laughed and pointed at Druscilla, who joined in the chuckles.

"Well," Lucia began, "if gargoyles are the topic, let me tell you a true tale of terror …"

The Knight's Watch

J. Brad Staal

The townsfolk of Baldock knew there was few things they could count on. The malt wagons carrying the day's shipment on the Great North Road headed for London. The deafening bells of Saint Mary the Virgin's cathedral that beckoned to them on Sunday. Then, there was Edwin Blair. He was the local lamplight, watchman and knocker-upper who always accompanied the setting and rising of the sun. It was a rarity to see Edwin outside after sunrise and the people of the town seemed to prefer it that way. Edwin had developed the same reputation as a black cat. It was considered bad luck to have him cross your path. It meant either you had trouble with the law or that your restful night had come to an end with the repeated rap-tap-tap of his knock on your door or window.

Edwin had been employed by the town as the lamplight and night watchman for as long as anyone could seem to recall. Like the sun and the moon, the light and the darkness, he was always there, always watching. It only seemed natural for the town's largest employer, Simpson's Brewery, to bring him on as the knocker-up shortly after they opened their doors. When the sun went down the town of Baldock belonged to Edwin Blair- bringing light to the darkness and watching from the shadows. Yet, in their wildest dreams and most bizarre nightmares, no one could really know just what it was that Edwin Blair was watching for other than Geoffrey the town drunk.

There was a lot about their nocturnal guardian that the town didn't know or chose not to know. Edwin, you see, was a Knight Templar, a member of an ancient secret society of crusader knights, who long ago vowed to protect this crossroads town and the church they founded at its center. After over a century of protecting and building the town there came that unlucky Friday the 13th in 1307. The knights that guarded the town and its secrets were scattered by the decree of Pope Clement. Most of them fled to Scotland, far out of the reach of the Pope's betrayal and stewardship of St. Mary's was given to the Knights Hospitaller.

It was 243 years later when Edwin and five other knights, descendants of the original stewards, were beckoned to Baldock after hearing rumor that St. Mary's had come under a dark and sinister presence. Upon arrival, they found that the market town founded by the Templars all those centuries ago had more than doubled in size and thrived. At its center, St. Mary the Virgin's church was now a cathedral which loomed over the entire town. Its three large bells, cast from smelted Pagan and Roman swords, could be heard for miles across the countryside. The Hospitallers had been busy expanding the church before mysteriously abandoning the project a few years earlier. The construction project was centered on the bell tower, the tallest structure in the town.

Grotesque granite gargoyles stood at the corners of the building, with more spread at even intervals in-between. Their mouths forever open, spouting gushes of water whenever it rained. Above the bell tower there stood a very different stone guardian, a larger spread-winged gargoyle with jagged teeth and fearsome claws that seemed to dig into the masonry. Its piercing eyes looked over the town. As if it was searching for - - something. This monolith was visible from every street, staring through those empty, carved eyes at all the buildings, and the townsfolk. Edwin and his companion knights inquired of the citizens of Baldock about the church. They learned that the construction had been completed ages ago, but the oversized, solitary gargoyle on the tower was a much more recent addition. And a most unwelcomed one, for it had replaced the large cross that originally topped the structure.

The rumor in town was that the addition of the highly detailed stone monster had drained the financial reserves of the previous occupants who subsequently fled town before repaying other debts that they could no longer afford. But other townsfolk, mostly elders, felt that something more sinister was afoot. No one, not a single person, had seen their neighbors leave. More ominous, they left their clothing scattered about and their food was left to spoil. Some of the children in town swore that the gargoyle, whom they nicknamed Pazu after the Babylonian demon, would change positions in the depths of the all-enveloping darkness of night. Mothers had even taken to using stories of the gargoyle to scare misbehaving children, telling them that children that wandered outside at night were taken by the stone monster never to be seen again. The story was told with some earnest as though there was some truth behind it.

Across from the town square was the stable where Edwin and his compatriots left their horses. The knights thought it was unusual for a community stable to be fitted with heavy oak doors that closed at night, secured with high-end iron locks and sliding bolts. The knights decided to take shelter in the church and planned to continue their investigations the next day.

As the sun set on Baldock, the Templars watched as everyone in the town began to hasten to their homes. There was a sense of some mild panic. By time the sun was completely gone, the doors of every home and the stable were locked tight. It was as if the celestial orb knew something they didn't and that even it feared the night.

The knights drew straws and set a schedule for standing guard. Edwin would take the early morning shift and so he began to settle in to his bedroll for the night. An hour passed without incident. The hour glass was turned over and the guard's replacement took a swig from his wine bottle before preparing to relieve his confederate. Suddenly, there was a loud commotion coming from outside of the church where the first knight stood watch. The Templar preparing for duty grabbed his sword and headed outside to investigate.

The night air fell silent as he got to the door. A strange noise punctuated the darkness. He froze in his tracks. Still, he needed to ensure his friend's safety. Edwin awoke and watched him slip out the door. The silence was soon replaced by shouting and then a blood curdling scream that pierced the night like an arrow. The remaining four knights grabbed a couple torches and their swords and rushed outside. They flung the church doors open, ready to face an army of assassins, but instead they found the lifeless corpse of their fellow Templar dismembered, mutilated. The knight's entrails were scattered across the sacred grounds. His head was missing altogether, torn from his neck by a ravenous beast. His arms had been ripped from their sockets and deep puncture wounds covered his torso. Yet, there was little blood and no tracks lead to or from the scene. No living soul could be found outside, nothing that could hold blame for this horrific act.

The Templars began patrolling the church grounds. The light from their torches was the only source of illumination. The new moon provided no aide to their task and the stars were mostly shrouded by a thick, greenish-gray cloud cover. John was the youngest of the remaining noble men. His only fighting experience had come from books and the practice grounds. His steps were slow and unsteady and he fell to the back of the group as the rest became caught up in looking for their brothers' attackers. His feet became shrouded in darkness and night mist as the lights of the torches got ahead of him. Unable to see where he was stepping he tripped over a root and was lost to the shadows.

There was a sudden great gust of malodorous wind over their heads and a muffled whimper buried within it. Edwin and the other two remaining Templars looked back and realized that the young knight was no longer in their fold … and found no sign of him. They shouted for him and scoured the church grounds, but there was nothing and no body.

"Perhaps John got tired and headed back in to the church," Edwin speculated or hoped. They nervously laughed and began to walk back to the church doors. If the boy had gone back to sleep, leaving them to patrol, he would be on midnight watch for a week.

The brothers rounded the corner of the building and saw a strange glistening on the great wood doors. They raised their torches and the orange flicker gave light to a ghastly visage. John's lifeless corpse hung on the door, puncture wounds covered his chest and sparse steams of blood flowed from the wounds. His bowels hung down to the stone below. The majority of his head was gone, only his lower jaw and flapping tongue remained above his neck, the rest was a midnight snack for a huge carnivorous beast.

One of the remaining knights, Peter, dropped his torch, losing his composure along with his supper, and took off in a sprint towards his brother. John was not simply his brother in arms, he was his flesh and blood and he had promised their mother his safe return. Peter fell to his knees in front of his brother. Sobs of anguish filled the air and the knights bowed their heads and prayed for the souls of their fallen companions ... and that this night of terror would end without more loss. That same sulfuric odor filled the air and it was as if a giant bird of prey loomed overhead.

Edwin raised his eyes along with his torch in time to see a shadow come down from the steeple and fly towards Peter. With its large wings spread and claws that glistened with fresh blood. It came down upon him like a hawk.

"Brother!" was all Edwin could get out before horror struck the band again. Peter looked back. Through his tears and saw Edwin pointing and then he looked up at the menacing shadow beast. He did not have time to scream or draw his sword. The unknown creature dug its claws deep into his flesh and pinned him down. It locked eyes with Edwin, its eyes glowed the same scarlet color as the blood it spilled. Before Edwin could move the creature flapped its great wings and left, disappearing into that unholy night with Peter's limp body in its grasp.

Of the six knights sent to investigate the town's ills, only Edwin and Willam remained .They moved closer and held their torches out as a ward. The creature, they theorized, seemed to prefer the shroud of darkness and they moved into the safety of the church and lit every candle and torch they could find. The knights left their fallen comrades and resolved to give Christian burials to their remains in the church cemetery in the safety of the daylight. Stranger still was the fact, they observed later, that not a single citizen came outside to see what the commotion was. Not a candle was it in any house. It was as if they no one dared challenge Pazu.

Sleep was not able to find the two Templars that night.

***

MORNING finally came in the shape of a giant fiery ball in the skies, vanquishing the evils of the night. The knights were prepared to pay their respects and pursue their investigations. They opened the door that held John's headless body that had been hung as bait. The door was clean and untarnished, not even a drop of his blood remained as evidence. Edwin and Willam rushed outside and looked around wildly. The people of the town had emerged from their homes and went about their business like cogs in a well maintained clock. It was as if the events of the wee hours had not happened at all. No one would acknowledge seeing or hearing anything unusual the night before.

The church yard betrayed them as well, there were no signs of the bloody massacre or of the remains of their friends. The menacing gargoyle on the clock tower was in his place with no evidence of change. From a distance it was difficult to see but Edwin swore he saw shades of scarlet on its claws When the Templars questioned the priests and townsfolk and brought up the shadowy creature they received a combination of blank stares and doors shut in their face. The looks of the children revealed a deeper truth, their eyes filled with horror, visible just before their parents yanked them inside and slammed the doors.

The brothers had been given a holy charge to investigate and protect this important crossroads town on the major trade route in the country. They could not leave this unknown and unholy demon to continue to terrorize the countryside. In their studies they had heard rumors, whispers and footnotes telling of magic aided by the ancient science of alchemy that could be used to fight demons and give light to the darkness. The elders shared stories of an old hermit alchemist named Richard who lived along the river near Baldock that had aided the earlier Templars who built the church. With few other options the knights headed off to search down the river in hopes that Richard had a resident descendent that could aid them in ridding the town of the flying terror.

Edwin and Willam rode for a few days until they came upon a small cottage along the river Ivel where the alchemist supposedly once lived. They approached the cottage cautiously, its walls were overgrown with roots and vines and they wondered if it was abandoned. Edwin approached the door and gave three solid knocks, when no immediate answer came they felt their assumption was confirmed. Just as they began to turn their backs the door creaked and moaned and they could see eyes peering suspiciously through the crack of the door.

"What do you want? There is no food or shelter here!" The voiced rasped from vocal cords that had not been used in years.

"Do you know of Richard the hermit? The stories say he lived here long ago. Are you one of his descendents?" Edwin inquired. A moment passed and he took the silence as confirmation enough to press further. "We are a part of the brotherhood of the Templar that he once helped ... Richard was a friend to us once, if he passed his knowledge on to you then we seek your aid."

Some time passed, long enough for them to question their plan. Perhaps the hermit has died as just that, a hermit without heirs. The old door opened wider and the vines that had grown over its corners snapped off. They peered inside but the dim fire inside revealed very little of the interior of the cottage.

"Thank you sir, I am Edwin and this is Willam my brother in arms." Edwin spoke politely.

"You may call me Richard." The hermit motioned them in. "Richard the Gray was ... my ancestor." He seemed a little paranoid trying to explain his connection to the hermit that lived here some 400 years ago.

"A family name?" Willam inquired with a joking tone.

The hermit shot a look back at him, Willam felt a hole being burned through him.

Richard brought them to the small table near the fireplace at the cottage's center and listened to the tale of horrors from their night in Baldock. The ominous gargoyle, the sulfuric and carrion odors and the horrific deaths of well-trained knights.

The hermit began pouring through his books and found what they described. He placed the open book in front of them, at first it appeared someone had spilled ink on the page. After a few moments the lines began to take a familiar shape. It was the grotesque creature that had slaughtered their friends. Vast wings and large claws with eyes that stared through the page, Willam stepped back and clutched his sword. It was Pazu!

The creature was an unspoken thing. Those children who nicknamed him did the town a disfavor for anyone that knew of it would never give it a name for fear of invoking the demon. It both saw and heard all that happened in the town below its perch on the great bell tower. The beast was the bastard child of Thanatos, death personified. The Templars had defeated it a thousand years ago, locking it inside a stone block and sealing it with mystic alchemical symbols. The Templars had the stone prison built into the foundation of the east end of Saint Mary the Virgin's church behind the holy altar. That was a secret that was guarded for centuries. But like many of their ancient secrets, the truth about the stone was lost when they were forced to flee the church. The renovations of the Hospitaller had largely expanded the east end and the old stone was recycled. Old carvings in the stone would have brought up talk of paganism and lead to calls for those symbols to be carved away.

Richard stood slowly, his old bones creaking and he went to his shelves and retrieved another book. He told them of the great power he could grant them with the sciences of alchemy. Edwin had heard enough about alchemy to know it often involved metal so pulled out his sword. He assumed Richard would be imbuing it with some new power, imagining Uriel's flaming sword beheading the son of Thanatos. The hermit paused and simply laughed at him, the alchemy was not for his sword but for the bearer of the sword.

Richard took the large volume and placed it in front of them. Dust from ages past remained on its cover. Through the dust they could see etched in the old leather was a golden symbol, a circle, inside a square, inside a triangle, inside a circle, alchemist's called it squaring the circle. "First I must teach you the science of alchemy. It will take time and nimble minds for you to master it."

Willam placed his hand on the enormous book and stood in front of the table staring at it. "If you had seen the evil that resides in Baldock you would know that we don't have time for this!" He pushed the heavy tome to the floor and it landed with a thud and a cloud of dust.

Edwin hesitated before moving to stand next to his fellow knight, "He is right. The people of the town cannot wait for us to go back to school. We need your help now or we will seek it elsewhere."

Richard sat in silence for a few moments, his eyes closed and his lips moving but making no sound before turning to a page about halfway through the book. He read it for a moment and turned to the next page, resting his hand on his scruffy grey chin. The two knights began to look impatient, ready to leave, until he looked up at Willam and locked eyes. The hermit had a very grave tone.

"A word of caution, perhaps. This is a power that cannot be taken back, once given it will be with you forever. It can be a blessing or a curse."

Edwin and Willam looked at each other and then back to the hermit. "Why should we ever want to give it up? We have vowed to fight until we die in battle or retire from old age." Edwin spoke with conviction. Richard smirked at the mention of old age, but wasted no more time with his impatient pupils and stood before them. He began tracing out strange symbols on their heads, arms and chests. Willam was the first to feel the marks begin to tingle quickly replaced by a burning pain as if he had been branded. The hermit began laughing like a madman as he saw his spells at work. Edwin stepped back, thinking that they had been tricked and he tried to get to the door as the burning sensation intensified. Before he could take three steps, he was over taken by the powerful spell and the world went pitch black.

When Edwin awoke, he found himself lying in a bed in the corner of the cottage. His limbs felt heavy and his head throbbed. Willam was lying in a bed a few feet away from him, still unconscious. The only light in the cottage came from the dying fire in the great stone fireplace which gave everything in the room an orange pallor. When he was finally able to lift his hand, he noticed his flesh had an unnatural tint. Edwin slowly sat up and placed his feet on the ground. They hit the floor like a blacksmith's hammer.

The hermit sat in the far corner of the cottage with his eyes locked on the knights. The dim light of the fire danced in his eyes. "How do you feel?" he asked. He didn't seem to just be inquiring out of courtesy.

Edwin took a moment to take an inventory of his faculties and replied, "Like a weight has been tied to my body and yet I feel stronger at the same time. What did you do to us?"

"I was prepared to teach you all about it, but you had no time for that." The hermit leapt up and threw another log on the fire before grabbing a polished piece of steel that was once a Roman breastplate. "Have a look for yourself!"

The light in the room began to grow brighter as the fire crackled and began to consume the new fuel. Edwin reached for the reflective metal. Even in this new light his hands were an unnatural bronze color. He grasped the edge of the steel and it crumpled like a piece of parchment, taken off guard Edwin dropped it with a clang. Richard grabbed the metal and pointed its mirror-like surface at the confused Templar.

Edwin had never had a soft or gentle face, but now the contours had become hard, angular and almost metallic, his skin matched his hands with the bronze pallor. The alchemical symbols were etched deeply into his flesh as if they were cast from molten gold. He quickly reached up to feel his face and there was the spark of metal striking metal. Edwin's eyes had been his only feature to ever receive any notice from women, described as a pale sky blue, they were now piercing dark blue, the color of hard rough cut sapphires. The knight was still taking things in when his eyes fell on Willam, "my friend? Why hasn't he awoken?"

"He came to a few hours ago, but just as I showed him his reflection he fainted, nearly broke the bed frame and shook the foundation!" Richard chuckled to himself. Edwin placed his hand down on his leg and there was a faint metallic clang. "What — what am I?"

The hermit looked as a parent being asked a silly question by a young child. "All the answers are in the book you haven't time to read, but I will explain everything after your friend wakes up," the hermit said as he motioned towards Willam. "I hate to say things twice." It was more than an hour later when Willam came to.

Richard told them their flesh was transmuted into an organic metal that could not be found in any mine and its hardness was without equal. Their strength would be that of nine men, but they must take caution as he referenced the steel that had bent so easily in Edwin's hand. They would never feel the pain of hunger or thirst again. He renewed his offer with earnest to teach them more to better prepare them for the battle to come.

Willam stomped his foot and the earth shook. The strength flowed through him. "No! We thank you for your help, but the Church of Saint Mary's and the town of Baldock cannot wait for your lessons." He gathered his things and stormed outside, the ground trembled with every step, a cup fell from a shelf and shattered.

Edwin watched his fellow knight head through the door. He looked back at Richard and then at the book. "I am sorry … you have done so much for us. We will return after the town is safe!"

Richard nodded as the knight turned and went to follow his friend. Edwin had no trouble finding Willam, he simply had to follow the one inch deep footprints. He was preparing the horses for the long ride back to town. Willam stepped into the stirrup and mounted the beast which let out a loud groan and attempted to buck the knight off, but could not for the weight.

"We seem to have put on a little weight," Edwin joked. They looked back and saw Richard cackling in the doorway. Willam dismounted and the horse breathed a sigh of relief and tried to run.

"I'm afraid you are going to have a hard time finding any beast that can handle the burden of your new selves," Richard advised through his laughter.

The knights looked to each other, "I suppose we walk then, perhaps this will give you time to find a lighter step." Edwin mused while looking at the trail behind Willam. He was quick to point out the similar one behind Edwin

They packed up their horses and prepared to walk alongside them. It was going to be a slow trip back to Baldock. The journey to see the hermit had taken only a few days, the walk back took a week. While they needed neither food nor water nor sleep, the steeds did. The knights found they could walk all day without tiring. They stopped to make camp out of habit and to rest the would-be mounts.

Willam led the way into Baldock and they found that the passive faces of the townsfolk were now filled with a combination wonder and fear at the sight of the bronze men. The two guardians of peace and justice stabled their horses and headed straight for the church preparing for the sunset. They were confident now that no demon would be a match for them. The sun set quickly that evening and the clouds rolled in over the countryside. The waxing moon would be of no help on the battlefield that foggy night. Edwin searched for a stone on which to sharpen his blade, but could find nothing. He looked down at his bronze flecked hand and began to run his finger along the blade and sparks flew as he honed his weapon.

Ominous clouds filled the night sky and the town of Baldock was swallowed whole by the pitch black darkness that could only harbor evil. The knights prepped their swords, soaked their torches in oil and headed outside to face their fates. Despite their new strength, Edwin still felt some unease. A piece of stone fell from the church wall and shattered on the ground. The knights turned quickly with their blades drawn prepared for battle. Edwin took a few steps forward and went to strike at a shadow that was moving. His sword stopped short when he saw the black cat on the wall, looking up at him with glowing green eyes.

Willam laughed at him before he joined his brother and began scouring the roof of the church for any signs of movement. An hour passed without incident before Willam took his torch and planted it in the ground. He took his sword in both hands and stepped out of the safety of the light. It was a short time before they saw movement on the roof of the church. The scent of their new flesh was alien to the beast that stalked them and it waited to make sure they were, in fact, viable prey and not some memorial statues for his most recent victims.

Willam gripped his sword tightly and heard a metallic creaking as his fingers ran together. Without warning the demon swooped down and grabbed hard at his chest and arms, knocking him back a few steps, but failing to inflict damage save for a rip in his tunic. The air was filled with a screeching sound as the phantom dragged its claws across his skin without success. Just as quickly as it struck the creature flew back into the black velvet sky. The sound it made sent a shiver through the night air. The failed attack filled them with more confidence. It gave the demon a challenge and with grim determination it knew this prey would be a unique kill.

Edwin set his torch down and went to join Willam. Soon the son of Thanatos, whom the town named Pazu swooped down from the clouds,

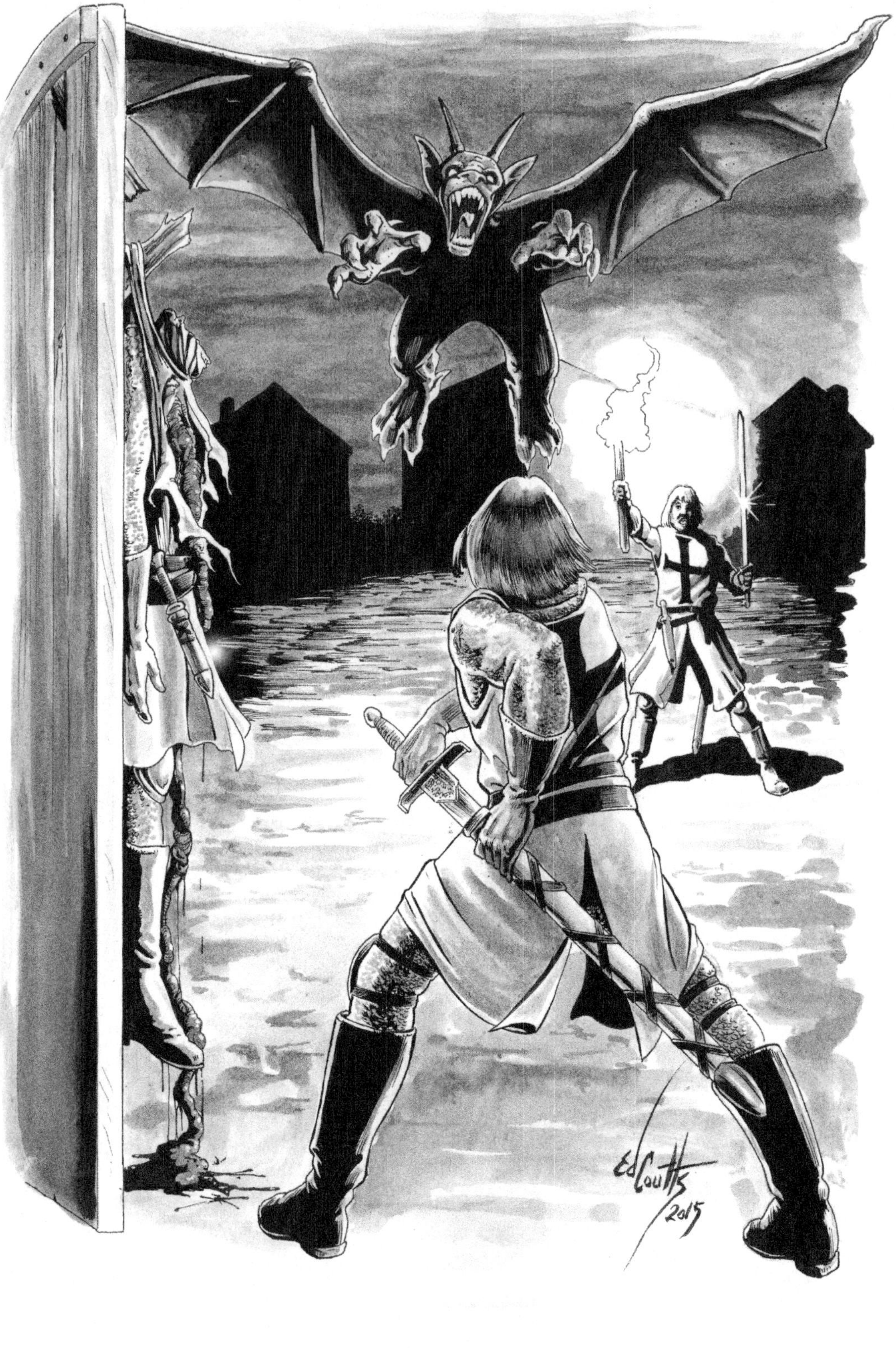
Ed Coutts
2015

attacking from behind. It found Edwin's skin to be just as impenetrable as Willam's. Frustrated and furious — thirsty for flesh and blood — it returned to the blackness. The Templars began to laugh and prepped for an offensive against the demon. Were the tables about to be turned on the bastard son of a demon?

It was a few moments before the shadow would strike again, trying to grab at Willam one more time. Edwin was prepared and struck out at the demon with his sword. He swung at it with his full strength, he felt it hit its mark and seemed to slice through like butter. At least that is what he thought, until he examined his sword and found the metal broken off inches above the hilt. He was a seemingly indestructible soldier but his sword was forged by a discount blacksmith named Gerald at a villa outside Perth. Edwin was stumped as to what to fight the beast with. Had he packed his mace?

Willam, however, was undeterred as he prepared his strike against the beast. Choosing to thrust at the flying nightmare when it attacked again. When the son of Thanatos struck at them again Willam lunged his sword hoping to hit the heart and found himself pushed back as if stabbing a wall. His sword shattered like frozen glass. Not only were their weapons of low quality it seems, but not made for such tasks as vanquishing demonic creatures of the night

The Templars were now without weapons as they gathered up their torches and tried to figure out another way to bring down the great flying evil. They could not know if the creature could hear them so they spoke in whispers, communicated in gestures. After a few moments, the knights walked to the center of the yard, Edwin handed his torch to Willam and waded into the darkness. Soon the winged demon came down on him again and as it grabbed at his arm and face Willam flung the torch at the center of the dark mass. The creature showed signs of discomfort and irritation as the torch bounced off it. Undeterred, the shadow - beast continued its attempts to rend the knight from the Earth without success. Both the demon and Edwin soon tired of the stalemate. The sound of the demon's claws grabbing at Edwin caused a high pitched, ear piercing sound like chalk on a black board. The knight thought he felt his new flesh begin to bend under the pressure. Willam ran at Pazu with the other torch and knocked it back with his shoulder. Willam looked at his fellow knight and saw a deep scratch in his face left by the demons claw, but there was no blood.

They could hear the beating of the creature's huge wings circling above their heads and they stood back to back prepared to fight. Willam threw down his torch. He had seen that it did them no good in the fight and they both stared up into the sky. They heard the demons call and knew that it was coming for them. Edwin was the first to see it this time as it swooped down in full attack mode. Just as it was about to strike there was a blinding light emanating from the church gate. It was like the sun at noon in the desert. The two knights knelt down and shielded their eyes as the light filled the sky.

"What are you waiting for?!" a familiar voice cried into the night.

The knights looked up and saw their savage attacker only feet from them with stone claws stretched out and mouth open, but not moving. In the light, the gargoyle was transformed back to stone, unable to continue his attacks. Edwin and Willam knew what they had to do, both of them making fists, bronze clubs striking at the beast with all their might. Willam's first punch took off the beast's left arm. His second blow plunged into the beats chest and caused his whole left side to crack into pebbles. Edwin came down on the beat's neck beheading it and crushed its horrible face to dust under his boot. The wings snapped off and fell to Earth with a thud and crumbled.

Even in this brilliant, holy light they could see a shadowy shape come out of the broken stone remnants and vanish upwards with a screech. The dark of night began to take back over again as the light faded. The two Templars waited for the dust to settle and looked back at the church gates and saw the old hermit Richard staring back at them through shaded spectacles. At his feet stood the black cat that had been hidden in the darkness earlier.

"Richard ... how did you ... ?" Willam looked bewildered.

"Third page of the old book you didn't have time to read." The alchemist laughed.

"So it's done? We defeated it?" Edwin asked.

"Driven back for now ... things like that have been around for a lot longer than we have. I suspect it will be around long after we're gone." Richard's tone turned from solemn to more light hearted when he looked to his cat. "By the way, have you met Jack? He's my eyes and ears in town." The cat sat at Richard's feet and stared at them unblinking. Edwin shook his head and laughed thinking back to the scare it had given them.

For the town's safety, and for a sense of justice for the fallen, the knights pulverized the remnants of the gargoyle into a fine dust. They gathered their belongings and joined the hermit back at his cottage. Over the next several years they would both become masters in the art and science of alchemy.

They returned to Baldock to act as its guardians, waiting for Pazu's return. It was a few decades later when Willam would find himself becoming restless. There was no sign of the demon and he had read every book available to them and believed he may have figured out an ancient puzzle. Willam was determined to find the location of the long sought after Holy Grail and return with it to the church of Saint Mary the Virgin where they could ensure its safety. He would leave Edwin to stand vigil as he sought out this prize. But that was a long, long time ago.

It was now autumn in the year 1766 C.E. and Edwin Blair remained as the town's sole guardian. Using the lessons taught to him by an ancient alchemist, he had been chief proponent and architect in the construction of the new gas lamps that stood along the streets. They would burn all night flooding the town with light while the sun rested. Each of these lamps was constructed with alchemical symbols etched in them to ward off demonic tampering and enhance the light they gave.

It had been two centuries since he had seen his friend Willam. That did not mean that Edwin was completely alone. He was accompanied each night by his companion, a light brown bulldog named Brutus. He wore a thick black leather collar and stood as tall as Edwin's waist. His right ear had a slight bend in it, a remnant from when he had earned his reputation as a champion bull baiter.

Edwin and Brutus were patrolling Stubcross Way when a shadow moved across the street. Brutus began to growl and the knight prepared for a fight, calling for his enemy to show itself. From the shadows jumped the black cat from that night all those years ago. Brutus stepped back a little, Jack was the only thing that seemed to scare him. The alchemist's familiar sat at the end of the street under one of the lamps. Edwin walked towards it and saw Richard come around the corner.

"Greetings old friend," he said, hoping Richard was simply paying a visit.

The old hermit looked back at him with a grave face. "It is good to see you Edwin, but we must talk of an urgent matter."

"Of course, what is it?"

"I bring word of Willam. He has found the Grail, but it may have come at a terrible price." Richard looked tired.

"Where is he?" Edwin asked as he gripped the hilt of his steel sword.

"The American colonies."

The Experiment Goes Wrong ...

It took almost half an hour before the effects of Ray's new cocktail concoction were evident. One by one, patrons at the bar, who also enjoyed the free libation Ray had provided excused themselves post haste to the restrooms, a favorite haunting ground for Elvis and his elfin entourage. The little buggers made a simple nature stop an ordeal.

"Have you noticed that more than half the crowd that was at the bar have crammed themselves into the restrooms?" Druscilla mentioned to Cher, who looked around and took notice.

"Let's skip whatever is in that pitcher and stick to the single mixed drinks," Cher replied.

"Good enough for me."

"I couldn't help overhearing you," one of the patrons said. "And, as a member of the barkeeping establishment myself, I can tell you that it's not unusual for people to react differently to the myriad libations we bartenders create. It's a hazard of the business. Let me enlighten you as to what goes on at my venue, unique in its' own right..."

B-9 Fate

A Murphy's Lore Tale

Patrick Thomas

I was in senior citizen heaven. Unfortunately, I was several decades too young to enjoy the experience. Truth be told, the hall was stifling hot, the climate that was more akin to how I felt about the place. The few fans they had around the room only moved the sultry air. There had been several apologies made for the broken air conditioner. In fact, they gave everyone a free card by way of apology.

No, I wasn't playing poker. Nor was I lucky enough to be at a greeting card convention. I was a long way from my duties bartending at Bulfinche's Pub, although several of our patrons were in attendance. It was a regular thing for some of them. Somehow, I had been suckered into going to a bingo hall. I'd had more fun at the dentist.

Still, I figured I might be missing something, considering who was here and appeared to be having a good time.

Or maybe it was fate, which was very possible, considering the ladies of the Manhattan Sewing Club, also known as the Norns and the Fates, were seated nearby. The three were avid bingo lovers, which didn't seem quite fair to me. And I said so.

"Maggie, couldn't you three just rig every hand so that you won?"

Maggie laughed, although in keeping with the crone stereotype it was really more of a cackle. I was happy to see she'd remembered to put her teeth in today. "Of course we could, Murphy, but where would the fun be in that? Before the game, we draw lots and only the one who gets the short thread governs what happens and she makes sure to not win. It's one of the few times we don't know exactly what's happening."

"So that's the thrill? Not knowing what's going to happen next?" I said.

"For us, that's a great deal," Maggie said, as she marked the last number that was called and gestured at my row of cards for me to do the same. "Although the not knowing is simply in regards to the game." Maggie looked sadly at a woman who was sitting diagonally across the way from me. She must have been in her late eighties, but she was playing the game, marking off her spaces, with the intensity of a teenager at her favorite sport.

"What's going on?" I asked, while another number was called.

Maggie shook her head and pointed again at my cards. "Just play the game, Murphy. In the long run, that's all any of us can do." Sitting directly across from me and taking up a good portion of the table, was Fred, who was attacking this new game with all his usual intensity and enthusiasm. The satyr must have had fifty cards on the table. He had a bingo marker in each hand and hadn't even bothered to sit down. He was running from one side of his cards to the other, marking off any numbers he might have.

"Murphy, I'm waiting," Fred said with a smile.

"Me, too. Waiting for this to be over," I said.

"Murphy, waiting means he needs one more number to win," said Demeter, goddess and head chief at Bulfinche's Pub, from where she was sitting on the other side of Maggie.

The older woman sitting diagonally across from me, whose name was Mildred, smiled and turned to Fred. "Congratulations. You're doing very well." Mildred had been tutoring the satyr in the game and seemed both proud of the young satyr and genuinely happy for him. Of course, Fred had his baseball cap and false feet on, so she thought he was just an ordinary guy. In some cases, it doesn't pay to advertise.

"Beginners luck," Fred said, but I noticed he was posed over that one card, ready to pounce with his bingo marker should that number be called out next.

The next number was called. It wasn't the one that Fred was waiting for.

"Shoot," Fred said, but he rushed to mark off his slew of cards. Down the table, there was a whooping and hollering. It was coming from Hercules and Main. No, it wasn't a street corner down in the village, but two divinities who apparently had just high-fived each other because the latest number put them into the waiting category as well. That had become close since beating a shadow stag that almost killed a bunch of us and started an imitation nuclear winter.

Sitting across from them, Coyote, in canine form, put his bingo marker back onto the table and muttered, "This is ridiculous. There's got to be some way to fix this game so it works better." Better meaning so he won. The god was working some kind of mojo that made sure people didn't think it odd that a canine was participating in the game.

Sue, the youngest of the Fates turned and looked Coyote straight in the eyes. "Don't even think about messing with this game."

Coyote muttered something under his breath and then said, "I never have this trouble on the reservations." He knew better than to mess with the ladies of the Manhattan Sewing Club. No one, not even the most foolhardy trickster, wants to end up on the wrong side of the Fates.

Another number was called.

"Ooh. I'm waiting!" Mildred said, practically bouncing up and down in her chair like a kid about to open a stack of birthday presents.

"I've been playing bingo for thirty years and I've never won the jackpot. I hope it happens before I die. I'm not getting any younger, you know," Mildred said, half joking.

All three of the Manhattan Sewing Club suddenly turned their eyes down and paid intense attention to their cards. That didn't bode well.

The sinking feeling I was getting in the pit of my stomach became an emotional Titanic as the next player sat down across from me, right between Fred and Mildred.

"John?!" I said. I wasn't happy to see John Thanatos. I don't think that I was ever exactly happy to see John outside of Bulfinche's Pub. Almost no one would imagine that the handsome man was in fact the Grim Reaper, although the ladies of the Manhattan Sewing Club didn't seem surprised to see him.

Death had a single bingo card and marker. He hadn't bought any cards for the later games.

"John, are you working?" I mouthed. John gave me a look that more than encouraged me to be careful. He enjoyed the time he spent in Bulfinche's Pub and didn't want to lose that. He also didn't want anyone at the table who wasn't already aware of his true nature to be let in on his secret identity.

Silently, I turned and pointed with my eyes at Mildred. John nodded. I then pointed to my watch and John held up one finger, then five. Mildred had fifteen minutes before her waiting would be over and her final number would come up.

I knew there was nothing I could do to change that. John and I had gone over this in private at the bar on more than one occasion. There are only certain circumstances in which life can be extended and for most, the action needs to be taken by the dying themselves, not another on their behalf. I knew John's argument. He was only doing his job. In some way, he was providing a service Mildred needed. He would point out she had lived a long and good life. Still, it didn't seem fair to me.

I turned and whispered in Maggie's ear. "Is she at least going to win?"

"No," Maggie said.

I lowered my voice even more. "C'mon, Maggie. The woman just made what turns out to be a dying wish. I'm not asking you to extend her life any, just let her win."

Apparently, I'd said that last part a little too loudly, at least around people with enhanced hearing, because Fred, Hercules, Main, Demeter, and Coyote all turned their eyes towards us. Fortunately, they assumed that Maggie had let me in on events, rather than suspecting John. That, or John was working his own mojo.

"It has already been woven," Maggie said.

"C'mon, you've got to be able to do something," I pleaded. Maggie smiled and it wasn't a pleasant one. While she had put her teeth in, it suddenly appeared she had been neglecting proper cleaning techniques for her dentures.

"So you wish her to win the game,
thus have her fifteen minutes of fame.
If you're willing to make a deal,
then with winner's delight she may yet squeal," said Maggie. I took it as a bad sign she was speaking in verse. She was on the clock now.

"What do you want?" I said. I admit I had some idea. I don't claim to be a super stud or the best looking man around, but Maggie was always pestering me for a kiss. I assumed it would be something along those lines.

"Destiny can sometimes be changed,
for a price fate rearranged.
I ask you once, even twice,
"*Murphy, are you willing to pay that price?"* Maggie whispered.
"Probably."
"I give you poetry,
I give you rhyme.
You answer only 'probably,'
are you wasting my time?" said Maggie.

"Give me some credit. I'm not going to blindly agree to do something without knowing what it is." For some reason, I felt bad that my answer hadn't rhymed.

Maggie nodded, as if I had passed some sort of test.

"To do before her final breath does seep,
I can tell you what you ask does not come cheap.
I can help this you with this,
but to succeed will cost more than a kiss."

Numbers continued to be called. Maggie continued to play, while I neglected my cards. Fred simply turned them around his way and marked them off for me.

"What price?" I asked.

"Bingo!" Fred shouted, waving one of his many cards in the air. The number he had been waiting for had come up. One of the runners in the hall picked up his card and started reading off the numbers. All of them had been called, so they caller announced, "We have a bingo."

Fred won fifty dollars. The game was continuing for the jackpot for the first person to fill up an entire card. That was the big jackpot.

"I have the answer you seek,
the price is one week," Maggie whispered.

"One week of what?"

"Of your hopes, your dreams,
your very breath,
because this week will bring
you one week closer to death."

"I give up a week of my life and Mildred wins her big jackpot?" Maggie nodded.

"How much time do I have?" Maggie just smiled. She rarely gave away any details about the future that didn't suit her purposes. "What if I don't have a week?"

"Then your days will be over,
ended by you pushing up clover.
Although this will make her spirit soar,
even a year would not buy her a minute more.
The time has come for you to say,
is this a price you are willing to pay?"

"Is the term negotiable?"

"No." Maggie looked at me.

"Oh Murphy, this is silly,
are you willing to die early
to give a thrill to Milly?
She's lead a good life,
been a grand old dame.
If you walk away,
no one will assign you the blame,
after all this is only a game."

"And all any of us can do is play the game, right?" I said. Maggie was absolutely correct. A week of my life just so some grandmother I just met could win a game that I didn't even like really didn't seem like a fair trade at all. There was no reason why I should do it, except maybe that I had hung out at Bulfinche's Pub too long. When I first found the place, there was no reason for Paddy to help me, especially after what I did to him. I tried to steal his pot of gold and had justified my actions by rationalizing it would get me out from under the control of a loan shark, who would have broken my legs, if not worse. The wrong that I'd done didn't matter to Paddy and he helped me. The boss continues to help others, even though sometimes it costs him dearly. If Paddy ever found out I had a chance to help someone and I didn't, he'd be disappointed in me. I would be ashamed of myself, because I'd done less than I could have. When I weighed things out, helping Mildred was more than worth the week.

"I'm in," I said. Maggie smiled a tartered grin. I realized she had probably been playing bingo with Mildred for years and had possibly arranged this whole thing, not that she'd ever admit it.

Across the way, Fred had followed the entire conversation.

"I'll take half of that week," Fred said. Both Maggie and John nodded, impressed by the satyr. John and Fred had developed a friendship of sorts. Fred didn't know John's true identity, but he could regularly beat John at chess, a game which Death is noted to be an expert at. It impressed the heck out of the Grim Reaper. Mildred, fortunately, was concentrating too hard on her cards to be paying any attention to the conversation. As the next number was called she exclaimed, "I'm waiting!"

I looked at Maggie. "Thanks."

She nodded. A moment later someone else climbed up to seat height, situating himself between Maggie and me.

"Look, I'm not into this nobility crap, but Murphy's doing the right thing. Why don't we just divide the time among the three of us," Coyote said.

From down the table Hercules waved. "Make it four."

"No, five," Main said. I guess heroes have pretty good hearing, too.

"Even better with six," said Demeter.

"Sorry, lads and lady. You know that your natures prevent you from making a deal like this and the matter at hand doesn't have enough time for us to reach an agreement. I'm afraid it's going to have to be split between Murphy and Fred," Maggie said, finally back to normal speak.

Mildred's number was called; she marked it and shouted "Bingo!"

The numbers were read and it was a bingo. Hercules and Main got up out of their chairs, picked up Mildred's chair and carried her to the front to collect her winnings. They brought her back and everyone congratulated her.

"I have to tell my daughter about this," Mildred said, pulling out a cell phone and dialing. John Thanatos began to reach out for her.

My head snapped up and I pleaded with my eyes. It got my point across. Looking in John's eyes was usually a very disturbing experience. There were things there that mortal men with time still left to live were not meant to see. It usually unnerved me, but this time, I didn't turn away. I simply fought hard not to shake from the chill that ran up and down my spine.

John looked at me in frustration. He understood my point, but threw up his hands. Then he looked towards the ladies of the Manhattan Sewing Club who, oddly enough, had chosen that moment to look at the ceiling and off to the sides and whistle. Behaving in a way that ensured they would be unable to see anything John did or didn't do.

Mildred kept the conversation brief. Bragged a little bit and told her daughter that she loved her and to pass it along to her grandchildren. She hung up the phone.

"Oh, that was wonderful. I waited thirty years. I thought that it would never happen," Mildred said.

John was wearing a cell phone, which chose that moment to go off. He looked at the screen and excused himself, saying there was some business he had to take care of. I was still wrestling with the implications of who was texting him. John didn't take his card or marker with him, instead handing them off to Fred.

"The two of you paid dearly for a moment of Milly's happiness. You deserve to see this. Each of you take one of my hands," Maggie said to Fred and me. We did and watched as Death returned to the bingo hall.

Death didn't come as John Thanatos. Neither did he come as the Grim Reaper. This time, Death came as a kindly older gentlemen with a bus driver's uniform and a cap. The emblem on the cap was a smiling skull. Apparently, Mildred saw Death as something of a tour guide.

"MILDRED, IT'S TIME TO GO."

"Who are ... " But Mildred didn't have to complete the sentence. She recognized Death. She wasn't afraid, but she did look a little sad. At that point, Mildred seemed to split into two. The more solid one fell to the table. The more ethereal one stood up.

"Can I take my pictures with me?" she asked.

"ALREADY DONE," said the tour guide Death, pointing to the spirit version of her purse, complete with photographs. She turned and looked down at her now-slumped body.

"What happened? Stroke?"

"YES."

"I finally won the big jackpot. I was beginning to think you'd come for me before it happened."

"I ALMOST DID. YOU HAVE THESE TWO GENTLEMEN TO THANK FOR YOUR GOOD FORTUNE."

"Really?" Spirit Mildred walked over to Fred and kissed him on the cheek. "Thank you."

"You're welcome," Fred said. "Thanks for helping teach me how to play."

"My pleasure." Mildred looked at the table and an impish grin came across her face. She turned towards Death and asked "Can I?"

The tour guide Death smiled. "YES."

Mildred walked through the table like it wasn't there and giggled like a school girl. She kissed me on the cheek as well. "Thank you."

"You're very welcome." She walked back through the table and over to Death. He extended an arm, which she took and held gently.

"So what happens now?"

"THAT DEPENDS A LARGE PART ON YOU. I HEAR THERE ARE A GOOD MANY FRIENDS AND FAMILY WAITING TO WELCOME YOU."

They headed out of the bingo hall, Mildred waving good-bye to the people at our table. The ladies of the Manhattan Sewing Club waved back. Maggie blew her a kiss. Mildred stopped and waved good-bye to several other people, but they couldn't see her. As they neared the exit, someone yelled for an ambulance. Maggie let go of our hands and the pair faded from view.

The Evening Marches on, the Strangers March in …

In a blink of an eye the stranger disappeared into the dining room just as the stage entertainment started. It was hard to hear the stand up comic who warmed up the audience before the singer came out because there were distinct click-clack sounds coming from one of the banquettes

"Look, some new guy has set up office space at that table," Cher pointed out to Druscilla, who was in mid-bite of her lobster claw. "He's got an old Underwood typewriter, like from the Fifties."

"Think maybe he's a writer?" Druscilla replied sarcastically as she popped a shrimp into the mouth.

"Just great," grumped Nick as he passed by. "First, that white-bearded author takes over a banquette as a sales outlet and now we have a young Hemingway taking up four seats to write a 'masterpiece.'

"Hey, Buddy, if you want to hog the space you owe us a story — a good one, something weird that goes with Ray's bubbly abominations."

He turned and said to the girls, *sotto voce*, "You should smell those restrooms. Now's that's Hell for ya!"

The young writer stopped typing and arose, spread his arms out to garner attention and started his delivery, pausing only now and then to pop a fried mozzarella nugget into his mouth and swallow it whole. He began …

Iris and Kayyalı: Beyond Trolltown

Patrick Loveland

"You mean Istanbul?" Iris asked, raising a thick, pink-speckled blue plastic tray up a bit to catch the mysterious stew that a pleasant looking churchgoer was ladling out.

"I mean Constantinople," Kayyali responded from within a thick, partible parka hood.

It bothered Iris that Kayyali almost never pulled his hood down, but that wasn't the only thing that did or anywhere near the worst. She didn't much like Kayyali, but they had both escaped from a rough situation and ended up looking out for each other. She didn't much care what he thought of her either but she suspected it was similar for him.

In a pidgin language they both knew but she was positive these church people wouldn't Iris said, *"How old are you anyway?"*

"Don't hold the line up," Kayyali said.

Iris took a few steps down the food line and an almost maniacally grinning pastor gently placed two warm dinner rolls, a pack of sealed plasticware, and a couple of wrapped butter pats on Iris's tray as Kayyali prepared to accept his stew. She balanced the tray in one hand and picked up an apple juice from an ice bath at the end of the line.

She tried to ignore an old lady posted just past the ice bath who was handing out religious pamphlets, but Kayyali cleared his throat in a way she knew meant she was being rude. Iris clamped the offered pamphlet casually between the top two fingers on her apple juice hand. She strode out of the way of Kayyali's path and that of three dozen homeless or otherwise downtrodden wretches still making their way down a row of banquet tables the churchgoers were using for their Christ-like generosity fest.

Iris wondered what the fenced-off square of gravel lot was used for when it wasn't the scene of a food line. Ten-foot wide canopies lined almost the entire square inner border of the lot which Iris decided was good because it was a misty evening and rain couldn't be far behind. In the short time they'd been in the pacific northwest of the United States, she'd picked up on some of the subtle idiosyncrasies of their cold, wet weather.

She and Kayyali were not so long ago in a place far to the north capable of having much colder weather, but there wasn't snow as far as the eye could see here, at least. No energy-sealed cages here either…

They had escaped a large underground facility in a region of the arctic they had never bothered to pinpoint after finally gaining their freedom. They never planned on returning, since the rest had made it out too and didn't need rescuing. Most of the rest had made it, would be more accurate.

Kayyali was one of the less obvious "deviations" in terms of outward appearance, as was Iris. That's how they had come to traverse mountains, ride freight trains, and walk in the open when many of their fellow "Deviants"—as they called each other as a play on their former captors' clinical label—had to move by night for more than one reason. She and Kayyali weren't much fond of the sun either, but they could stand it when necessary.

Even now, though, Iris looked up from the questionable contents of her tray and watched as the fine churchgoers gave Kayyali sideways looks and the ladler's hand shook as she did her volunteer duty. He nodded and thanked her politely and advanced to receive his rolls and such and the pastor's grin was only half as maniacal for Kayyali.

Kayyali looked more normal than your average Deviant, but he was covered in scar tissue, some of it overlapping in almost obscene looking folds and crevices. Also a bit unsettling, his eyes were a pale blue-gray which contrasted strongly with his dark-olive skin and they seemed slightly clouded over, but his vision was perfect.

Kayyali took a pamphlet from the last churchgoer and followed Iris to a plastic table and chair set along the fence line perpendicular to the food line and under the canopies. They sat and started to eat.

"So, maybe we should think about finding a more permanent setup... again. I hear there are whole chunks of mostly unused underground city in Moscow," Iris said.

Kayyali frowned like he was trying to think of a better way of saying what he was thinking but went ahead anyway and said, "Your black skin and homosexuality would not go so well there, from what I remember. Even among the cast-downs and throwaways. My past there would make it even worse. Even living in the shadows below would not keep you safe I don't think."

Iris watched the line of homeless and poor zip up coats and throw up their hoods as it started sprinkling.

"Paris then? I hear there's a lot of underground there."

Kayyali thought a moment and replied, "I say that we stay fluid until maybe the rest find a new home and then we join them. Also, our scouting has been fruitless thus far, but we could still find something down here... or even further south. It is important to remember, though, that underground only meets one requirement," then he switched to the pidgin the Deviants had developed in captivity to communicate secretly as a well-bundled hobo cradling a plate approached and sat near them.

"We are... monsters to these people. That is why the bad ones like them took and studied us. We are as different to each other as all of us are to them, but what we share is that difference and it binds us. We should be with our own, and only our own. It just might take some time," he finished in English.

The bundled hobo seemed to notice their cautiousness and said, "Name's Rich. I'm nothin' to worry about. Just here to eat."

"Your name is Rich? Ironic, right?" Iris said and chuckled.

Rich sighed and said, "Yeah, hilarious."

Kayyali gently elbowed Iris. She scowled at him but stopped upon receiving what she always thought of as his all-business face. She sheepishly looked back at Rich and said, "Hey, no offense."

Rich said, "Not worried about it."

A round of yelling met with cautious complaints near the open fences of the lot entrance drew their attention away from Rich's unfortunate name and Iris's insensitivity.

Eight or nine scraggly, mean looking men strode into the lot with purpose. They looked like freight-hoppers and wore packs and hobo ensembles of denim and warm layers and coats. The only thing that was the same on all of them was a black bandana around each of their necks, at least on the ones where that area was visible. More black bandanas were worn around legs, arms, or curling out from a jeans back pocket, and the meanest looking one in the front wore another tied as a thick headband from his brow line up to almost the top of his head. They moved down the food line, pulling back hobo's hoods, getting real close, and examining everyone. No one was happy about it, but no one protested real strongly.

Rich let out a soft, "Shit" to himself.

Kayyali asked, "What is happening?"

"FTRA shakedown or some shit. They don't usually make their presence so obvious."

"FTRA?" Iris asked.

Rich said, "You don't look new to riding the rails. You never heard of 'em? They're kinda like… bikers without bikes? Gang'uh burnouts, racists, tweakers, and scuzzy bastards who ride the rails too, only they're like king shit riders. Hey, just don't piss 'em off, for both our sakes, huh?"

The gang of unwholesome freight-riders ignored over-gentle protests from the church group as they made their way past the food line and along the line of plastic tables and chairs under the canopies. Unsatisfied by the hobos and vagrants on that side, they followed the corner around toward Rich, Kayyali, and Iris, the only ones sitting on the back row.

The leader sauntered up to them and stopped, so the rest of them did too. Some of them kept scanning all around while the others looked hard at the three diners because the leader was.

Headband, as Iris decided to think of him, bent over and cocked his head to get a look at Kayyali under his hood and winced a bit. Noticing this, one of the minions stepped forward to pull the hood off of Kayyali's head but Headband grabbed the grungy man's outstretched arm.

"I can see it ain't the kid, fuckin' moron," Headband growled then pulled the minion away from Kayyali and handed him back his arm as he straightened back up. Kayyali nodded in acknowledgement of what could be perceived as something like politeness.

Headband said, "We're lookin' for a young guy." He made a point of looking at Iris and winking as he said, "White…" then to Kayyali and Rich, "…leather jacket with that punk shit all over it—bright green Mohawk if he's stupid enough to still have it. He's our problem an' not worth a shit of trouble for nobody else."

Rich said, "I haven't seen 'im."

Headband glared at Rich but his tone was calm and even as he said, "Well, if you do, you'll send it on down the grapevine, right?"

Iris was pretty sure Headband was really high on something but didn't care to guess what. These types didn't scare her, but she knew all too well what happened if too many more normals found out about her and Kayyali's *special attributes*.

Plus: she knew Kayyali had a strict no-show policy on their true selves unless absolutely necessary. In fact, Iris hadn't actually seen Kayyali's true form for herself and she wasn't sure she wanted to. In any other circumstances Iris wouldn't give two shits about that or someone's opinion of her actions, but even the Examiners—the name they had for the pseudoscientific paramilitary goons who had held them—seemed to be afraid of, or at least nervous around, Kayyali, and that wasn't an easily earned honor.

"W-will do," Rich stammered. Kayyali nodded his answer and Iris did the same after a long moment.

"Sounds *great!* Enjoy your food," Headband said and strolled away with his gang in tow. They made their way out of the gravel lot and were quickly out of sight in the thickening sprinkles.

Rich spat at the ground and said, "Pieces'uh shit."

"But they seemed so nice," Iris said.

"Hey, you guys sleepin' out?" Rich asked.

"Yes," Kayyali replied.

"I can't recommend that, 'specially with those jackasses roamin' around. Might wake up dead. I can get you into *Trolltown*."

Kayyali and Iris just looked at him.

"It's a shanty camp under a big river overpass a little ways into the woods. Don't worry, it's just a name—no real monsters there."

"Oh man, I'm glad you said that. I was worried," Iris said, deadpan enough that Rich took a second to decide how to take it.

"Cute. Anyway, if I'm with you, should be fine gettin' in."

They looked at each other and Kayyali nodded his approval. Iris thought a bit longer, then nodded and said, "Sure. Thanks."

Rich said, "Wealth isn't always about money I guess."

Iris wasn't sure what that meant but he was half-smiling as he said it so she decided she was forgiven.

***

After finishing their meals, Iris and Kayyali slung their packs and followed Rich through the rain-battered town and into the forest on its eastern edge.

A little less than a mile into the woods, Iris noticed the sound of cars on a highway. A quarter mile after that, she heard the sounds of a river. Just a bit further and they could see both. The highway rose and curved away from them over the decent-sized river, and, in the dark under the bridge overpass and behind a high fence which stopped a ways into rushing river water, Iris could make out the shanties, tents, and draped cloth and tarp of what could only be 'Trolltown'.

Rich led them through knee-high overgrown grass to a cutout in the fence that had been re-attached with zip-ties to create a kind of hinged action across the top, allowing it to be used for entry without looking like it could.

"It's like a doggie door…" Iris said.

Rich said, "It serves its purpose. Not too worried about people's feelings or conceptions here if it's functional." He crouched down and went through it then stood and held it for them. After Kayyali and Iris were through and up, Rich let the door of fence patch fall back into place. It made a tinny scraping and tinkling sound as it made contact which set Iris's teeth on edge.

They followed Rich through more tall grass the short distance into the "town square" at the rough center of the makeshift housing Iris had seen from their approach. She noticed a kind looking—possibly Native American—woman lighting candles placed in cheap Chinese paper lanterns hung in about a dozen spots. The lanterns were almost all different and some even had the shape of cute, cartoonish animals and must've be for children. Another resembled a Jack-o-lantern. Their multi-colored glow was comforting in the darkness under the overpass, if Iris was being honest with herself.

Iris heard a generator being pull-started somewhere out of sight on the other end of the camp and once it kicked on, roots reggae music and strings of bluish-white Christmas lights strung between the tops of tent poles and hooks on shanty walls came on in sections and twinkled a little over head level all around the camp. She smiled, which was rare for her, and caught a little gleam in Kayyali's murky eyes as he looked around at the lights.

Rich was out of sight in what must've been his tent for just a moment and upon returning he produced a large bag of what looked like juice with big chunks of fruit half-dissolved in it.

He said, "We got dinner out of the way..." In his other hand was a stack of bright blue and red plastic cups. "...so let's get to dessert!"

***

Of course, the bag of juice was powerful fermented fruit alcohol, also known as "pruno". It was actually a pretty drinkable batch and/or recipe in general and Iris and Kayyali—not wanting to be rude—drank their fair share. They drank with Rich, the Native American girl Hope, the generator starter Dave, a dwarf called "Chicago", and a colorful band of more nameless misfits and loners. A rare fun time was had and Iris almost wished these normals were real monsters so that she and Kayyali could finally settle down... again.

***

Something woke Iris up from a dream about an alternate Trolltown filled with those real monsters and some of her own creature friends from "The Bottle"—their former home and prison. She'd had worse hangovers, but she definitely didn't feel spectacular.

The rain was steady and the sound mixed with the running river to create a soothing effect, so for a few moments she just watched Kayyali sleep a few feet from her across Trolltown's square—they opted for using their own sleeping bags since the townies had made a fire anyway. The fire was just brilliant embers now and most of the Chinese lanterns had flicked out, as had the generator, so the Christmas lights were out too.

In the faint light of the last few lanterns and the embers, Iris could make out Kayyali's face fluttering a bit under his draped parka hood almost like the layered wings of an insect spreading out and folding back together—but it was layers of flesh, not little wings and there was a strange glow from somewhere deep within that was mostly obscured by all the folds. She was no beauty when she showed herself either, but she could only imagine what his real face was like. The Examiners had always taken Kayyali into sealed surgery and observation theaters to study him so Iris and the others had never seen his truer form. She looked around to see if any normals could see this but everyone was down for the count.

A shriek and tinny clang of thin metal colliding drew her focus. *The doggie door?*

Iris crawled to Kayyali and shook him awake. His face fused entirely upon waking to look like the scar pattern Iris was used to seeing and his eyes blinked open.

"What?"

"I heard that gate door open and close," Iris said.

Kayyali locked eyes with her and, despite their differences, his trust in her instincts negated any need to question her further. He threw open his unzipped sleeping bag and only stopped to rub his temples and groan before hauling himself up to his feet. Without having to discuss it, they both rolled their bags up and attached them to their packs in case they needed to leave quickly.

They took heavy foot-long flashlights from sheathes on the sides of their packs and headed for the fence without turning them on. They didn't actually need them to see in the dark but they made for good truncheons when necessary.

As they approached the fence line, they half-crouched and went silent. There was no one in sight, but that just made them more cautious. The steady-falling rain just past the fence line went from soothing to the opposite due to its ability to interfere with their heightened sense of hearing.

Kayyali abruptly stopped so Iris did. She smelled what he must have: blood. They looked at each other and scanned the area again. Iris noticed a patch of bright, artificial green amidst the tall grass and made a gesture to get Kayyali's attention then pointed at the green.

They advanced carefully and stopped again at the sound of a tortured moan. Closing the final distance revealed a young white man with 'punk shit' all over his leather jacket and a bright green currently-limp Mohawk he was apparently stupid enough to still have.

The 'kid' started moaning and crying into the long grass as he clutched his abdomen with bloody hands. Kayyali touched his shoulder and said, "Do not be alarmed," which had the opposite effect and sent the kid flailing and crawling away from them back toward the hinged section in the fence.

As the kid forced himself up to a crouch to get through the doggie door, a suppressed gunshot was heard out in the dark woods. The bullet grazed the fence, just missed the kid's shoulder, and ended up going between two of Kayyali's ribs only to hit one on the other side of his ribcage interior before ricocheting more languidly into his left lung. Iris dropped all the way down to the grass out of instinct, as did the kid, but his dropping was only half intentional. Kayyali sunk roughly onto his butt in the grass and breathed in repeatedly like he'd only had the wind knocked out of him.

From the woods Headband yelled, "Do not help that kid! He's our business! I'll burn that whole place!"

"Fuh-hngk-F-fuck *you!*" the kid forced out, flinging blood spittle from his lips.

"That you, Jake? Hey, is it gettin' hard t'breath yet? And walk? If you'd just taken it in the head like you should'a, I could've made this a lot less painful."

Jake the kid tried to curse Headband again but just coughed and moaned instead.

Iris crawled to Kayyali and grabbed his arm gently but firmly to get him to look at her. He smiled mirthlessly and nodded.

"I'm fine."

"I figured. So let's get out of here already," Iris said.

Kayyali gestured toward Jake and said, "And him?"

"What about him? He's a dead punk we don't owe shit."

Iris heard rustling and cracking from the tree line through the sounds of rain and river.

"Are you a *monster?*" Kayyali asked of Iris.

"What the hell?"

"Yes or no?!" he now demanded.

"No!"

"You act like one!"

Iris said, "It's a fucking word! I'm not normal… What's the difference, old man? If I showed myself, it would be a small difference…"

"And yet for him it could be everything. Not to mention… how can we blame what you call normals for hating us if we truly are monsters, in flesh or otherwise."

Iris listened to the sounds of approach and hated Kayyali real hard for a moment before rising to a crouch, crawling to Jake, and hooking her arm under him.

"I s'pose you won't give us a pass on the no-show, huh?"

Kayyali shook his head.

"Okay, but if we're doing this, you need to get off your old ass."

Kayyali got to his feet as Iris half-dragged/half-assisted Jake's stumbling toward Trolltown square. He followed her to their packs, put his on and helped her with hers, also re-sheathing their flashlights.

Rich came out of his tent rubbing his eyes and kneaded his crotch like he was heading to the river to piss. He saw them in the dim light of the last lanterns and fire embers and said, "Jesus! What's goin' on? Is that blood?!"

Iris said, "That gang is here for their kid." She nodded to her charge.

"Y-you've gotta go!"

Kayyali coughed and said, "We know. Is there another fence opening on that side?"

"Nobody comes from that direction so we just go over or around the fence. Shit—I'll help you but get him out of here."

They all rushed as best they could through Trolltown to the far fence. Kayyali effortlessly hopped up onto it and climbed with one hand while pulling his rolled sleeping bag out of its straps. He placed it across the top of the fence and straddled it.

Iris climbed onto the fence one-handed as well while handing Jake up to Kayyali like a sack of groceries. Rich went slack-jawed upon witnessing their incredible and unexpected agility.

Kayyali noticed and said, "We get good exercise on the road."

"I guess you do..." Rich said.

Iris was up and over the fence in an instant then dropped the twelve feet to the grass on the other side into a crouch. She rose back up and took Jake's half-conscious bulk from Kayyali like it was almost nothing. Kayyali dropped too and his legs absorbed the shock but as he came up he coughed and groaned.

Iris said, "Are you—"

"Let's go."

Without acknowledging Rich again, they rushed through the rain for the tree line ahead of them, Iris with Jake's arm hooked behind her neck and her fingers down in his belt loops.

Just before they reached the eastern woods, they heard yelling and sounds of struggle back in Trolltown so they stopped. Kayyali must've been thinking but Iris couldn't see his face in his dark parka hood. Then he turned, grabbed her flashlight from the side of her pack, crooked his elbow to grab his own, and flicked them both on.

Kayyali waved the bright flashlights back and forth over his head as a flight deck worker would and whistled high and loud like you might to a distant dog. He started flicking the lights off and on as he waved them and fluttered the whistle too, trying not to go unnoticed.

A bullet whizzed through the rain and hit a tree about ten feet to their right.

Kayyali turned off the lights and headed into the deep shadows of the tree cover and Iris followed, but he stopped several feet in, turned back, and watched Trolltown and the overpass. Iris wasn't entirely sure what he was up to but she trusted him enough not to ask.

After less than a minute, she could see several of the black bandana wearing gang members hopping the high fence and helping each other over, then a few ran across the overpass between a late night driver here and there.

When all nine of them were in view, Kayyali turned and advanced through the dark forest. Iris realized he was trying to lure them away from the relative innocents in Trolltown, but she wouldn't have bothered so it had taken her a bit to get that.

Headband taunted from a distance behind them but the rain and fluttering trees masked the words. Kayyali just silently trudged forward as Iris followed and helped Jake do the same.

"What's your plan?" Iris asked.

"From my memory of the local maps, there is a town with a hospital this direction. We just have to stay ahead of them."

"They'll c-catch ush-hngk…" Jake spat out.

"Kayyali, if we keep our hands tied, he's probably right."

"And?"

"So I say we set him down for a minute, take out the trash, then go to the hospital."

Kayyali said, "Not while he is awake, which we must keep him if he is to live."

Iris scoffed and shook her head.

"You can leave if you like. I will take him there."

Iris stopped and said, "No foolin'? *You shall release me?* Oh thank you, infallible master."

Kayyali stopped and looked back at her with a dark—even in darkness—expression on a face which fluttered at the scar-seams.

"If you want to make this petty and personal, I will oblige you. Just not now… and not here."

Jake swayed at the end of Iris's loosened grip and mumbled, "Can we knh-keep goin'?"

Iris weighed her options. She really wanted to drop this punk kid and go some rounds just to see what Kayyali was made of once and for all. It occurred to her, though, that she might not win and—if she was being honest with herself—she would probably get really lonely without him if she *did*, condescending asshole or not.

A train horn sounded in the woods behind them in the distance to their left. Iris and Kayyali looked at the trees in the direction of the sound then locked back on each other. They nodded in silent agreement and rushed forward and to the left of their original path.

After a few minutes of hurried hiking, they could see tracks through the trees. They made their way to the border between the trees and gravel of a slight rise the tracks were installed upon.

The freight train was coming but fast.

Jake mumbled, "Too nhn-fasht… Goin'toofast…"

"Maybe for you, kid," Iris said.

They let the train engine car pass and—since it appeared to be a long one—they waited in the downpour edge for a good spot to hop on nearer to the end.

Kayyali and Iris started to run at pace with the train and Kayyali leapt up and onto the ladder at the rear of a freight car. Iris matched pace with the speeding train and handed Jake up to Kayyali who climbed one-handed to the roof of that car with Jake on his back. Iris jumped on and climbed up to join them.

"NnhWhatthafuckwasthatshitt…" Jake drawled out but Iris doubted he'd remember much of this part and assumed Kayyali had decided the same if he was alright with that little show of ability.

A bullet ricocheted off the side of the freight car they were resting atop and Kayyali and Iris saw Headband and several of his crew standing at the edge of the gravel track rise near where they had just waited.

Headband fired again, grazing a round off of the freight car's upper lip, so Iris and Kayyali dropped against the roof surface. Jake was already there.

Iris groaned in annoyance more than anything else. They let the train go a bit further before looking again. The train curved to the right, giving them a clear view of the last snaking length of its hind section.

Headband, most of his crew, and whatever larger gang they belonged to had apparently earned at least some of the fear and respect they seemed to have garnered from the freight-hopping hobo community: they hopped the second to last car and the reversed rear engine car at speed by grabbing any available hand and foot holds and enduring the joint-ripping force of it. One of the gang wasn't as legendary and ended up severed and messy in the wheels.

"So... do we just 'stay in front of them'?!" Iris yelled over the machine roar of the train and the now pounding, diagonal rain.

Kayyali watched Headband and his gang crawl and climb all over the last two cars and thought. He looked down at the barely conscious Jake, then back at the end of the train.

***

Headband—also known as "Splitter" to his "Freight Train Riders of America"/"Fuck The Reagan Administration" cronies—climbed confidently onto the rain-slick roof of the empty rear engine car—*rain and speed be damned*—with silenced revolver in hand.

Too bad about Dank gettin' lunched by the train, but Jake needs to bite it or the rest of us are all lookin' at decades inside. He took a headcount: *Chonch, Popper, Tits, Monk, and Zippy made it on.*

Splitter could just make out Jake—aka "Vanilla"—and the two good Samaritans' dim forms through the darkness and rain several cars down. He was feeling his sweet smoke real strong so he ran across the engine roof and jumped for the next car. He landed just right and strutted into the wind and rain across the last freight car toward his prey.

With only a few stops to crouch for balance from the train rocking and such, he made it across two more cars before realizing the three soon-to-be-victims hadn't moved yet. They must not have seen him even though he was only two cars down now. *This won't be nearly as fun if they just sit there and eat some bullets real easy. And they better not think they can reason with me or some shit. Not an option. Better make that clear.*

Splitter fired a round toward Jake and the two hobos without really trying to hit them. They grabbed Jake and helped him along toward the front of the train. *That seemed to get 'em energetic!* He hooted and called out nonsense words to spook his prey and hurried along atop the cars after them. He looked back and saw Monk and Zippy right behind him and Chonch, Tits, and Popper not far behind.

One of the prey must be hit—other than Jake who already was. They're movin' pretty slow.

Splitter gained on the trio and heard Monk and Zippy close behind him. The train went around a bend and rocked pretty hard so they all crouched down and grabbed handholds. Splitter looked up from his holds and could swear he only saw two of his prey now: Jake and the bigger hobo. Splitter narrowed his eyes and studied the cars ahead, remembering something his awful uncle and surrogate father used to say about wounded, scared animals being the most dangerous.

The hobo with Jake started descending out of sight a couple cars down between two boxcars, hefting Jake down with less difficulty than Splitter would've expected, *but I've got the gun, so fuck him.*

Splitter, Monk, and Zippy made it to the cars Jake and the hobo went down between but didn't see them down in the junction. Splitter leaned over the sides and saw the boxcar toward the front of the train had a mangled lock and was partially open. *How the fuck did he get it open? He's carrying Jake, this train is hauling ass, and that's the hardest one to pop—even when it's sittin' still. I still have the advantage, what with this hunk of deadly on me.*

"Awright—let's get these shits, boys."

Splitter tucked the suppressed pistol in his waste and started climbing down to the car junction well with Zippy and Monk ready to follow.

***

Chonch led Tits and Popper down the rain-battered freight car roofs. They were going slower due to Chonch and Popper having a touch of trouble getting on the train intact. *Hell, I think my shoulder almost popped out and Popper tweaked his ankle somethin' fierce. Splitter's*

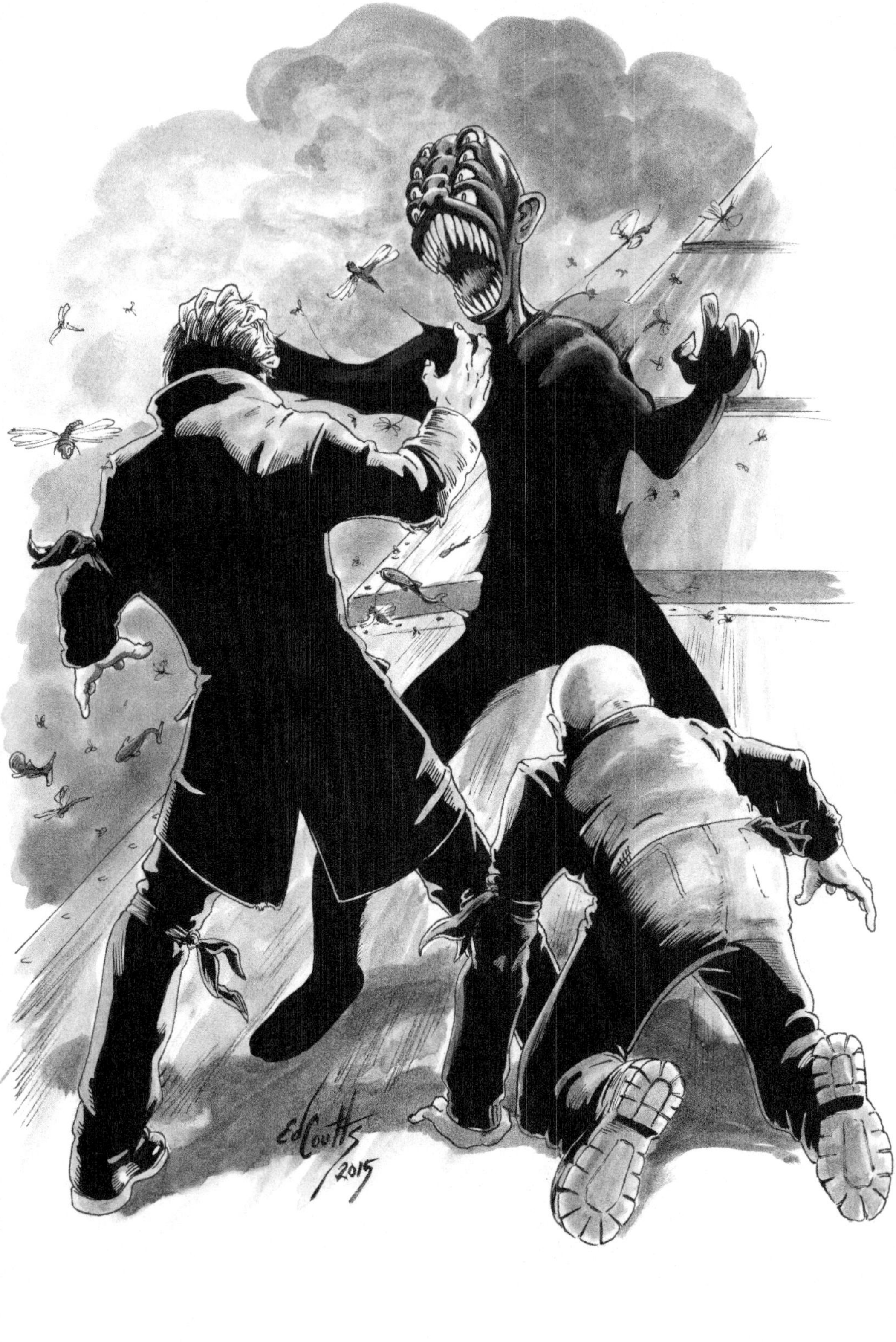
Ed Coutts
2015

losin' it, jumpin' a train this fast! Jake's gonna die from his gut shot any-damn-way! Now we gotta grease two unknowns for no reason along with him.

Splitter started to climb down between two boxcars a few cars up and Chonch wished he could ask Splitter what was going on. The wind and rain whipped up real powerfully and Chonch couldn't see for a moment—Popper yelled, "How the *hell?!*"

Chonch tried to rub the water out of his eyes and opened them on a smiling black woman in hobo clothes.

"Hi," the woman said with a gleam in her eyes.

She broke apart into a whipping flurry of glowing, warped insects, fish, and bird-like beasts of varying sizes. These abominations swarmed around Chonch but only to pass him. He looked back in time to see the woman reform with more eyes running up along her temples and more holes running up her nose. Her mouth broke open, a gaping chasm of obsidian shark teeth, and she tore into Popper's neck where it met his shoulder and came away with most of it in a meaty spray.

Tits jolted and threw himself back to avoid being next but slipped on the slick surface of the roof and fell back off the train and down into the wheels.

Chonch was too confused and terrified to scream, but that didn't stop Popper.

***

Splitter was climbing across the sliding channel for the graffiti-covered boxcar door when he heard something like a scream back down the train a few cars. *I better not have lost another idiot to this train. This is what we do. Can't let it get out that my crew can't even ride some freight.*

He made it to the opening and swung himself into the inky black interior of the boxcar. He steadied himself and immediately took out his revolver and his zippo lighter. He flicked the lighter a few times with no results while Monk and Zippy were climbing into the car behind him. Monk took out a wrench he carried and set it in the door channel so they couldn't get locked in by the train shifting. They took out their own pistols to play the backup role. They didn't have suppressors, but in here that shouldn't matter.

The lighter ignited and flickered, throwing shadows up around the crate and palette filled boxcar. There were narrow channels between the ceiling-high contents and Splitter tried to peer into darkness past his flame to the left and right.

Jake moaned quietly to the left.

Ha!

Splitter aimed the pistol toward the source of the sound and crept toward the far end of the car. He saw two hobo packs against the far wall and Jake's legs along the boxcar floor like he was lying down, *and hopefully bleeding out.*

The big hobo stepped into view at the end of the channel. His hood was down enough that Splitter couldn't see much of his face, but his eyes were reflecting the flickering lighter in a strange way. It was eerie and made Splitter anxious to be done with this.

The big hobo said, "You can't have him."

Splitter chuckled through his fear and said, "If I were askin' that might mean somethin'," and he aimed his revolver between the almost glowing eyes in the dark.

"So, I am correct to infer…" the hobo started as he stepped down the channel and pulled back his hood to reveal a heavily scarred head and face, "that you intend…" he opened his parka, lifted it a bit, then let it fall down his arms and off his body, "to do me harm?"

His cutoff shirt sleeves revealed more of the thick, heavy scarring shared with his head, and dense, intricate tattoos all up and down his arms.

Without answering, Splitter shot the big hobo between the eyes dead-on.

The large man's head was thrown back and his body swayed around once like it was going to topple—but his head snapped back laughing and he threw his arms wide out from his sides.

The shock of just that caused Splitter to drop his lighter and they were back in almost total darkness. Then there was a metallic sound back by the door as the wrench was removed and the door slammed shut.

The big hobo unraveled then flapped and spread open, filling the boxcar with an otherworldly and ineffable luminescence followed by a neon and tar mixture of organic chaos which poured into the space Splitter, Monk, and Zippy were taking up.

Were taking up.

***

Iris heard and saw enough coming out of the cracks from her hanging position outside the door to decide for certain that she didn't need to ever see Kayyali's true form for herself. Plus, she finally got some *real* food, so things might be looking up for them.

***

The nurses and doctors gave Iris and Kayyali suspicious and fearful looks as they deposited Jake's unconscious but still-living form onto a gurney. Most of them wheeled him into the trauma ward and got right to work, but one nurse tried to intimidate them into waiting for the police and gestured to the armed guard near the entrance who was already watching them closely. Kayyali gave her his all-business face from within his draped parka hood and politely explained that they were leaving but the police should have more than a little interest in what Jake could have to say about crime and gangs in the area.

Iris and Kayyali walked out of the emergency area unmolested and kept going until they were across the street and past the periphery of the hospital lights.

Kayyali stopped and looked back so Iris did the same.

Iris said, "He'll be fine. *In good hands* and all that."

"I didn't think you cared."

"Well, not much. It is nice not to be a 'monster' for once, though. That was pretty cheap, though…"

"It got you moving, right?"

"Sure. Hey, anyway… You gotta admit that was more than a little fun. We should be like… monster vigilantes or something."

Kayyali smiled and shook his head.

"Maybe… If we don't kill each other first."

Lucia Joins In and Things Get Weird

"That was quite a story," said L:ucia D'Amore, who was on break from hostessing. "I like shapeshifter stories. Remember that old TV show *Science Fiction Theater*?

Everyone shook their heads.

"No one remembers? There was one episode there a guy was able to change his face when he got a genie to grant a wish and the 'gift' messed up his life. He wound up getting possessed by the genie. Oh, wow. Well it reminded me of the rash of possessions and exorcisms I witnessed years ago. It was an epidemic."

"That must have been scary," Cher said.

"More than scary. It can happen to just about anyone — except us,that is," and she laughed.

Nick chuckled. "I've always had a big headache with possessions. There are a lot of rogue demons and old ancient supernaturals who like to mess up human's minds. It's an evil pleasure now reserved for politicians."

"I only have a few minutes left on my break but, I can condense this story." Lucia pulled up an empty chair from the nearby table.

Personal Demons

Jean Marie Ward

"You can't not help them. It's a textbook case of possession." Deborah Paxton set the mugs on the lacquer tray with a double thump. It was Deb's idea of punctuation — double period, subject closed, nothing more to be said.

Which was just as well since Anita didn't trust herself not to scream. She wanted to grab her lover by the shoulders and shake her until her perfectly bleached, perfectly straightened teeth rattled in her head. How could you ambush me like this? This is my home, the one place I felt safe.

But that was the problem. The two-story bungalow clinging to the hill below Alexandria's Masonic Memorial belonged to Deb. Anita only lived here — and the way things were going, not for much longer. The thought cut like broken glass and hurt worse.

She peered through the kitchen doorway at the man and thirteen-year-old girl perched on either side of Deb's sleek leather and chrome sofa. Rob Garcia's mouth widened in a smile composed of equal parts hope, embarrassment, and pure terror. In contrast, his daughter Julie seemed unnaturally poised, her pale eyes opaque.

Like basalt … no, not rock — obsidian … oily … lightless … and very, very old.

A bad sign.

Part of her disagreed.

She turned her attention back to her lover. "It's not that simple, Deb. If the girl's possessed by a ... (she couldn't bring herself to say 'demon') If she's really possessed, we're talking sorcery. The real thing, gods and devils here, with us, on the material plane. You have no idea what that means."

"I think I do. It means you still haven't forgiven me for the Psychology Today article." Deb shot Anita a wounded puppy look across the bag of Florentines. The grapefruit top notes of her perfume filled Anita's nose, turning the comforting aroma of brewing coffee into something bitter. "Have you?"

"Not now. The Garcias — "

"Can wait. This can't." She slid the cookies onto the plate. Rustle, rustle, thud, thud, thud. "We've got to talk about it sometime."

Why? You're doing enough talking for both of us. Anita kept the thought to herself. Deb read any kind of response as encouragement.

"Don't go all stoic on me, Anita. The way you keep running from the issue isn't healthy — for either of us. It feels like you're running away from me, and it's tearing me apart.

"I never thought the clinic would fire you for being a tantrika. It's not as if you were practicing on their precious patients. They would've been better off if you had. God knows," Deb said, "modern medicine hasn't done the Garcias any good."

"The clinic didn't fire me. They didn't renew my contract. There's a difference. Besides, it's not as if nursing jobs are hard to find. I'm just looking for something that doesn't involve shift work."

"Right, and I'm Mother Theresa. No, wait," Deb said, touching her forefinger to the center of her chin, "that's you!"

Her mouth puckered as if for a kiss. There'd been precious few of those lately — to say nothing of what when along with them. And whose fault is that? Anita dug her toes into her slip-ons, fighting the urge to slam the counter. She wouldn't give Deb the satisfaction.

"Look, I admit I shouldn't have asked the Garcias here without consulting you, but you've been so miserable. So defeated. I had to do something. I thought if you could help them it would give you something better than your old job. It could be the start of a whole new career. With your R.N. and this, you could write your own ticket."

Ticket to what? A new career as a board certified nurse practitioner with a subspecialty in exorcisms? Anita could see the sign on the door now: Anita Lung, Witch Clinician, Demon De-Possession by Appointment Only. The image was like a double shot of migraine pumped straight to her frontal lobes.

And Deb was smiling. She plainly thought she'd come up with the perfect solution to everything. Anita didn't need telepathy to hear the mental italics, either. All she needed was that painfully supportive smile. Her partner — of all people! — still didn't get it.

That Psychology Today article was the professional equivalent of outing her against her will. Sure, it wasn't supposed to happen that way. Sure, the photos only showed her altar, her equipment or her hands. But who needs to see your face when they know where you live and who you live with?

She'd have been better off if Deb had outed her. Her sexual orientation didn't reflect on her professionalism or her judgment. Her former employers would've ignored it rather than face the prospect of a fat settlement and the perfect storm of bad publicity that would've followed. What they couldn't ignore was the revelation that one of their nurse practitioners — an "educated person" with access to dangerous drugs and medical machinery — practiced "black magic mumbo jumbo" in her free time. There was no way to turn it into an opportunity, either. The new line might be "Thou shalt not suffer a witch to earn a living," but that didn't make it any less deadly.

It was a miracle Garcia hadn't reported Deb the minute she suggested a tantric sorceress. He must be crazy, desperate, or desperately crazy. Unfortunately, he didn't look crazy. He looked like the poor schmuck stuck behind door number two with the five hundred pound Siberian tiger.

Just because he's desperate doesn't mean it isn't something simple, something Ms. Fix-It ignored in her rush to make good. Holding tight to that thought, Anita searched the view framed by the kitchen window for a better omen than her pounding head and the sinking feeling in her gut. Nothing appeared in the green-handed arms of the maple trees. The gray afternoon sky was as dim and flat as on old mirror. There wasn't even a cloud to misinterpret.

The gods must be seriously pissed at her.

Garcia jumped to his feet as soon as she left the kitchen. "Ms. Lung, you'll help?"

"Call me Anita, and I'll do my best." She shook the hand he offered. His grip was firm without making it a contest. Score one for Rob. "Please, sit. Deb will be out with the coffee in a minute. So, Julie, what's your take on all of this?"

No response.

Anita sat on the smoke-tinted Lucite chair across from the girl and tried to ignore the way the designer plastic stuck to the back of her knees. Julie stared at her. Anita couldn't decide if the girl was looking at her or if she just happened to drop into her line of sight.

"Didn't Dr. Paxton explain? Julie stopped speaking three days ago," Garcia said. "She'll do everything you tell her, but she doesn't say anything. She just stares."

Anita sensed as much as heard Deb exit the kitchen, unobtrusive and completely professional now that the "consultation" had begun. She set the tray on the burnished metal coffee table, the hem of her skirt brushing Anita's calf in a quick, so-not-accidental caress that managed to be both arousing and infuriating at the same time. Anita's sex drive had withered with her job prospects. Damn it for flaring now, when she couldn't afford the distraction.

"Julie hasn't spoken to you," Deb corrected gently. "Try to relax, Rob. Let Anita do her thing."

Garcia frowned at his daughter and clamped his lips together. He didn't appear to be hiding anything. Leaning forward, hands clasped loosely between his legs — he wasn't protecting his heart and belly chakras in any way. Anita suspected he was wide open on a number of other levels as well.

The girl was another matter. Anita never met a thirteen-year-old who didn't react to food, if only to wrinkle her nose in disgust and say how much she didn't like it. Julie didn't appear to notice the cookies or the soda Garcia said was her favorite.

"Now, who ordered what?" Deb chirped. "Double sugar, right, Rob? And for you ... "

She plunked two mugs of coffee, one black and one heavily creamed, between Anita and the girl. A series of rapid blinks telegraphed Julie's confusion. Her upper arms tensed against her side. She wasn't expecting two cups of coffee, not when her dad had asked for soda, especially when there was a can of soda sitting right there on the tray. Deb's actions made no sense, and the girl didn't know how to react. Not even to ask a question.

Deb flicked a sharp glance in her lover's direction and Anita tipped her head in acknowledgment. Grudging pride twisted Anita's insides tighter. How long had Deb's first session with the Garcias lasted — twenty minutes? Glutton for publication she might be, she'd still found the key anomaly in the girl's behavior, and a perfect way to demonstrate it. Julie's answering glower was almost reptilian.

Anita's skin prickled with a chill that had nothing to do with the air conditioning. The part of her that refused to dismiss the girl's problem as some sad but ordinary teenage trauma was growing stronger, stretching its muscles like a psychic cat. She whispered a brief prayer and lowered the mental barriers she used to separate her physical and spiritual senses.

"Let's try again," she said, easing power into the words. "We'll start by trading names. People call me Anita, but my real name is Anitya — transience. What's yours?"

The girl's chin wobbled as she struggled not to speak. Her gaze crashed into Anita's, surprised and furious.

"Na-na-na-na ... Julie!" she shouted.

Garcia flinched. Fear for his child scoured Anita's enhanced senses like hot, wind-whipped sand. His aura sputtered in angry crimson bursts over the fluid rainbow veils of physical and spiritual health. She picked out a few darks threads of guilt — enough to show he was normal, but nothing that would poison a child's spirit to the brink of catatonia.

Enthroned in the matching Lucite chair to Anita's left, Deb was haloed in crackling candy red, eager orange and lemony yellow. The shifting, iridescent static made it hard to detect weaker emanations — like the pale, almost colorless flutters of light lapping Julie's body. No — beating it, pounding it like waves hammering a levee that refused to break.

Anita shook her head. That was inside out. Auras emanated from living things. They were the visible energy produced by every physical and emotional act of living. Julie's body was a lightless husk surrounded by fading glimmers trying to push their way back in.

But her body wasn't dead. Her chest rose and fell in the normal rhythm of a child at rest. With Garcia's permission, Anita took her pulse. Her heart beat steadily beneath soft, warm skin that smelled faintly of soap. Yet she generated less of an aura than a coma patient. Her hand weighed heavy in Anita's grasp. The sorceress thought again of rock, black glass, and the weight of great age.

Meanwhile, the being behind the child's eyes appeared to be assessing her. Anita didn't expect it to be impressed. She was short, close-faced, and her hair badly needed a trim. Her shorts and faded T-shirt were one step up the mood indicator scale from pajamas, but only because she hadn't slept in them yet. She wished she could read it that easily. The entity didn't behave like other demons she'd met or the ones she'd studied during her apprenticeship.

Not that it mattered. Deb was right: she couldn't not help. It was part of all her job descriptions, nurse and tantrika.

"Tell me everything, from the beginning."

"Julie and her friend Katie had a summer assignment to research the life of a soldier buried at Arlington. They picked a guy who died in World War I. He was supposed to be a poet." Garcia shook his head. "So Julie got the idea to read some of his poetry over his grave. Like a memorial service."

The wan radiance of Julie's spirit blazed as if her father's words were a trigger. A vision created from her memories unfurled in Anita's mind.

Two girls in short, patterned skirts and sandals stood in a field of close-cropped grass planted with row upon row of identical headstones. Julie clutched a few sheets of white paper to her chest. The other girl…

Katie held a bouquet of bright flowers wrapped in plastic. The stone at their feet listed to the left, as if the occupant of the grave had grown restless.

They waited, exchanging furtive glances, until a middle-aged woman carrying an identical bouquet moved to the next field of stones. Katie lowered the flowers to the grave sideways, bending her knees as little as possible in case she had to run.

"Chicken," Julie taunted fondly.

"I'm just being smart. The vibes here are all wrong. Forget the poems. It's not like we have to do a video. All we need is a picture of the headstone."

"No. I chickened out when my mom was in the hospital. I got all squicked by the tubes coming out of her chest, and I ran out of the room. I ran! That was the night she died."

"Julie, this guy's been dead a hundred years. He doesn't care."

"But I do. I'm never running again." Julie moistened her lips and started reading from the papers. Her voice stumbled over the line: "Who so dismisseth flesh shall obtain possession of it yet, by thy black hand, Naberius."

Katie winced and rubbed her arms. She looked like she wanted to say something else but decided against it. Julie continued:

"Perdition's hordes are thine,
"As I am thine, Naberius."

The wings of a large fly glittered as it struck the polished stone. Julie gasped and collapsed on the flowers. Katie called out her name.

"Katie's mom thought it was the heat. By the time I got home from work, everybody was fine. Only she wasn't." Garcia swallowed. "Two o'clock in the morning, Julie ran into my bedroom crying. She said: 'Daddy, there's somebody in my head, and he's pushing me out.' I thought she'd had a nightmare. I sat her down on the bed and tried to tell her it was just a bad dream, but it wasn't. I saw her face change right in front of me and I couldn't stop it. I couldn't do anything."

He smacked the flat arm of the sofa. "It's my fault. I should've read those damn poems. But I didn't think I needed to. God ... The priest at Georgetown told me Naberius led nineteen legions of demons and was supposed to make people better speakers. But would he do anything to help? No. It isn't serious until somebody's puking pea soup and their head's spinning around their neck. He said that it was a prank. She'd get over it. You'd think he'd been taking lessons from that damned child psychologist!

"Oh damn," he groaned, realizing his error. "Sorry. I didn't mean you," he said to Deb.

"I've been called worse."

Amusement sweetened the music of her voice. She winked at Anita over the rim of her coffee cup, then blinked at the girl. The pattern of Julie's freckles shifted across her face like ants repositioning themselves over a soda spill.

"Shit," Garcia said, "not again."

"Are you a good Catholic, Rob?" Anita asked sharply.

"What does that have to do with anything?"

"I need to know. My gods are different from yours, and I can't heal your daughter without their help. Most priests, even the Jesuits of Georgetown, would call that trafficking with the Devil. They'd call it a mortal sin. If you want to go somewhere else — "

"No. I don't care what you do as long as you save Julie."

"My Master requires an offering. Give me something you treasure. Something blue."

Garcia started to pull his blue shirt out of his chinos, then thought better of it. He fished in his left pocket and withdrew a shiny brass money clip set with a large sodalite. "Julie gave it to me for Father's Day."

Deb's approval and relief followed Anita across the front hall to the house's original living room, as tangible as a warm hand against the small of her back. Pride demanded she shrug it off. No matter how real the need, she hated being manipulated. But the sky had darkened since she left the kitchen, casting a pall over the room's view of Old Town and the Potomac at its back. Now the omens appear. She snorted in disgust.

A hammered silver offering bowl waited on the sideboard where she stored her supplies. Because she wanted to throw something, she laid the clip inside the bowl with extra care. She needed to release all the resentment and sense of betrayal festering inside her before she started the ritual. But it wouldn't be easy, even with the familiar mantras of the Medicine Buddha already whispering from her lips. The room and everything it represented wouldn't let go.

With its east-facing windows and usually cheery light, this was supposed to be Deb's office, but the previous owner ran a dance studio. The old barre was bolted to the studs of the room's load-bearing wall through a giant mirror that was too expensive to remove and impossible for Deb to finesse. In the giddy days after she moved in, Anita interpreted the mirror as a symbol of their love, reflecting light from outside and within. For once she didn't need to hide anything.

The banners of white, blue, red, yellow, and green she hung on the walls were as much about the rainbow flag as the rainbow body of Buddhahood. Deb pushed her to refinish the old floorboards and paint the blueprints for her mandalas over the varnish. Between the windows, Anita had raised her small altar so the brilliant blue statuette of her Master, the Medicine Buddha, was higher than the barre on the opposite wall. His mirror image glittered as brightly as the original, magnifying his presence in the room and throughout the house, transforming it into her sanctuary, the nexus where all the worlds she inhabited could coexist in harmony — Tibetan and American, sorceress and nurse, lover and beloved.

But mirrors were deceivers by nature; their reflections, backward semblances of semblances. Instead of viewing it as a lesson, she'd fallen in. She'd confused her desire for her lover with her lover's desires, and what had happened? She'd lost her job and her credibility, while Deb's peers gushed over her "sensitive treatment of non-traditional beliefs" and upped her lecture fees.

"Why are you being so stubborn? Let me call in some favors."

"The last thing I need is a pity job. They never work out."

It's not as if she could say to her partner: Stop trying to make it better. Meddling will only make it worse. Or worse yet — Deb might succeed, turning Anita into her dependent.

She had to stop herself from yanking the top drawer of the sideboard off its slides. For a minute she blanked on the incense she needed, then banged her knuckles prying the crumpled box from the back of the drawer. She reached for the knob to the compartment where she kept her bottles of purified water and the bowl she used to rinse her hands and mouth.

Her prayers stilled. Her lines, the sacred geometry she used to build her mandalas were scuffed thin. It'd be a miracle if they survived the ceremony.

She couldn't blame that on Deb. She couldn't blame it on the article or post-employment depression either. The worn and peeling paint didn't lie. She'd been distancing herself from her magic for months, maybe longer. So long, she choked on the word "demon." She couldn't bring herself say it out loud.

She pressed her bruised knuckle against her lips. As the servant of gods who demanded truth, she was a master at self-deception. She didn't want to be a tantrika anymore.

Oh, she said her prayers and meditated and floated flowers in bowls on her Master's altar. But the hard things, the ugly things she'd wrestled with since she was a little girl — she didn't want anything to do with them. She wanted to live the rest of her life with a smart, beautiful woman in a cute little American bungalow surrounded by its very own picket fence, bringing flowers to a quaint blue statue, not fighting monsters no one else could see.

Did some part of her think putting her rites on paper, hammering them with scientific skepticism, would break their power over her? Was she feeling betrayed and sorry for herself because of what happened — or what hadn't?

Was she still a sorceress? After all, she'd forgotten which incense she needed.

Anita braced her arms against the sideboard, riding out the aftershocks of understanding and the doubt that came with them. She had to be. Julie and Rob needed her skills. The Buddha would take care of the rest.

The thought steadied her. She rinsed her mouth with the stale-tasting water, spat it into the white porcelain bowl, and finished purifying herself. Chanting her mantras in earnest, she placed Rob's offering on the altar and lit the censer shaped like Mount Meru. She covered the painted lotus in the middle of the floor with a small pillow of life-sustaining barley and crowned it with the eight-sided mirror representing this world. With dark blue sand, she sketched her Master's secret symbol close to the small mirror and gingerly positioned a red felt cushion over the design. She drew a different form of his name on the opposite side of the mirror, centering a silver bowl containing more barley over the sand.

Then she retrieved the basket containing her prayer wheel and five squeeze bottles filled with colored sand. "In the holy name of the Perfectly Enlightened Medicine Buddha Lapis Lazuli Radiance, enter and be healed."

"Daddy, I'm scared," the being in Julie whined.

The pewter sky growled as Rob assured her there was nothing to be frightened of. He sounded like he didn't believe it himself.

Deb, bless her, didn't have that problem. She led the others into the room with her chin held high and the faintest hint of a strut in her graceful, long-legged stride. No wasted motion. No tics or punctuating noise. She paused in front of Anita, lush lower lip caught between her teeth. Anita's breath hitched. She ached to tell her everything was all right — they were all right. The Medicine Buddha had revealed her stupidity and false pride for what they were, and the ritual hadn't even started yet. But she couldn't, not with Rob and it watching their every move.

It didn't matter. For that one moment, Deb seemed to possess some special kind of lover's telepathy. A hesitant smile at odds with the confident, slightly bossy woman Anita had fallen in love with bloomed across her face. It was so unexpected, so perfect, Anita wanted to cheer. She wanted to kiss it just to prove she wasn't imagining it.

Caught up in Deb, she almost missed Garcia's sigh of relief. No matter what Deb told him, he probably expected crosses, Bibles, maybe restraints. Instead he found a mostly empty room lit by ordinary overhead fixtures. The incense was a mix of sandalwood, cinnamon, juniper, and cumin. It smelled more like curry than frankincense and myrrh. The exorcist wasn't scary either, just an ordinary woman with a basket full of sand.

Julie ignored her, studying the big mirror with something akin to predatory calculation. The mental equivalent of an ice shower yanked

Anita back to reality. Nothing like the sudden realization of what eighty-four square feet of shattered glass could do to four unprotected human bodies to focus a nurse's mind. Anita's lips thinned in a grim smile. That wasn't happening on her watch. She wouldn't let it.

"This is a ceremony to cure body, mind, heart, and soul," she explained briskly. "Since the offering was made in your name, Julie Garcia, the cushion is yours. Kneel on it and close your eyes."

Smug as a lizard, the girl obeyed. A flicker of anger toughened Anita's resolve. Her walls would hold. Her sanctuary would stand.

"Rob, your job here is to strengthen Julie. Kneel to her right so you're facing the sideboard. No matter how strange things get, try not to say anything until the ceremony ends. If I get distracted … "

Garcia drew a deep breath. Several long seconds later, he exhaled and nodded slowly.

"Deb." Deb beamed, practically glowing with faith in her partner and her partner's skill. It was almost as frightening as the prospect of the mirror breaking. Anita swallowed. "Kneel on the floor to Julie's left so you're facing Rob. You're there to boost his courage. Concentrate on him no matter what you think you see in the circle or out of the corner of your eyes."

Her mouth hung open, ready to continue, but the words wouldn't come. Deb believed in psychological truth. She thought Anita's gods and devils were metaphors. It was better that way. All she had to do was stay put and think good thoughts — which was a given, because she was Deb. Then don't tell her anything. Deb and Rob aren't the only ones with ears in here. True, but ducking the hard stuff was a lousy way to start an exorcism.

Deb nodded. Her aura vibrated with anticipation.

Anita grabbed her hand, squeezing the bones beneath the warm silk of her skin. "No. Deb, this is important. Before we're done, you could see, hear, maybe even taste things that don't exist in this world. Some of them are more seductive than you could possibly imagine, and some of them are awful beyond belief. Whatever happens, promise me you'll stay where you are until we're finished. As long as you do that, I swear nothing bad can touch you."

"It's all right. I promise."

Deb gave their joined hands an earnest little shake. The corners of Julie's mouth twitched. Anita said another prayer.

She let the whispered words fade into silence. The circle in which she would build her mandala was a sacred space, a pure realm with no room for illusions, even those she cherished most. Her breathing slowed, drawing in, pushing out, until she was empty, a vessel made of flesh. A different chant sprang from her lips, its notes cut crystal sharp. With a quick, sure strokes she drew the gods' double thunderbolt in green sand behind Deb, a red flower behind the girl's sneakers, a golden jewel behind her father, and her Master's blue scepter behind the space where she would kneel. Working from the outside in, she threaded colored sand along the four largest circles, sealing each round wall with her strongest enchantments before beginning the next. Finally, she picked up her prayer wheel and set the basket on the floor between herself and Deb.

Her tendons protested as she knelt in front of the scepter, yet another sign she'd coasted too long. Couldn't be helped now. Muttering the final incantations more sharply than usual, she released the full measure of her power. It rushed into the void she'd created, sparking bone, nerve and flesh. Both hands clutching the handle, she twirled the prayer wheel over the bowl of barley. Of their own accord, the seeds jumped from the bowl and rained on the eight-sided mirror in the center of the mandala.

"Open your eyes," she ordered Julie.

The demon in the girl took its time obeying. Hail clattered against the porch roof and upstairs windows.

"This is it?" the demon asked a voice little too deep for Julie's age, but otherwise unremarkable.

"It's enough. Look into the mirror and tell me truly what you see. There can be no falsehood in the house of the gods," Anita said.

"Why not?"

"Because it angers them."

The girl arched an eyebrow. The gesture, like the voice, was older than her face. "I see that which finds the secrets of the earth and unlocks every door."

The image of a blackened, mummified hand formed in the ether over the girl's head. Deb gasped. Ignore it, Deb. Keep your promise. Don't look.

She wasn't as empty as she was supposed to be. The counterweight on the prayer wheel rapped her bruised knuckles in warning. The demon in Julie smirked.

"What is it?" Anita asked.

"You're the witch. You tell me."

"I can't."

"Liar!" The girl's head jerked back. "You saw it! I showed it to you!"

"I saw a phantom conjured from ether." It's the truth, Deb. "I don't know what you saw in the mirror. I've been watching you."

The demon in the girl glared her. "It's the Hand of Glory," she answered sullenly.

"The severed hand of a hanged man made into a candelabrum," Anita mused. "That's an odd thing for a girl your age to see. How'd you find out about it?"

"I read about it on the Web."

"You read it on the Web?" Anita's gaze locked with that of the demon peering out of Julie's eyes. "You lie."

"Julie read it on the Web," the demon amended.

"Then who are you?" Anita asked.

"Arthur Howard Whateley."

"What!" Garcia erupted.

"Is that the name of the poet?"

"Yes, but —"

"Good," Anita said.

"What do you mean 'good'? My daughter just announced she's been possessed by a hundred-year-old Satanist!"

"Silence!" Her command roared through the room, whipping the ether with centrifugal force. Garcia staggered as if fighting a windstorm only he could feel. As suddenly as it attacked, the power died.

"The demon in your daughter said its name was Arthur Howard Whateley. That's its second lie in the house of the gods," she said.

"That'll cost you," the demon taunted.

Garcia struggled for breath. Deb panted fast and shallow. Anita whispered, "I know."

"Give up," it said.

She shook her head. "I won't."

"You should. That old priest was right, you know. Mommy's dead. She's with the angels and I'm all alone at my time. I'm supposed to act out. It gives me a sense of control over my life. Give it a few weeks and everything will settle down."

"Settle down?" Anita laughed. "What makes you think you can pull that off? Julie's father is sitting right next to you."

"I've learned a lot in the last few days."

No lie in that. Anita felt pride swell the demon's soul, and something else. Need hummed in the ether between them. How very peculiar. "Why would you bother? What's so special about this girl?"

The girl sank back on her haunches, eyeing Anita warily. "Nothing. Anybody would've done as well, although her youth is an advantage."

"It seems odd that a demon of your rank would care so little about its host. How do you plan to use the body? What do you need it for?"

The demon contemplated the girl's hands as if the peeling polish on her stubby nails might yet be saved.

"Come on. You have to answer eventually. You can't leave the circle until you do."

"Your gods haven't bound me yet." The girl pushed the toes of her sneakers against the floor. And didn't move. She shifted her weight from leg to leg. Her calves and thighs strained against the denim of her jeans. But the fabric under her knees had fused with the felt of the cushion, and the cushion had bonded to the floor.

"What do you want?" Anita said.

The girl moaned, rocking back and forth in a desperate effort to free her body from the magic holding it in place. But nothing worked. The hand of the Buddha held her fast. The next turn of the prayer wheel was a hymn of thanksgiving. The mirror would remain unbroken. The demon would answer to the sorceress's gods. Anita felt their presence whisper along the light downy hairs of her arms. At their command she released her right hand from the wheel's handle and squeezed it into a fist.

The girl gasped. Her eyes bulged and shoulders hunched as if the gods were squeezing her.

"Power!" the girl forced through gritted teeth.

"Power for what? To open the gates of Hell? To raise the dead and set them over the living?" Anita demanded.

"YES!"

No. The unspoken word spun between girl and sorceress like the endless note of a singing bowl. The girl screamed. Volleys of hail pounded the house with the force of a thousand rifles firing at once. Tiny pops echoed within the room as bubbles opened in the ceiling and rained roaches, flies, and silverfish over the group.

Deb shrieked and covered her head with her hands. Garcia swore.

Anita turned the wheel faster. The stream of vermin rolled away from the circle like rain off the peaked roof of a temple. A network of immaterial gutters carried the flow in an ever-gathering momentum to the edge of the mandala. Before the first rush struck the sand, the outer circle ignited in rainbow flames that consumed every trace.

"I did it to live!" the demon screamed. "I can raise the dead and hold sway over legions, but they're dead. I'm dead! Without sense or sensation. I know every secret, but all fruit is forbidden to me. I don't even know the feel of burning flesh or why its memory torments the damned. I want this!" The demon clasped its hands and shook them in Anita's face. "I want life!"

"Then you are mine, Naberius. The life of the flesh is the greatest lie of all."

The purifying fire died. Sandalwood- and cinnamon-scented smoke wafted towards the painted corners of the mandala and coalesced into its guardian spirits. Their bulbous faces and tiger teeth grew more horrible as they gathered substance.

The demon bawled something that didn't sound human. Vapors thicker than smoke unfurled from the girl's eyes, ears, nose, and mouth. They coalesced into a shape that was vaguely man-like, but purple-black and disfigured by death.

Anita thrust the prayer wheel into the bowl and scrambled to her feet. If Naberius couldn't have Julie's body, it would seek another host. For the sake of everyone gathered in the circle, it needed to choose hers. She needn't have worried. The enraged demon swarmed her like a cloud of moths. Millions of cottony wings struck their separate blows. Anita felt them all. The soul dust they left behind smothered her skin and sifted through her clothes. She moaned, only to choke on Naberius's mildew-sweet scent. The demon pressed himself against her, inside her, buffeting flesh and nerves with delicious, deadly sensations. But the possession wasn't complete. Anita's arms encircled the man-sized cloud. Her fingers raked the darkness.

The violence of Naberius's next attack nearly lifted her from the floor. The demon hammered into her, front and back, top and bottom, as if its blows could drive her from her flesh. The force of the thrusts arched her back. Her mouth stretched so wide it felt like her cheeks would rip in two. It was almost too much for Anita to absorb.

Almost.

Naberius didn't comprehend that until far too late.

A devil's fistful of hail strafed the windows, shredding the screens and pulverizing glass. But it couldn't breach the adamantine wall of sand and spirit. Even if it had, it wouldn't have mattered to Naberius or her.

She was the Great Bell of Nothingness, the vessel forged and tempered to carry the power of gods, the living portal to their realm.

Naberius tried to pull away. She wouldn't let go. The harder Naberius fought, the better it felt. She wished they could be locked in their struggle forever. She would never be empty. Never reviled. Never apart. Never alone.

A dark star of pleasure exploded inside her. The power of the Lapis Lazuli Radiance streamed through the weak fabric of her flesh. Anita wailed in ecstasy. The Master's soul light burst through the pores of her skin. The Master's power swirled around the barley-strewn mirror, gathering strength and speed as it spiraled outward.

Julie's body collapsed with a whimper as the Master poured her spirit back into its mortal home. Sand rose from the floor, recreating the

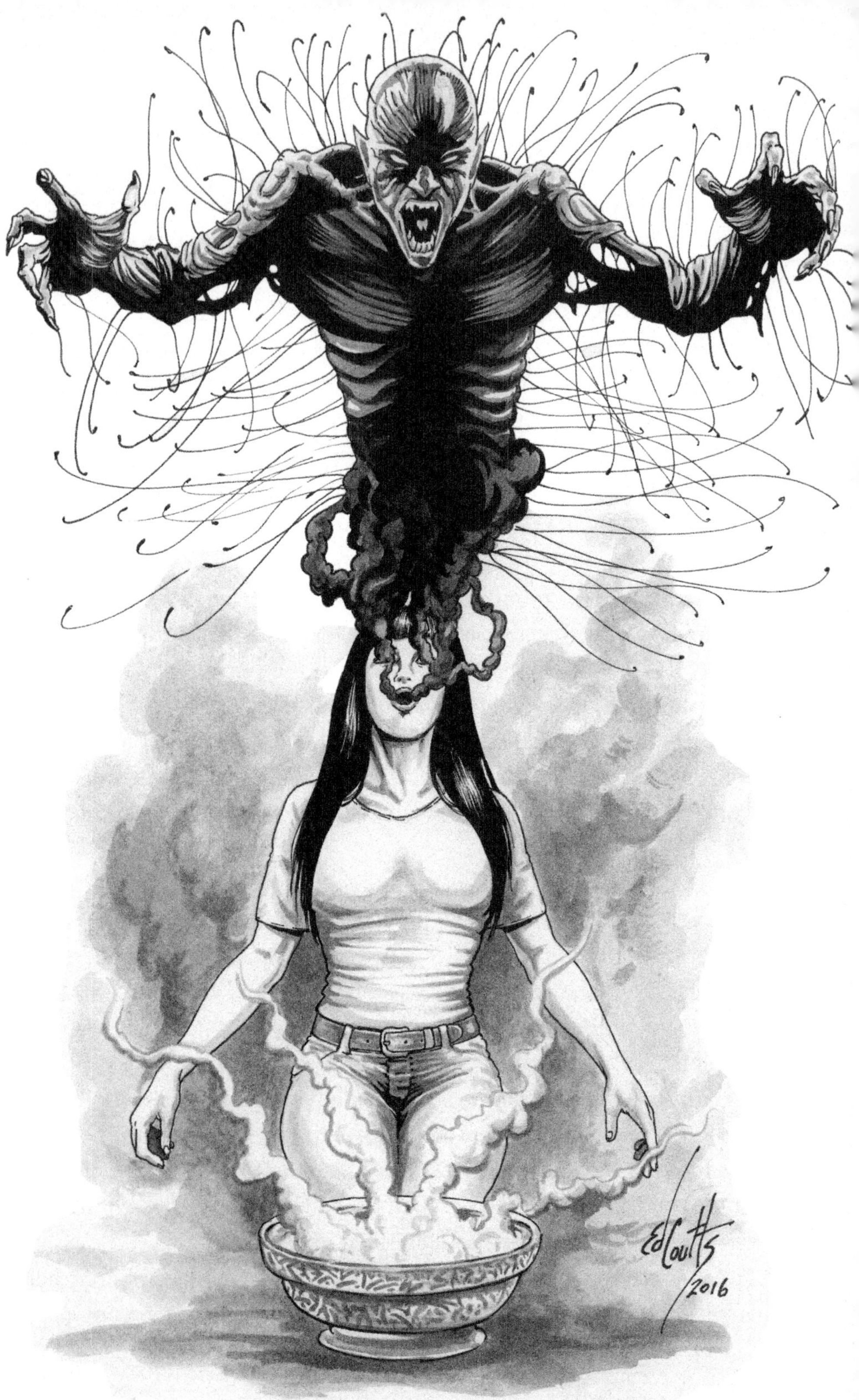
Ed Coutts
2016

mandala's walls and the sacred objects of the gods in the material plane. Scepter, thunderbolt, jewel, and lotus spun in space until captured by the Master's cleansing wind. A mile downhill from the spire of the Masonic Memorial, the air released its burden, and the blessing sand flowed into the Potomac River.

***

By the time Anita recovered from the Master's touch, Deb had vanished from the room. Garcia and his daughter hugged and sobbed reassurances at each other. Their auras shimmered with the clear, safe colors of normal lives: yellow for balance, green for life, and the Master's healing blue.

The usual unspoken agreement applied. Nobody wanted to talk about what just happened — the first step in rationalizing it away. It was better that way. Julie didn't need any more trauma. Anita told them to check in with their family doctor and showed them the door.

The rumble of their car's engine faded until it was indistinguishable from the storm. Anita closed the door, and raced upstairs, ignoring both her aching legs and the rain blowing in the mirrored room's windows. Despite the lingering effervescence of spirit, her brain was clear. The Garcias were Deb's clients. She should've been the one to send them home.

The sound of the shower met her at the foot of the stairs. Grapefruit-scented steam billowed out of the open door to the master bath. Condensed moisture fogged the medicine cabinet mirror and trickled down her cheeks. Deb hadn't drawn the shower curtain. The water hissed against the tub, silvering her lithe curves and the high, ripe swell of her ass. Magnifying the raw pink patches on the backs of her thighs that weren't there last night.

"Deb, what happened?"

Deb screamed, dropping soap and loofah. The delicate, peach blossom skin of her breasts, her mound, and the insides of her thighs was scraped lobster red. Sympathetic fire burned across Anita's breasts and thrust a flaming brand between her legs. Pushing her fading energies to the limit, she scanned Deb's aura. She must have been more tired than she realized. She could barely see Deb through the haze of frightened brown and poisoned green.

"Oh, Deb, you didn't need to do that. Demons aren't contagious. Turn off the shower. I'll get something for your skin."

Deb's hands flashed to her breast and groin, shielding them from her lover as if from a threat. "Leave me alone!"

"But you're hurting yourself for no reason. You were never in any danger from Naberius. I took care of him."

Deb's answering laugh was one fingernail on a blackboard shy of hysterical. "I'll say you did. You fucked that rotting bastard right in front of me."

"I didn't. It's not like that." But a part of it was. Anita shoved the thought away. "That's how I banish demons — and anything else that doesn't belong on the material plane. I'm a portal to the Void."

"How can you say that with a straight face? I was there. I saw you. I heard you. You think I don't know what you sound like when you come?"

Deb slammed the side of her fist against the tile surround. Anita flinched at the sound, the flash of agony contorting Deb's face, and the throat-clenching, soul-killing fear of worse to follow.

"To think I spent months blaming myself, hating myself for hurting you. I would've crawled on broken glass to go back the way it was before. I loved you," Deb sobbed.

Loved. Past tense. Anita grabbed the doorjamb to keep from falling. This couldn't be happening. She'd just figured everything out. She'd defeated the demon. She'd earned the right to fix things with her lover.

Who's fixing now? The water in the bungalow's old pipes burbled in wicked delight. She would've liked to blame it on the demon, but she knew better. According to the sages, desire was the root of all suffering. Even her name was a lesson. Tout passe, tout casse, tout lasse. Everything passes, everything breaks, everything palls.

Not like this.

Anita forced her jelly legs to stand and marched the three steps to the towel warmer. She grabbed the plush gray bath towel off the top rack and slung it over her shoulder. She would've preferred blue — or fresh olive branch green — but gray would have to do. She closed the taps.

The shower curtain rings squealed over the rod as Deb yanked the curtain between them. "Get out!" she screamed. "I want you and your filthy monsters out of my house!"

"Not until I'm sure you're all right."

Deb glared at her over her flimsy shield, a cornered she-wolf baring her teeth. "What are you going to do, cast a spell on me?"

Anita ignored the gush of pain. A wounded, frightened animal couldn't help but bite. She draped the towel over her upturned palms, presenting it as if it were an offering. "I haven't yet. I don't plan to start now. But I'm stubborn. I won't move 'til I'm ready. You should know; you've been pushing me for months."

Deb sniffed. Anita chose to see that as a good sign. At the moment, though, the bar for omens was pretty low.

"I'm sorry," Anita said. "I know it's not enough, but it's all I've got. All the magic in the world can't fix the past. Trying only makes it worse. Look at what happened to Julie. I'd rather look ahead. I want a future with you, Deb. Even when I'm hurting, even when I'm so mad I'm stupid with it, I can't turn away from you. I love you."

"Is that supposed to make everything right?" Slowly Deb shook her head. "You are so full of demon shit. I was there, remember. The lie of the flesh is the greatest lie of all!"

"So what if it is," Anita replied. "It's the one we live."

Wouldn't Be a Friday Night Without a Cat Story

"I had one run-in with a demon a few years ago," said Druscilla as she looked at Nick. "Remember the Warlock Murders?"

"Yeah, that was a nice case you handled. London, right?"

"Scotland Yard assignment. Working with the demons and the dead is a challenge"

"The dearly departed are always unpredictable, replied Nick,"as unpredictable as the hereafter itself. At least in Hell you know what's happening."

"How do you mean?"

"Well, every recently deceased who does not end up in my realm sometimes has his own private hereafter."

"Really?"

"OK, get a grasp on this. There's this guy, Frank … .who had a real deal adjusting to his demise. I got this story second hand so the details may be a bit fuzzy … listen …"

And the Cat Came Back

Danielle Ackley-McPhail

BEING dead was a pain.
 Yeah, kind of ironic, but it was, in every sense of the word. All the pain-in-the-ass things Frank LoCosta thought he'd eventually get away from when, at some perpetually-in-the-future date, he died — like hunger, exhaustion, physical pain, even … well … everything — would no longer be a problem … well, guess again …

Or maybe it was just Frank's kind of dead, after all, there weren't a lot of people around like him, not like you would expect if this was all there was. The others must go somewhere. He wished he had … He'd give a heck of a lot to see pearly gates somewhere at this point, or even not so pearly ones.

Okay, so he exaggerated, there had to be worse things than where he was, but since he expected he was pretty much trapped here, he didn't have to worry about them. Of course, he never stopped to consider that those "worse things" might actually be here!

Frank pushed the thoughts away in favor of remembering what led to them: he was starving! Robbed of his chance of getting answers out of Nutjob — it bothered him too much to think of the guy as Quinlan Mack, given the last time he saw him — Frank had taken up aimlessly wandering the city. At least, that's what he'd thought he was doing; an endless circuit haunted by the undead and memories of when such places meant something to him. Of course, by the time he found himself sitting at his favorite table at Café du Monde it sunk in that what he was doing was haunting all the places he and Nicky ... well ... used to haunt together. They had a little more appeal in the other life than they did in the after life, but Frank supposed that wasn't what drew him here anyway. He had to admit he was looking for Nick. With his own future put paid to, it was desperately important that he find his partner wasn't in the same fix. After all, Nick was the only one left that gave a damn about a man named Frank LoCosta, wasn't he? If Nick had bought it too, who would be left to care what had happened to Frank?

A glimpse of Maya wouldn't hurt ... or it would, but only because she wouldn't draw near. From time to time he caught sight of his wife flitting along the edges of his new existence, but she always disappeared before he could reach her. The question was: Why? He couldn't answer that any more than he could the thousands of other questions banging against his brain, and it was driving him nuts.

Frank shut down his thoughts, refusing to think about anything of consequence, he just sat there and breathed in deep, immersing himself in the pseudo-Cajun feel of Dani Beaufont's little café. She'd done a good job, actually, considering they weren't within a thousand miles of New Orleans; spice and flavor didn't just describe her food, though he'd die again for just a taste of her crawfish jambalaya and jalapeno cornbread ... heck, even just for her dirty rice. Instead he sat here tortured by the enticing aroma while he listened to the newest thing in Creole music drifting out from under the green and white striped awning, with laughter and life weaving itself in harmony.

He purposely ignored the undead eating at the tables surrounding him, exerting considerable effort to look at anything except heavily laden forks sliding into mouths other than his, but his stomach roared in protest and treated him to a sucker punch from the inside. It wasn't any happier than he was. Tune it out, LoCosta ... tune it out! But it was no good. He sat there, with his gut wrapping itself around his spine, watching people leave, sated and draped in strands of Mardi Gras beads. A flung-back tumble of chestnut curls and a deep, throaty laugh launched Frank into another unwanted flashback. The three of them, Nicky, Maya,

And the Black Cat Came Back

and himself, had come here just days before the day ... the day Maya was killed. That night had been glorious; great food, better company, and much joy ... Maya had walked out with so many strands of beads you could barely see the front of her shirt. The entire evening had been supercharged with life; yet soon after, Maya had lost hers. That pain was worse than the hunger he battled now, and just as unrelenting. He pushed the thoughts away, burying them deep, as always, but they'd be back.

The sound of reverberating metal was his first realization that he'd vented his anger and frustration, that and the gasp of every undead patron around. Even the transplanted musician stopped playing his horn. Everyone was looking confused ... except for the horn player.

What Nutjob had told him the second time they'd met rose in Frank's thoughts: You might have enough focused energy and anger to actually flip that guy around. Well, apparently he'd had enough to thump a café table too. As the white aluminum stopped vibrating and the violent clatter faded to an unsettling memory, the black man's warm, caramel-color eyes locked with his and Frank felt an overwhelming desire to shrink back.

But he shouldn't be able to see me, was Frank's first thought. No one else can see me.

Then he considered all the new-age cranks he used to deal with back when he was a patrolman on the force. Could the old guy be one of those ... what did they call them? ... Mediums? A flash of memory came to Frank's mind ... of that "I talk to dead people" guy from cable television. For a moment, the old man's grizzled face superimposed itself over the cable guy's make-up artist masterpiece and Frank couldn't help the laugh that was startled out of him.

Those caramel eyes looked ancient and disgusted, the tight, silver-laced curls glittered in the sunlight as the guy shook his head slowly. Frank was sharply reminded of how his father used to look ... each and every time Frank, as a young man, proved his faith was misplaced on a punk kid without a lick of sense. The memory was not an easy one. It had occurred way too often, before he'd gotten his head on straight.

Frank didn't like that this stranger could reduce him back to feeling like that punk kid again. He was about to tell him so when the musician disappeared, leaving behind the soulful wail of his horn and an uninterrupted stream of sunlight.

Shit! Shit! Frank was ready to slam the table again, but this time with his head. How could he be so dense? Only now, when the guy was gone, did he realize what he should have caught right away: he hadn't heard one single thought from the musician, though from the look on his face there would have been plenty to hear. That only meant one thing, as far as Frank knew, that this guy was in the same boat as he was. Dead. Yeah, shit was right. He'd just let his second chance to figure out the rules disappear in a disgusted flash.

"Sorry, horn-man," he whispered. "Please come back." He wasn't expecting that to work, but it depressed him just the same when it didn't. Hunger wasn't a problem anymore. Now Frank was nauseous.

Getting up from the table, he didn't really know where he would go from here, but staying wasn't an option. As he made his way through the sidewalk traffic a movement from the café caught his eye. Char. His shadow. Back once more. With a grim expression on his face, Frank dodged and ducked through the side streets and alleyways, watching his back to see if she followed. He could have just blinked himself somewhere else, only where did he have to go? And it wasn't as if his time was valuable. He had way too much time on his hands, might as well use some of it up. What better way than finding out what the little punk was up to? He tucked into a doorway and waited for her to pass.

She moved with boneless grace, fast and fluid. She couldn't have been more than thirteen ... maybe fourteen. Her eyes were ancient. Kids were growing up way too quick these days ... and dying just as quickly. And lately, every time Frank turned around, there she was. Silently he stepped out of the shadow.

"Hey kid, what's the deal? You following me again?" From beneath mottled bangs of multicolored hair she just turned those eternal green eyes on him and slowly blinked. There was no other expression. The look on her face said it all and he almost believed it: He was beneath her notice and any attention she bestowed upon him was gracious of her. Yeah, almost. Again with that boneless grace as she turned and sauntered away, hips swaying and her nose in the air.

"Yo, I said, what's the deal?" He started to grab her arm and reality tilted on its axis. Moving faster than he could even acknowledge the girl whirled, leapt, and snapped at his chin, her teeth clicking sharply just millimeters from his stubble as he jerked back. She was gone just as quickly, loping away, weaving through the foot traffic until the only sign of her was her rapidly disappearing wake.

Damn! The kicker was he was sure she'd only missed on purpose. And he doubted he'd truly taken her by surprise. He rubbed his jaw and puzzled over the girl who'd so easily ditched him. What the heck was going on here? And how could he get out of it?

"Dat girl, she ain't quite de same as you an' me."

Frank jumped, reaching for his gun, but not drawing it. It was hard to fight years of training. He didn't bother trying, even though he didn't think the gun would do him a blasted bit of good. Would it even work here? Or was it just a prop his mind filled in because it was supposed to be there? Hell if he wanted to have to find out!

"You let all dis get to you, it make you sloppy, do all of de rest of us a world of harm."

Horn-man's voice was as smooth and smoky as his music, his Cajun cadence sounding just a little eerie given their current state and all. Frank was pretty sure the guy's second comment had more to do with earlier at the café than with the shadow girl or Frank's reaching for his weapon.

"I meant it … in case you heard me before … I'm sorry." Frank stood straighter, more respectful, and shoved his hands in his pocket. He wasn't sure himself if he did it because there wasn't anything better to do with them, or because it was the direct opposite of almost drawing on the guy. "I was afraid you wouldn't come back, and everyone else has been ignoring me."

"Not ignorin', watchin'. Dey need to know you ain't comin' out of de dark at 'em. A lot of things in de dark; most of dem you don't want leavin' it."

That took a moment to sink in. Was that supposed to be figurative, or literal? Either way, Frank had a much better understanding of the wariness in the others' eyes. It wasn't like he had any idea what they could be afraid of, but given his luck with everything else, it only stood to reason there would be a bogeyman or two on this side of the looking glass.

"She lookin' out for you, you know," Horn-man continued on his original track. There was no doubt he spoke of the shadow girl. "She might walk in de dark sometimes, but she ain't a part of it."

A shiver shot down Frank's spine at the thought of Char flirting with danger. He had seen a lot in his years of service, but the broken children — be it their bodies or their spirits — had always hit him the hardest. It was uncomfortable thinking of even a dead girl putting herself in harm's way.

"I told you, she ain't quite like us, de dark slide off her skin like it ain't nothin'. You do better worryin' about you and what mischief you is courtin'." With those last words Horn-man turned and started to walk away, his instrument pursed between his lips and the jazz beginning to wail. Frank wanted to wail right along with it; his answers were getting away again!

"Hey!" Frank called after him, "Hey! Wait!"

Horn-man didn't blink away like before, but he didn't stop either.

"Damn it! How the heck can I stop this courting you're talking about if I don't know what you mean or anything? I need answers, not warnings!"

The words drifted back like the notes of the music, soulful and final. "I'm done talkin' to you today, got things I need to be doin'. You, you need to be thinkin' some."

"Thinking some!?" Frank vibrated with frustration. "Now just what do you suppose I've been doing since I got here?"

The musician stopped and looked over his shoulder, his odd eyes pinning Frank where he stood. "Thinkin' about the wrong things, that what you been doin'. You think on what I said about dat shadow girl and fixin' your attitude. I be back when you is ready."

"Wait!"

"Again with de waitin'! I got things to do, son, and so do you."

He could hear the impatience in Horn-man's voice, could see it in the set of his shoulders, but Frank couldn't help himself; he needed even just that tentative normalcy that came with knowing someone's name.

"Please ... just tell me what I should call you."

Again that disappointed look Frank had first inspired back at the café.

"Boy, ain't you already figured out de harm in knowin' a name? You got a lot to learn. Stick to Horn-man, cause I ain't givin' no one de kind of power over me dat comes with knowin' my name." Without another word, he blinked out.

For a long, depressed moment, Frank stood there looking at the spot where the old man disappeared. He was never going to get any answers, was he? Unless, of course, he found them himself. What did Horn-man say Frank had to think about? The girl ... the girl and changing his attitude ... Well, both seemed as difficult to figure out as a Chinese puzzle box so, as he never was very good at self-reflection, the girl it was.

She followed him a lot — he would be a piss-poor detective if he hadn't noticed that right away — but she mostly never drew close, and rarely said a word when she did. There was something about her that struck a cord with him, as if he should know her. But he'd never pinned her down long enough to figure it out. All he ever saw of his shadow was a cool indifference that sometimes slid over into contempt when Frank did something she considered particularly dense: like trying to eat the leavings off the plates at Du Monde, or reaching out to help one of the undead.

He pushed the girl from his thoughts. It wasn't like he needed the extra reminder of his own inadequacy. What could he say, he would never get use to being ... different, and hunger and ingrained manners had a way of running a man's life.

It was getting late and dark. Not many undead around — mostly vagrants — but more than a few cats wandered in his wake. That made him think about his cat, Charly, which made him think of home. He missed both of them. Hell, he didn't even know what happened to her. Poor thing ... left all alone. It was too much to hope that his neighbor, Miz Krantz, would have taken her in.

Anyway, now he knew where he was going, instead of wandering aimlessly, hoping to catch a glimpse of Nick among the undead. Frank headed for Coleman Street. He'd feel much better in his own place. For a while he could forget everything. He was beyond tired and looking forward to his overstuffed couch and the comfort of being in his own space.

Thinking about home got him thinking about Shadow Girl again. Was she bedding down in one of these alleys he was passing, maybe a flophouse somewhere? Did she have a home where people missed her? Or was she alone in the world? Frank wasn't comfortable with that thought. He and Maya hadn't had kids, but they'd wanted them desperately. Just the thought of a fourteen-year-old girl bunking on the streets threw Frank's parental instincts into overdrive, even if she was already dead.

As he cut across the vacant lot on Brooks he looked for his shadow. He didn't spot her, but he did have a flashback of that disgusted look she reserved for him. The ones saved for when he did something dumb. Frank stopped short. Doing something dumb ...

With a growl he drove tense fingers through his auburn hair and his dark brown eyes deepened even further. There wasn't anything he could do about the punk kid even if he found her. He was tired. He was hungry. He damn well wanted to be home. Now.

Shaking off his tension and unease, Frank clung to that last though, let the cluttered images of his tiny three-room apartment form in his mind, and took a deep breath. His eyes drifted closed. He took another deep breath. If he concentrated any harder, his ectoplasmic head was going to burst — yeah, so he'd seen Ghostbusters one too many times, but it wasn't like he had much else but movies to go on when it came to being dead. Slowly he peeled one eye open. He was still new at this blinking deal; it didn't always work right.

This time it did.

He was standing in his living room, a tumbled pile of books spread across the floor in front of him and mountains of books and junk mail on every surface. Home ... haven. He let out his last breath and his stomach rumbled. Damn! He didn't know what to do. It was driving him nuts. Frank wandered into the kitchen. He was so desperate his mouth was watering just at the thought of food.

He wanted to scream. He'd give anything for something he could eat. It was no good, though; going through the motions didn't get him anywhere. He might feel like he still had all the working parts, and everything certainly tasted great, but eating did nothing to alleviate his hunger.

Flicking on the light, Frank almost indulged himself in that scream he'd been thinking about just a moment ago. There, crouched on his counter, was his shadow cirl, Char, pawing through the piles of junk. In front of her was a little pile of questionable foodstuff.

"What … ? How … ? Hell!" Frank sputtered through his rage. Here he'd been worried about the little punk and she was safe and sound, squatting in his apartment! How the hell did she get into his apartment? He was about to vent all his considerable frustration on her when something registered past all his high emotion.

The girl perched on his countertop — previously normal, if radical in appearance — was twitching a three-foot long tail. It was impressive, actually. Long and full, with tortoiseshell markings … markings that set his nerves jangling in recognition. Superimposed over Shadow Girl and her new anime sportage was a memory as vivid and jagged as a bad dream: His last day on earth as an undead, climbing through the window and out onto the fire escape, an agitated Charly heading up the steps before him, her tail bottle brushed and twitching … Oh crap … Char … Charly …

She began to purr, her tail lashing in a lazy, relaxed sort of way that Frank knew too well. Her expression could only be described as smug. Through the looking glass, in deed, only there was no little bottle or cake in sight to alter his perception. Frank LoCosta was stuck in this fractured reality.

He was shaking.

Across the room, Charly must have decided she'd given him enough of her attention because she turned her back on him and began to eat her gleanings.

Watching her was torture … until Frank realized the edge slowly being taken off of his hunger. Dumfounded, he dropped into his usual chair at the small round kitchen table and locked his gaze on Charly. The apartment behind him could have imploded and he wouldn't have taken his eyes of her. It was heaven! Just like he was doing the eating himself, only the gamy flavor of the dubious fair didn't bother him like it normally would. They were both silent until the last morsel was gone and Frank no longer felt like he was battling his digestive system.

"Why didn't you tell me?" Frank practically breathed the words, as if anything louder would bring back reality as he'd known it just minutes before, but his stomach remained quiet and uncomplaining while Charly looked at him with one of her indecipherable expressions.

The tension of the moment began to build and Frank shifted uncomfortably, his jaw clenching and his temper beginning to flare. She should have told him ... he was her ... um ... person — owner just didn't feel right anymore, not with her looking all too human — he'd cared for her and fed her and allowed her to wrap him around her paw, and how was she treating him now? As if he was of no consequence. As if ...

That stopped Frank in mid thought; she treated him as if she were a cat and he a lowly human. Why the heck was he surprised? He reined in his attitude and tried again. "Why?"

One of those slow, languid blinks. One of those put-upon sighs cats pull off very well. Then she looked at him straight in the eye and uttered, quite simply, "You weren't ready."

"Excuse me?" He knew she was right, but still it stung.

"You can't even accept your deal, how could you grasp mine?"

"I'm ... dead, what else is there to grasp?"

"Oh come on," Charly's inflection was a curious melding of punk kid and quintessential cat. "Maybe you say the words ... barely, but you don't really believe them."

The ghost of Horn-man's voice drifted through Frank's thoughts: he had to think of Shadow Girl ... or rather Charly, and he had to change his attitude. Well, now was the time then. He already knew how difficult it was to deal with her when she was still a cat; the experience was intensified now that she could really tell him what she thought of him.

"My name is Francis Robert LoCosta, and I am dead." It was like an AA parody, but Frank said the words. It made his stomach a little queasy to realize that he did believe them. Nothing else happened. No celestial music or light bridges ... no shadow demons swarming to drag him to hell ... nothing. Well, except for Charly giving him a considering look, her head nodding as if he'd confirmed something she was rather hoping he wouldn't.

But he thought that was what she'd wanted! His stomach roiled a bit more. Apparently stress was another thing that didn't go away because you were dead.

Why was he confused? He hadn't been able to make sense of Charly as a cat, why should now be any different? "Aw, forget it. I'm tired and I'm going to sleep."

Frank turned without another word and stalked into the other room. Ignoring everything around him, he stretched out on the couch, which still looked as if he'd just climbed out of it, and pulled the blankets over his head.

What had he learned about his new state today? That it was a bad idea to bang on tables, or anything else that might react, around the undead; That it was more satisfying to watch someone else eat, than it was to try it on his own; and, oh yeah, being dead sucked! He tried to push everything back out of his thoughts, blanking his mind and courting oblivion. Fortunately, being a detective, he was good at this, having had lots of practice grabbing odd naps as he could in the middle of an intense case. His gut gave him a bit of a problem, but Frank dealt with it. He was just about to drift into unconsciousness when another set of instincts kicked in, throwing him into crystal-clear alertness. A sudden weight straddled his hips and dainty hands began gently kneading his stomach.

A razor-sharp memory of his last time with Maya rushed past his defenses until Frank's hands — along with the rest of him — moved nearly faster than thought. He slammed the memory back where it belonged and sat up abruptly, his grip locking around the delicate wrists as he simultaneously pushed those lithe, firm thighs back off where they sat provocatively across his hips. A thump that could only be a tail lashed lazily against his legs. Frank was breathing fast, his blood pounding with adrenaline, and he had to consciously tell himself not to tighten his hold.

"What the hell do you think you're doing?" He was more than tempted to toss her off the couch, as he had hundreds of times before when she'd been smaller ... and covered in fur.

Another one of those looks; the ones that said, "poor, feeble-minded human."

"What ... do you think ... you were doing?" he repeated, his teeth clenching and the rest of him absolutely still. As if there was any doubt.

"In your dreams, monkey-boy."

Frank couldn't see her expression, but he heard derision and pity in that irreverent reply. Part of him was startled out of his anger and confusion by her obvious movie reference, though he shouldn't be surprised, she'd been his steady companion through any number of midnight movie marathons and there was nothing like Buckaroo Bonzai to convey a sense of the ridiculous.

"There's something wrong ... there." Charly didn't try to extract her hands from his hold, instead she used her foot in a yoga-like move to point at his stomach ... a move unconsciously sensual enough to confuse the matter just a little further, not to mention add to Frank's discomfort. "I was making it go away."

Neither of them moved. Frank felt really foolish. He didn't quite get what she meant by "wrong" and "making it go away," but despite her display of flexibility it was clear nothing about her attitude was or had been intentionally sexual. Should he apologize, or should he just accept what she said and go on? The thought alone took no time at all. The decision hardly longer than that. Charly never had struck him as having much of an interest in apologies. It didn't matter, though; before Frank could respond the weight across his legs was gone and his hands were holding empty air.

He lay there cursing himself, alone in his apartment, wide awake, with an ever-sharpening pain in his gut.

Weary beyond words, he curled in a ball on the couch, clutching his stomach. He groaned and could feel clammy sweat beading his forehead. Stomach problems had been the one thing he'd never worried about in his other life; he wished he could say the same now. Pretty ironic that in ten years as a cop he hadn't developed the standard-issue ulcer. By the feel of things he was making up for it. Either that, or something Charly ate had turned, if it was even possible for a vicarious meal to give him a tummy ache.

Well, lying around wasn't getting him anywhere. Better for him to try and track down Horn-man, or at least put himself where the guy could find him. He wasn't even going to try to track down Charly. She would come back around when she was ready and not before; she always had.

With a though, he left the apartment, appearing instantaneously at Café Du Monde. Handy trick, that. Frank was beginning to appreciate it more and more as he got the hang of it. He could only go places he had been, but that hardly mattered. What, was he going to do, become a tourist now that he was dead? He didn't think so.

He scanned the café, trying not to watch too long as people ate Dani's finest Cajun faire. Frank's gut twisted sharply until he looked away and it settled into a dull ache. His stomach was still in a knot and he didn't know what all that spice would do to it. Now wasn't the time to find out the hard way.

No, he was here to find Horn-man. Only that seemed as futile as looking for Charly right now. It was midnight, and even at this hour the place was packed with the after-theatre crowd and those who just didn't know when to call it a night. Despite the mob inside Du Monde and out, there was no sign of the musician. Frank would just have to wait here because he had no idea where else to look for Horn-man and he was as likely to turn up here as anywhere else.

There was someone sitting at his table drinking a savory cup of chicory coffee and people-watching. The guy looked like he was settling in for a while but Frank figured what the hell and sat down anyway. What was the guy going to do, tell him to buzz off? He wouldn't even know Frank was there.

Frank lasted maybe ten minutes. He didn't know if it was all the food around, which he tried real hard to not watch people eat, or if the smells alone were enough of a problem, but his stomach ache had gone beyond a dull annoying discomfort right into acute abdominal agony.

What the hell good was it being dead?! Pain should not be a part of the afterlife. A sudden jab worse than all the others and he reflexively curled around his gut, his arms wrapped around and his knees jerked up, as if going fetal somehow would ease the pain. Ha! As if!

The people-watcher yipped and scrambled away from the table Frank's knees had slammed into when he went into his impersonation of a pill bug. Even without trying Frank seemed to have a knack for unsettling the undead. Damn! Horn-man wasn't going to be happy with him. No, not at all. He'd be lucky if the man showed up any time before Armageddon now. Of course, Frank wasn't in any shape to ask questions, anyway, so it was just as well.

Oh man ... he was dying ... again!

"No ... no ... you jus' wishin' you be."

Well ... he'd come back to Cafe Du Monde to find a man. Here he was. Sweat dripped into Frank's eyes as he looked up into a familiar, warm-caramel gaze. The sight wavered and he wondered if his vision was going too until he realized Horn-man was slowly shaking his head. Yeah, he was clearly disappointed.

"Sorry." Frank muttered and curled back around himself. He didn't have the energy to keep his head up, let alone to continue apologizing. Apparently being newly dead was like going through puberty again: a second change to experience being a screw-up. Only his old man had nothing on Horn-man when it came to "the Look". Frank felt worse now than he had the time he'd gotten caught puking up his first smoke. Damn if he didn't feel like he was about to cry, even.

That realization was like a blast of frigid air down his shirt. No way was he going to cry in front of this guy. The only thing worse for Frank's self-esteem would be to lose it in front of Charly's unforgiving gaze.

"You have enough yet?" The voice wasn't Horn-man's. It wasn't even male.

Oh great! If he wanted to find her he would have been out of luck, but all he had to do is think about how much he didn't want Charly around, and poof! there she was! Frank groaned and curled into a tighter ball. Maybe she was a hallucination brought on by whatever was killing him.

No such luck. He cracked one eye and peered past Horn-man's shoulder. Charly was perched on top of a decorative cask stamped "moonshine", her eyes open wide and innocent, though her smirk was anything but. The tail was gone, but Frank thought he could see the very tips of a set of cat ears poking through her spiked hair. He closed his eye again and rested his head on his knees. It was hard to think of anything but the pain for very long.

"What you playin' at, bijou?" Clearly Horn-man wasn't talking to him. Of course, he might as well not have been talking to anyone because Charly merely made a rude noise as her only answer.

"Who said your name, boy?" This time the question was aimed at Frank, but he couldn't answer. It was all he could do not to scream. "Dis from de other life, someone say your name, dey bring down on you de way you was before you died, good or bad, but most always bad. You stuck dat way until you go beyond or someone take it away. Not too many got dat mojo goin' on."

What Horn-man said slowly sank in and the memory of Quinlan Mack surfaced in Frank's thoughts. The whole while he'd been calling him Nutjob because he didn't know the guy's name. Every time Frank had seen him he expected to see evidence of a fight that was never there; a black eye, a split lip, that kind of thing, but there was never a blemish … until Frank said the man's name. Once he remembered Nutjob's name it summoned him and the damage was done. The uninjured appearance faded away and became the beat-up image from the photograph Frank had from the other life. Watching Quinlan go through all that again had been rough. He never would have wished that on the guy the first time, let alone want to make him go through it twice, but that was what had happened, until the man died again. Now Frank understood the true severity of the situation. If he hadn't told Quinlan the details of his death he would have gone on suffering from all the injuries he'd gotten before the fatal one.

If at all humanly … ghostly possible, Frank went even paler. He didn't know how he died! He didn't know! The pain wouldn't end.

Charly made another rude noise. "He said his name … and he's still this way by his own choice."

Frank stared at her, horrified. She'd tried to end this. Somehow she could take away the pain. Only he'd stopped her! He hadn't understood. He was confused. Was it his fault he didn't know all the rules of the game yet? He tried to apologize yet again only his whole body began to spasm. The table rattled horribly and some bizarrely twisted part of Frank's mind had to laugh. Dani would be lucky if anyone ever sat at this table again by the time Frank was done with it. Children would run by and touch it on a dare, but everyone else would watch it sideways from the corner of their eye.

Oh god! He hurt ... he really hurt. He couldn't imagine that it had taken anything more than this to kill him the first time, even though there must have been something else, because after all, he was still friggin' here! Oh god!

"Enough, Charlene, you do what you do for him, he don't need to suffer no more." Horn-man was stern but he wasn't a match for that cat. Still, he must have caught her on a good day. Frank fought his eyes open just in time to see Charly unfold herself from the top of the cask and saunter over to where he huddled. He didn't just tremble, he shook, and he couldn't say if it was whatever ailed him that caused it, or a reaction to the intent look in her glowing green eyes as she drew nearer.

They say the eyes are the windows to the soul: Charly had opened the blinds and Frank was astounded by what he saw there ... no that word was not strong enough, no word was strong enough for the complexity of what he felt. He hadn't yet run into a deity in the afterlife, but right now he was gazing on one even he couldn't dispute was god-touched. And even as he realized it, she reached out to touch him.

His first reaction was to tense, but he was already tighter than the spring on an obsessive-compulsive's watch. He couldn't flinch or move even if he'd intended to, not that he would make that mistake twice. Only sheer determination kept his eyes open, though, as Charly knelt before him and slowly ran her hands over him; first up and down his bent legs, soothing and straightening them as if they were nothing but folded paper. From there she went to feather-light touches over his arms until they fell away from her goal. Again, as earlier, she began to knead his tortured stomach. Cramped, icy flesh gave way to intense warmth until bit by bit the agony leached away. Frank found himself weak, but well. Astounded ... yes, again with the astounded ... he looked up into her eyes felling some uncomfortable mix between worship and wariness.

Charly stared back at him and bit by bit the revealing glow of moments before dimmed and faded all together until Frank looked once more into the unfathomable depths of cat's eyes in an all-too-human looking face. The only mirrors left in that gaze reflected back his own image ... it was humbling.

As Frank was grappling with the transformation, his eyes registered a blur of motion mere moments before his chin telegraphed a stinging pain to his brain. In a flash, Charly was gone, but she'd left him with a reminder of her affection. His laugh was a little weak, but he leaned back in his favorite chair to watch the undead patrons eat in comfortable silence while Horn-man picked up his instrument and began to play. From the corner of his eye he thought he saw a flicker of chestnut hair, but now wasn't the time to chase snipes. There would be time enough for answers later, after Frank got his strength back. Now was the time to indulge himself in some vicarious Cajun cuisine.

Time for a Monster Story

"See what I mean?" Nick said. He smiled coyly and silently got up and returned to the dining room.

"I'll take demons anytime," commented Druscilla as she waved to Lucia.

"There are things worse than death."

"Oh, yes, I know," Druscilla replied. "Sometimes reality can be as terrifying as a new plane of existence. That reminds me of a place I visited once and the mysterious happenings at the local pond ...

Willow Pond

April Grey

By that point, my mother was no longer among the living, and so, there was no one to warn me about Willow Pond.

I never married or had children, and I suppose Aunt Margot chose to leave her worldly goods to me simply because, like her, I was alone. She could have just as easily given the money to the local dog pound, a place where she had donated her services well into her eighties. Something is to be said for pity, as I was planning an early semi-retirement; and her place, an old farmhouse sitting next to a pond surrounded by ancient willows, would serve me well.

Upon her attorney mailing me the house keys, I courageously rented a car. I rarely drove and had never driven a manual. So, it was my misfortune that the only compact available on the lot was a stick shift. Still my spirits were high as I travelled down small country lanes and through quaint villages still unacquainted with the likes of Walmart or Kentucky Fried Chicken. In fact, I was wondering exactly how desolate the area was when I spotted a gas station complete with a convenience store attached. I heaved a sigh of relief, grateful that some vestige of civilization remained in this rural outpost. I fueled up the tank, bought some supplies, and checked my directions to the property. The station attendant gave good directions, and within three quarters of an hour ,I turned into a drive, quite overgrown, but recognizable for the statues of lions guarding the gates on the stone wall.

I hadn't been there since a young child, and though I remembered that some unpleasantness had unfolded there, I couldn't remember exactly what. My mother preferred not to discuss my father's side of the family, understandable after the divorce, and so I never sought out the story of my one visitation with Aunt Margot.

The house was smaller than I remembered it; of course, when I was last there, I was much smaller. Warned that the front door's lock was difficult, I headed round the back to the screened in porch facing the glade that revealed the pond. The sun was still high in the sky this late afternoon of a rather warm midsummer's day. I couldn't help but think that, all too soon, the sun would drop behind those massive willows, and the prolonged gloaming would come.

The lands were overgrown, no doubt due to my grand-aunt's infirmity toward the end. In rural areas, there is little that one can keep private, and the service station attendant — a thin, bucolic man with a lopsided grin — certainly remembered her.

"She was as mad as a hatter towards the end," he said as he rung me up. "Adult services got called in, but she died before they could place her in a home." He laughed to himself and shook his head. "She'd tell the darnedest stories, she did. Things in the water, and she wouldn't drink anything from the well. Came here for bottled water nearly every day. And when she got too old she asked my cousin to bring her bottled water and groceries." He sighed. "She was good about recycling, too."

I smiled. She had loved dogs and cared about the environment. And she had cared to give me a home, too. I felt bad about not being there for her. But Philadelphia was a world apart, and she never contacted me to let me know she needed help.

I wondered if her dying in her own home was a blessing. My own mother spent several years in a nursing home before her death, and being a dutiful daughter, I visited her twice weekly, listening to her reminisce and regret that she was no longer on her own. I should think it much nicer to die in familiar surroundings than an institution where choice was often removed for the convenience of those who ran the place.

My thoughts continued to ramble. But as I caught my first glimpse of the pond, my stomach turned, and I trembled as if my body were covered in fine cobwebs. The trees were still bigger than life, with a couple uprooted and rotting. The pond itself, while not overly large, contained a black stillness, as if the depths were far greater than the length or width. Something in the water ... and then the thought fled. The leaves of the willows dangled, giving the impression of being in the South where Spanish moss adorned the boughs of trees. The color of the leaves was a soft sage green, an unnaturally muted shade reminding me of fungus. I felt very cold now, with a shiver heading down my back and spreading through my extremities.

The path to the front door was completely lost in overgrown shrubs. However, the path to the back of the house facing the pond was open and easy to walk in spite of the weeds. I took out the keys and slipped them into the old style lock on the back porch. Piles of newspapers tied for recycling, and never collected, towered all around me. A glance at the date showed that that one particular pile had been awaiting its fate for the past decade. The newspaper canyons filled the back porch, effectively blocking off the natural light. The kitchen door easily swung open, and I prepared myself for a barrage of smells. But there were none. The fridge was unplugged and cleaned out — who had taken the liberty to be so helpful? Perhaps the attorney had paid someone, more than likely so. Yet the newspapers had been left — too burdensome to remove? I walked over to the kitchen tap, the style of which was mid-1950s, and turned it on.

After a few burbles of air, rusty water gushed out. At the convenience store, I had picked up bottled water along with a can of beef stew and some fresh fruit. In places like this, people could get heavy metal poisoning from the water pipes or become ill from a polluted well. Aunt Margot had been wise enough to take precautions, hadn't she? Still, I was glad for the running water. I rinsed off my face and patted it on the back of my neck, removing the stickiness accumulated during my long drive. Looking through the window over the kitchen sink, I spotted the pond through the willows. Already the trees were blocking out the setting sun, leaving the world dark with the sky still a bright light blue.

I walked through the small dining room to the hallway. A cozy living room faced me, and to my left, the hall ran back to the stairs for the upper floor. I felt some apprehension about going up those stairs. The original farmhouse was colonial and the ceilings quite low, making me feel claustrophobic. Those stairs were even more cramped, and I resisted my curiosity to see the upper floor while the shadows were gathering. Perhaps tomorrow morning, I would be in a more suitable frame of mind to explore? I went around turning on the lights. For all the pile up of newspapers, the downstairs was tidy, Spartan even. The living room had a large modern couch, quite out of fashion with the rest of the building, but it was wide and long enough for me to sleep on.

I sat and turned on the television. There was no cable box, and snow rained on the stations. I turned off the set but stayed there. Crickets chirped in my ears, and then a screeching sound ... cicadas, I thought. Having lived most of my adult life in the city, I could not be sure if the annoying clicking sound was indeed insect-made. With the dwindling of the light, the fauna of the area began its evening serenade. Exhausted by the long drive, I closed my eyes and picked out the low sound of bullfrogs calling to each other. People complain of the incessant noise of the cities, but here, deep in the country, life presented its own racket as every species croaked or shrieked its own cacophony of lust.

I dosed off and awoke with a start at the crack of lightning and then the dull roar of thunder. It was the heavy, dense feel of heat lightning rather than an actual storm. I was glad I had turned on the lights before my nap; waking in a strange place in the dark would have worked nerves that were already acting up. I had forgotten how noisy the great outdoors could be, but also how strange to have the awareness that not another person was around for miles.

I headed to the kitchen to make some dinner for myself. Clean plates sat neatly stacked in a rack near the sink. I located a saucepot in a cabinet near the old white porcelain stove and heated up my can of stew. I sat in the dining room wishing that the television worked and regretting that my purse was in the car with the library paperback still inside; I didn't feel like heading out in the dark to the driveway to find it. Perhaps if I found a flashlight, but then I yawned and realized that the long drive, the excitement of a change of scenery and the fresh air combined to create a sleeping pill far superior to anything put out by the pharmaceutical companies. I wouldn't need a book to help me sleep after all.

As I washed the saucepan and dish, another crack of lightning and roar of thunder hit. In the flash of light, I could have sworn I saw movement out by the pond. The dish fell from my shocked, suddenly numb hands and broke. Swallowing, trying hard not to panic, I turned off the water as my thoughts careened.

My mind presented me with a long-forgotten old nightmare from my childhood: blackish-brown muddy appendages all tangled with algae reaching up, grabbing my ankles, and then a sharp tug. I fell and was pulled down under the black glass surface. The pond was shallow at that end, but I remember the light above me retreating as I was towed to the muck below.

My parents had only been a few yards away. Recovery was swift, and I remember shaking as they put me into an old enameled bathtub filled with hot water. My mother clucked over me, admonishing me that I shouldn't have gone so close to the edge. Was it a dream or memory? No, it was memory. That part of the visit, so blissfully repressed, became even more strongly felt, bursting through with greater vigor due to the years it has been so deeply submerged.

Movement and the ripples of the deadly black waters taught me that my imagination had not played my memory false. I knew what was down there now: something with silver, reflective eyes, craving my flesh.

Though my flesh was no longer young, I did not hesitate to run from the house as fast as I could. My keys were by the back door, and I was loathe to waste time trying to go out through the front, even though it meant going nearer to it, them, whatever it was that had waited so patiently for my return.

Stacks of newspaper wobbled, and then fell behind me as I careened through the canyons of paper. The door creaked behind me. Roots and uneven patches of turf nearly tripped me as I made my way through the overgrowth to the drive. The car keys were in my hand as I yanked open the unlocked door, but another crack of lightning showed me further movement coming from the water's edge. Amorphous shapes crawled along the ground: amphibian-like in their glossy luminosity. I didn't

Willow Pond

know how many because the smothering dark had returned after the lightning flash. They might be humanoid and on all fours, but I thought not. The eyes did not seem to be in pairs but rather cast all over their bodies. I kept thinking that it was a host of infernal beings. But, what if it was simply one huge mass of flesh covered by eyes?

My hands shook so badly that the keys dropped to the floor of the car. A deadly silence fell, no crickets or frogs made their mating cries. It was too dark to find the keys, and I fumbled for the interior light switch, cursing my unfamiliarity with the rental's dashboard. Another flash of lightning lit up the sky, again giving me a gut-wrenching glimpse at whatever it was, out there, glistening in the dark. It had already crossed by half the expanse between me and the pond. My fingers touched something metallic, and I found the keys. My entire body was palsied with fear, and after two attempts, I managed to get the keys into the lock.

A sound, a slurping as if one was walking on the gooey thick sludge of a bay at low tide, reached me. With the sound came a smell of dead leaves fetid with mold such as one would smell at the end of November. I gagged and ground the key in the lock. I feared that I would flood the unfamiliar car.

My hands refused to obey me as I continued to turn the motor over. The cloying smell of gas and the terror of a potentially flooded engine assailed me. Beyond the sounds and the smell of the car it was out there. I did a quick count and turned the key again. The engine caught with a feeble protest, just as something landed on the hood. I whimpered and sent the car crashing into reverse, destroying a forsythia bush or two as I drove at as high a speed as I dared. I hadn't even put the headlights on — didn't want to see if they were following. In blind panic, I drove straight backwards until I came to the end of the long driveway. Even then, I did not stop to check for cars but slammed into forward and safety.

I wasn't able to catch my breath even as the miles sped under me, and the tremor in my hands never diminished but rather grew greater until I feared I would lose control of them entirely.

My plans for early, partial retirement are replaced by disability payments. I never returned to Willow Pond, and rather than allow others to suffer my fate, I had the building razed and the pond drained and filled.

Anxiously I awaited reports of what they would find there in the muck. What vile creatures would be revealed? On the phone, my demands to know what they found were met by a polite silence.

The tremors continued to spread through my body, making it nearly impossible to hold a pencil or work on a computer.

I can no longer dress or feed myself. A night attendant helps me navigate the hours after dark. As the illness worsens, I fear I shall have to move to some hospice or institution to live out my days. Perhaps I should kill myself.

I laugh when doctors tell me I have sudden onset multiple sclerosis.

I know it was the pond. Its miasma contained some toxin that wreaks havoc on the brain and nervous system, creating illness and hallucinations. I have no other explanation since the workers I employed to drain that deadly water found no creatures.

Yet my memories, both from my childhood and that singular night, taunt me. When my eyelids droop from exhaustion, the image of a myriad of shining eyes comes before me, and I jerk awake, shrieking.

Days and nights merge, I am never quite awake and never fully asleep. There is no respite.

"The water, the water … " I scream and grasp her hand, as the visiting nurse sedates me.

Here, Things Take a Turn

Lucia winced and tossed off a "That why I swim in pools." As she returned to the main dining room.

"I'll stick to the hot tub," Cher commented. Druscilla nodded in agreement.

Ray came over with a small plate of mini-sandwiches. "Who's the glum guy at the small table overt there? Never seen him before."

"He's a gumshoe,"Nick answered sotto voce. "He just came off a tough case and he came here because the case was so bizarre he needed a different atmosphere to get hammered."

"Tough case?" Druscilla asked. "Not a supernatural thing, is it?"

"It was in the news some time ago. Here, I'll explain …"

Clean and Pure

John L. French

SOMEONE killed her sister. Knifed her and left her for dead. Just who it was, the police couldn't or wouldn't say.

Sarah found out when a city detective knocked on her door at eleven on a Tuesday night. She knew right away it was bad news. That time of night, cops don't drive all the way from Baltimore to bring you glad tidings.

The detective who came out was young and very kind. She gently explained how Gayle's body was found in a back yard behind some row home in the eastern part of the city. It was now at the Medical Examiners and after tomorrow it could be released to a funeral home.

"Is there any other family?" the detective asked gently, "Other siblings, parents … "

"I'm all Gayle has, had," Sarah replied. "I'll make the arrangements. Do you need me to identify her?"

Detective Michaels shook her head. "We did that through fingerprints."

"So Gayle had a record?"

Michaels nodded and when Sarah asked, "Drugs?" softly replied, "And other things."

Sarah knew what those "other things" were. Larceny, shoplifting, other kinds of theft and probably hooking as well. She'd been there, done it all and more and was lucky to have escaped. Her memory was blessedly hazy, but she knew that in those dark times she did whatever she had to to get her jolt and that once it hit she didn't care who did what to her. More than once she'd wakened with a needle in her arm and stranger on top of her.

"Any idea who might have done it?" Sarah had to ask the question. She already knew the answer. Any given user, dealer, street ho or pimp. And for any reason at all or no reason whatsoever. Gayle may have stolen someone's money or man, may have taken the last bit of stuff or drank the last diet soda. Any slight, any show of disrespect could be a death sentence.

But while anyone could have killed her sister, there would be no one specific person. Detective Michaels confirmed this.

"We have what we think is the weapon used. But there were no prints, maybe DNA off the handle if we're lucky. And someone could always come forward."

Both women knew the chances of that. "Coming forward" was a quick way of waking up dead. "Stop Snitching" was more than a DVD; it was a rigidly enforced code. Dealing yourself out of jail was one thing, but dropping a dime would get you a firebomb through your window. As for getting lucky with DNA, luck and the Eastside had nothing to do with each other.

Thanking Michaels for her kindness, Sarah took her card and accepted the detective's promise to keep in touch and advise her of any developments. She closed the door knowing that was the last she'd see of any police. She knew the score. When she was on the street she heard the cops themselves talking. "Misdemeanor homicide" they called it. "NHI - no human involved." In a city with a rising crime rate, Gayle's death was just another number, a name on a folder, to be filed and forgotten when the next body fell.

"Damn you, Gayle!" Sarah yelled once her door was closed and locked. "Damn you to hell," she shouted again, knowing full well that her sister might already be there. She was grateful for thick walls and living alone, glad that no one could hear her rage and anger over her sister's death and that later there'd be no one to see her cry.

Three in the morning and Sarah still had not slept, her mind continuing to turn over all she had told her sister about her past life. Had she said something to make her time in hell seem glamorous or desirable? She didn't think so. She clearly recalled telling Gayle of all the remembered horrors she'd endured so as to keep her from the same mistakes. But if it wasn't her fault, whose was it? Who was to blame for her sister's death?

Not her parents. They had given all they had, had done all that they could. While not overly religious, they had raised both their girls to lead the good life. "Be clean and pure," Sarah remembered her father saying. "Be clean and pure in this life or face the cleansing fires in the next." It wasn't their fault that Sarah had fallen in with a wild crowd at school and made every wrong choice she could. Just as it wasn't Sarah's fault that Gayle had refused to heed her warnings and learn from her sister's mistakes.

I should never have let her go to school in the city, Sarah said to herself as the night slowly shifted into a cloudy day; should never have let her quit either. I should have driven down there and dragged her ass back here or else sent her to one of those small town colleges in Pennsylvania where two stolen cars and a break-in are called a crime wave.

It wouldn't have worked, Sarah admitted to herself, not for her, just like it didn't work for me when Daddy tried it. Gayle would have lasted a day, maybe two, maybe even a week then the demons inside her would have driven her right back to Baltimore, probably with half my stuff.

But, she decided sadly, at least I would have tried. Now all I can do for my little sister is to bury what's left of her. In the back of her mind she knew that something else might need doing as well, but she'd wait and see what the police did before listening to a part of her she'd thought long gone.

The funeral was a small affair, just Sarah, her friends, members of her parish and some people from her work. No one who knew Gayle came.

Detective Michaels made an appearance, some kind of cop courtesy, Sarah supposed, as the woman had no further news about Gayle's murder. No suspects, no leads, and from the way she talked, damn little chance of developing any.

"If you think of anything, of anyone," Michaels said as she was leaving the Belair Funeral Home, "give me a call."

Although she didn't realize it at the time, there was something different about Michaels's voice. It was later, after her sister was hours in the ground and Sarah was getting ready for bed, that she remembered the tone. She hadn't heard it in some time, not since before she left the city. It was the way cops talked to suspects, or people who had been or would one day be a suspect in something.

"Guess she looked up my record," Sarah said to herself, "and figured once on the street always on the street."

She should have been mad and was surprised she wasn't. To herself she admitted there was some truth in it. Ever since she heard of Gayle's death Sarah had felt something inside her, something she had thought long gone. It was her street sense, the outrage that came from someone taking something, someone from you. No matter you didn't need it or want it. No matter that you hadn't seen her for a month or talked to her in weeks. She was family, she was yours, and no one but you had the right.

Sarah knew what she'd do, what she would have already done, had she still been out there. While the cops would never hear it, word would have reached her. Blood called for blood and Sarah would have drawn her share or seen that it was done. Even now, a county and ten miles away, Sarah felt the growing need to do right by her baby sister. She'd thought, she'd hoped the police would do it for her. She knew this was not going to happen, not now, not for another dead junkie, not for a ho whose death had made the city that much nicer. Justice for Gayle would have to come from somewhere else.

In with these thoughts Sarah heard the voice of her father.

"Leave it in God's hands," he would have said to her had he been there. "He will see it right, if not in this world then the next. All will pay, all will be cleansed. And those who commit great sins will burn the longest before they are pure."

Even as she acknowledged that her father was a better person than she'd ever be, Sarah felt the past five years start to slip away.

Sunlight burned bright. Sarah woke and instantly regretted it.

"Shit!" she said out loud as reality chased away already forgotten dreams.

She had thought that a night's sleep would burn away her anger, but as her feet hit the floor and she reached for her robe she found that it was still with her. Not as strong, but still there, reminding her that Gayle was dead, her killer was not and nobody gave a damn but her.

"I have a life," she told herself, trying to talk away the idea forming in the back of her mind.

Not much of one, she realized, thinking of the funeral and those who came. People who came out of charity or duty, "friends" with whom she shared dinner and drinks but nothing else, a couple of guys she'd screwed and who kept in touch in the hopes she'd do them again. There was no one close, no one who offered to stay over and share her sadness, no one like family, like her parents who died or the sister she'd lost.

"I have a job." Again, not much of one. She was a mid-level cubicle dweller, pushing papers that came from God knows where over to who gives a damn. It paid for the condo she lived in, the food she ate and the clothes she wore. She could quit it tomorrow and not miss it at all and chances are those she worked with would forget her name inside of a month.

"I've got a home." No, she had a high priced apartment she'd paid for once then kept paying for in the form of condo association fees and dues. It was worse than rent and all for a big box to go to when she was done working in her little box.

And at the end of it all, Sarah thought as she sat in her fuzzy slippers and cotton robe drinking coffee, at the end of it all an even smaller box is waiting for me. And she'd be damned if she could think of six people who'd be willing to carry it to her grave.

"I got nothing," she finally admitted. She started making plans.

***

The Eastside had changed. Some of it was gone. Everything north of Hopkins Hospital and east of Broadway had been dug up or torn down to make room for research buildings, shops, new homes and apartments.

The people who lived there were gone too. Bought or thrown out to make room for the new construction. They would not be back. Not when the houses yet to be built were being advertised as selling for more than the entire area was worth back when Sarah was using. Her father would have liked it, she thought, once the building was done. Everything would be clean and pure.

And they'd keep it that way. The city would make sure that all the streetlights worked and there would be video cameras on every corner. Police patrols would increase. And of course the new owners would no doubt have their own security force, a private army made up of ex-cops who didn't have to follow as many rules. There'd be no deaths there like her sister's, no vacant yards or dirty alleys in which to leave a body. And those who were killed would draw the politicians, the news and the full force of the law, none of whom would rest until someone, innocent or not, was locked up.

Turning her back on this brave new world, Sarah crossed Broadway into her old haunts. West on Chase St, then into Billie Holliday Ct. It was there, across the alley, in one of the yards in the rear of Caroline that her sister was found. Which one she didn't know, not yet.

Sarah felt the eyes of the neighborhood on her. She was a stranger, an unknown. They might make her for a cop, but not likely. Chances were the ones who had to know knew everyone of them, even the undercovers.

She sat on part of a crumbling wall and waited. For what she didn't know but for now, with nothing to do and nowhere to go, she was content to wait and watch.

Nothing happened the first day, or the second. Sarah had a room at a rundown hotel on Pulaski. Once a part of a major chain, it now changed names every six months or so, its only tenants hookers, cons just out of the Pen and tourists who didn't know any better. But the rooms were cheap with good locks, cable was free and with the mirrors on the ceiling she didn't have to get out of bed to put on her makeup.

"Whatchoo want?"

It was the middle of her third day of waiting. From her place on the wall Sarah looked down at a young child, a girl no more than ten, one whose curiosity had overcome her fear of the strange and different.

"Whatchoo want?" the girl said again when Sarah didn't answer. This time she pointed to the back of the houses on Caroline St.

"Where was the girl killed?"

"Which one?"

"That's what I want to know. Which house?"

"No," this was said with a child's impatience for the denseness of adults, "which girl?"

"The one that was cut."

The young girl thought for but a moment then, "Which one? The one this week or the one last week? Before that they be mostly shot."

Sarah knew she'd been too long off the street when she found herself stunned by the casual way the child accepted violent death.

Quickly shaking off her shock, Sarah said, "Last week."

The young girl nodded and pointed to a yard in the middle of the block before running away.

And soon they'll all know why I'm here, Sarah said to herself. Good.

The police came next, a blue and white cruiser pulling into and blocking the alley. Two white cops got out. One stayed with the car, scanning the houses, watching the neighbors, protecting his partner. The other approached Sarah.

"Good morning, Ma'am."

Had she been in Perry Hall, Sarah would have returned the greeting. But city rules were different. She ignored the officer and kept on looking at the back yards of Caroline St.

"Ma'am, do you have any identification?"

This time Sarah deigned to answer.

"Yes."

"May I please see it?"

"No."

Without turning around, Sarah knew exactly what was happening behind her. The neighborhood was turning out to watch the show. They'd start at their windows, balconies and doorways but they'd come closer and closer as her exchange with the officer kept on, stopping at the invisible but well understood boundary line that separated audience from players.

As the officer's polite, community-policing demeanor started to fade, Sarah knew him to be in a dilemma. Why he had chosen her to bother she did not know, but now that he had, he had to resolve the situation quickly. He had to choose between backing down and losing face or arresting her and risk angering and possibly inciting the gathering crowd. For her part, Sarah now had much the same problem, give in or go to jail. She made her decision with the next question.

"Ma'am, can you identify yourself?"

Sarah looked up at the officer. "Certainly," she said, smiling as if seeing him for the first time. As the officer visibly relaxed she tapped her chest and said, "I'd know me anywhere."

As if on cue the patrol wagon appeared at the other end of the alley, blocking it off. The cop's partner, who must have called the wagon in when he saw how things were going, moved himself between her and the crowd. As uniformed back-up arrived Sarah was professionally and, considering how quickly a crowd could turn from spectators to participants, gently handcuffed and driven away.

To her surprise, Sarah was not taken to Central Booking. Instead she found herself in an interview room of the Homicide Unit, staring at herself in a mirrored window. As she wondered if anyone was on the other side, she studied the woman she could see.

Yeah, that's me, she thought, thinking back to her exchange with the officer. But it's not the same me who left Perry Hall. That woman had forgotten what it had been like, what it was like. That woman had a sister, thought she had a home, career and friends. That woman was a fool.

The woman on this side, the "me" I am now, is awake again after a five year nap. In just a few more days, maybe a week or two, just by watching and listening, she'll know things – where the dogs are fought, where the drugs are stashed, where the users shoot up and where they run to when the cops come. Maybe she'll learn who killed her sister and why. And maybe she won't and keep sitting on her wall until she gives up, goes crazy or gets knifed. Whatever happens, that woman, this woman, is a fool as well.

When the door opened and Detective Michaels walked in Sarah knew exactly what happened and felt a third kind of fool.

"You sent them to bring me in. Whatever I said, whatever I did, they were going to bring me here."

Michaels nodded. "I thought that would be better, and safer, than talking to you in public. Now just what the hell are you doing out there?"

The first rule on the street is you don't talk to cops. The second is you don't explain your own business. Sarah broke them both.

"What you can't, or won't."

"You think sitting on a crumbling wall is going to find your sister's killer?"

"More than you're doing."

"You don't know what I'm … " Michaels stopped. The second of the two rules also applied to cops. Instead she asked, "What are you going to do if you find him? Call me or shoot him yourself?"

"I hadn't thought that far ahead, but thanks for the idea. Now if you're not gonna lock me up, can I go?"

Refusing the detective's offer of a ride, Sarah caught the 23 bus and rode it back to the Hopkins garage. She hadn't been on a bus in a long time and had forgotten how soothing it could be, riding and not driving, looking out the window and watching things go by, worrying only about missing your stop. She decided to start taking the bus instead of paying to park.

The next day, back on her post, Sarah did not expect to find things any different. While some would accept her more for having being hassled and locked up, others would suspect her for that very reason, thinking her a plant among them.

As she sat, Detective Michaels's question came back to her. "What are you doing out here?" And she had to admit she didn't know. On the day she left Perry Hall it had seemed a good idea. Now, she wasn't so sure but she could think of nothing else to do. Her initial plan – wait, watch, learn – had become a vigil to her sister's memory and somehow Sarah felt she would know when it was over, when it was time to go home.

It was somewhat after noon when a young man came up and sat beside her. Dressed in the street uniform of white t-shirt, baggy jeans with boxers showing and heavy work boots, he waited for Sarah to relax and accept his presence.

"You okay?" he asked, not looking her way but copying her stare at the houses across the alley.

"Yeah. Thanks."

"Cops didn't mess with you?"

"They had shit and knew it. States Attorney cut me loose no sooner than I got settled, right after dinner hour."

The young man nodded and was quiet for a time. Finally he asked, "You her kin or something?"

"Kin to who?"

"The girl who got cut last week."

"My sister."

Another nod. "So why you here?"

"Somebody has to be. This is where she died. This is where I mourn." As she said it Sarah knew it was true and didn't feel so much the fool.

"I can respect that." He moved to leave.

She wanted desperately to ask the young man next to her what he knew about her sister's death, what the word was on how she died. But she didn't dare, not right then. She couldn't force it. When it was time she would know.

The next day came and went, as did the day after. On the third day Sarah found someone sitting on what she had come to regard as "her wall." It was a woman in her early twenties, close enough to Gayle's age that they may have known each other.

"He dead," the young woman said abruptly.

"Who?" Sarah knew the answer but needed to hear the words.

"The one that done cut your sister. He dead."

Sarah grabbed her wall as a sudden spell of vertigo hit her. "How, where, when?"

The young woman pointed to a yard several houses north of them. "Dat house up there. OD'd sometime back. Dogs got to him and everything."

Sarah studied the woman on the wall, searching her face for a lie and seeing nothing by the truth. Not knowing what to do or say, she just stood there until the woman gave up her place.

"Now you know so you can leave. Ain't nothing for you here anymore."

The woman walked away, leaving Sarah alone.

The all too sudden ending left Sarah adrift. She didn't want to leave, not like this. Where was the justice, the confrontation? She'd been half joking when she thanked Michaels for the idea of a gun. The thought of shooting the bastard down filled half her fantasies of how it should end, the other half being calling Michaels and watching him taken away in cuffs or killed while resisting. But to find that he'd been dead all this time, this wasted time …

Sarah reeled. The vertigo came back even harder and she grabbed the wall to keep from falling.

She knew she should leave. There was nothing left for her to do. But there was nothing left for her anywhere else. Maybe her place was still on the wall, watching and waiting for something that would never come.

Gunshots. The sudden cry of a young child closely followed by shouts of "My baby, my baby." People running both toward and from whatever happened. Sarah joined the latter crowd and soon found herself walking away from Billie Holliday Ct, across Broadway and into the soon to be new Eastside.

At the sounds of sirens she turned and looked west and saw police cars with lights flashing converging on where she had just been.

And she knew it would always be that way. People would die; their sisters, sons and daughters would die and keep on dying and there was nothing anyone could do. Sarah looked around at the construction and vacant lots that would soon be offices, shops, homes and apartments and she knew what was needed.

***

As old and neglected as they were, it did not take long for the fire to race through the houses on Caroline St before jumping over to set the homes on Billie Holliday Ct ablaze..

Engines and trucks from all available city fire units and some from the county responded but were unable to prevent massive property damage and a tragic loss of several lives.

Still smelling of the gasoline that she had so far been unable to wash off, Sarah sat in her cheap hotel room and watched the fire-fighting efforts live and late-breaking on the news. She wondered if Detective Michaels would make the connection. If she did, fine. The Pen was as good a place as any to wait and watch. And if not, there were other walls in other neighborhoods in a city that was far from being clean and pure.

What Was in Those Drinks?

"Now I remember that story," Druscilla said.

At that moment, Lucia returned with a warning. "Ray's been experimenting with the cocktails again."

"We know," Druscilla said.

"That's why I am on lemonade tonight, lemonade with vodka, that is," Cher added and giggled. "Hey, the writer went to the restroom. Let's take a peek at what he's working on."

So, Druscilla, Cher and Lucia calmly walked over to the banquet and this is what they saw neatly typed out, double spaced and steaming hot …

Conception Monkeys

KT Pinto

"There is a correlation between the creative and the screwball. So we must suffer the screwball gladly."
Kingman Brewster

THE TV flickered as I got comfortable on the couch and felt the cold medicine taking effect. Begrudgingly, I closed my eyes and let my thoughts drift. I saw various shades of gray as I wandered through the depths of my psyche. Then I noticed it: a bright, white light that cut through the darkness like a steel knife.

It was from that light that she emerged. Long brown hair hung down to her small waist, and her almond-shaped eyes sparkled knowingly as if she had been waiting for me. She was dressed in black spandex shorts with a shiny black skirt and more than 10 yards of hot pink crinoline draped over the shorts to hide any flaws. Her shocking pink half-shirt with a dancing monkey on it revealed soft tanned skin below large breasts. She was wearing pink high top sneakers with two pairs (one set black, one pink) socks, and had a pink scarf tied around her thick, curly hair. Cherry-colored lipstick covered full lips, and her outlandish eye make-up gave her multi-tiered cat's eyes. She had a simple silver charm around her neck, which struck me as odd considering the rest of her outfit ... and the rest of her jewelry.

Covering both her forearms were bangle bracelets: big, chunky, plastic jewelry in a rainbow of colors that rattled and clicked every time she moved. Some had charms on them that jingled like bells, making her sound like a gypsy dancer when she waved for me to come to her.

She stood quietly for a few moments while I looked her over again. "A picture would last longer," she said by way of greeting.

I blushed and cleared my throat in embarrassment. "I'm sorry I ... what are you doing here?"

She shrugged, her large pink and silver earrings shining through her hair. "I'm not really sure. I must've taken a wrong turn in the E-wing."

I blinked in confusion, positive that I had missed something during the short conversation. "E-wing? What's an E-wing?"

"You know, where the automotive hangers are."

I suppose she believed that she had cleared up everything for me, but I was even more baffled now than I was before. It must have shown on my face, because the girl's features softened and she held out her hand with a loud clatter of bangles.

"C'mon," she urged, "I'll show you."

I really didn't have much of a choice as she grabbed my hand and pulled me down what I could only describe as a long, dark hallway. I began to have a feeling that we had left my mind some time ago. My fears were confirmed as we stepped out onto a football field, a warm breeze caressing my face as we walked towards the bleachers. I glanced behind me and was slightly nervous to see only a brick wall where we had entered.

"Um ... the hall ... "

She shot me a sparkling smile, but didn't respond. She continued to pull me towards the bleachers, and that's when I noticed that I was wearing blue parachute pants and a matching jacket, with a purple sports bra with a smiling monkey face underneath. My high tops were purple and white, with purple and white socks. I tentatively touched my hair, relieved to find that at least it was still short and hairspray free.

I noticed that the football field was occupied by teens dressed in various forms of casual clothing, from denim shorts and T-shirts to pretty spring dresses of various lengths. I noticed that all of them had some sort of monkey on their clothes. I nudged my companion, who had paused at the first row of bleachers. "I assume that this isn't the football team?"

She shook her head as she pulled a banged-up instrument from its case and started to put it together. "Nope," she responded, closing the case, "Marching band."

My confusion grew as I realized what instrument she held. "Why do you have a bassoon?"

She grinned. "Stupid, huh? It is my preferred instrument, but I do play others. The conductor won't hear of it. He apparently has it in for me. Of course, the fact that I'm really late won't help. I hope Scott covered for me ... "

"Uh huh," I was trying to understand ... really, I was, "and so this is the E-wing you were talking about?"

She looked back at me in confusion as she stepped onto the field. "Huh? Oh, no. The E-wing's in there."

I glanced to where she was pointing and saw a huge gray building that I could have sworn was a prison. I turned back and watched my companion, who was trying to slide into her position on the field without being spotted by the conductor. She paused for a moment to thank a dark haired kid wearing mirrored glasses and holding a trombone. I assumed that he was Scott, and returned his cocky, three-fingered salute.

Urged on by the attention, he wandered over to where I stood. He leaned brazenly against the fence that surrounded the field and grinned. I realized that this child was used to getting what he wanted from women. I'm not sure if the disgust I had for people like him registered on my face, but I don't think he would have noticed it anyway.

He looked me over like a dog does a bone (I think he was actually salivating), "I know band practice isn't as titillating to the mere mortal as it is to us band geeks, so you have to be from the newspaper."

I really didn't understand that logic, so I responded as intelligently as possible, "Um, OK."

"Well, I'm Scott Hankowitz, with two t's and a z. I'm head of the trombone section. We're practicing for the upcoming competition in New Jersey ... Um, shouldn't you be writing this down?"

I tapped my head, not wanting to admit I had tuned him out. "Photographic memory," I responded.

"Uh huh." It seemed like Scott had tuned me out this time. "So, as I was saying … " I guess we had spoken about me for too long.

"Hankowitz," the director yelled, "Get back in formation!"

Scott gave me what I guess he thought was an endearing smile and walked back out onto the field, leaving me once again alone. It was then that I started to wonder what the heck I was supposed to do next.

"You look confused," said a deep voice behind me.

I turned and looked up into the deepest, bluest eyes I had ever seen. It took a bit of effort to pull my attention back to the entire face, but it was worth it. Soft white skin, high cheekbones, a chiseled chin, and a perfect ski-slope nose. Straight blonde hair flopped boyishly across a modest forehead and into those gorgeous eyes. And then the adjective hit me … "boyishly". This boy was almost half my age. I took a step back and was amazed by this child's broad shoulders, large chest and small waist. It took me a moment before I was able to respond something that could have possibly been English.

He gave me a smile that made me wish there weren't laws against the things that I was thinking. "My name's Denny. Are you a freshman?"

Now, I know I look younger than my age, but this boy deserved a kiss. "I'm here with a friend. I'm just trying to find the E-wing."

Denny's smile faltered slightly. "You're standing in it."

I glanced around, noticing for the first time that, number one, I was indoors and, number two, that there were little E's painted along the walls opposite the lockers. "Oh," I answered intelligently.

"Was there any place you were looking for in particular?"

I turned around slowly, trying to figure out what had just happened. "Actually my friend had mentioned the … "

I stopped speaking when I realized I wasn't in the E-wing anymore. I was in a garage … and the gorgeous Denny was no where in sight. In the middle of the garage was a yellow Dodge Aspen from — and this was just a guess — the 1970s. It was big, it was ugly, and it had a bunch of monkeys jumping out of a barrel painted on the hood. I walked slowly around the car, glancing through the windows to figure out whose car it may be.

I had just figured out, from the big pink fuzzy dice hanging on the mirror, the zebra print seat covers and the little disco ball hanging from the keys in the ignition, that the owner had to be my colorful companion, when I tripped over the legs of the man working under the car. I fell heavily on my hands and knees as the mechanic rolled himself out from under the Aspen. I felt strong hands slip under my arms and help me slowly to my feet. I turned to thank and apologize to him, when I found myself looking at yet another handsome teenager.

He was a redhead, with blue-green eyes that never seemed to stop changing color. He had a sprinkling of freckles across his button nose, and a curl of auburn hair that brushed his forehead. He, like Denny, had a large chest and chiseled arms, but looked much more innocent than the blonde ever could.

"Are you all right?" he asked.

Again, I had seemed to lose my knack for the English language. You would think I had never spoken to a handsome high school senior … "Good … I'm good." OK, so maybe I was a little out of practice …

"Can I help you with anything?"

I looked at him quietly for a moment, trying to guess how insane he would actually think I was. "Did you ever have a feeling that you were in a dream but then, you pinch yourself, and you're still exactly where you were?"

So, maybe he did think I was crazy, but he was kind enough not to say so out loud. "Let me guess, it's your first day of school, right?"

I touched my cheek in silent amazement. I have got to thank my Avon lady for that age defying cream! "I am still in the school? Oh good!"

He smiled slightly, my sanity much more in question. "I guess the automotive hanger kinda threw you, huh?"

So this was the hanger! Now if I could just figure out how to find the pathway back to my own mind. I assumed asking him that question would have him calling the men in the white coats. "Um, can you tell me where the marching band meets?"

"Sure," he responded, obviously relieved that he wasn't the one I had been looking for, "Go right out these doors, make a left, and go out the second set of doors on your right." He looked at me with a bit of his concern on his face. "Are you sure you can handle that?"

I didn't know if he was kidding or not, until I looked at his face. I never saw eyes twinkle like that before. "You're a riot," I responded, pleased with myself that I remembered some comebacks from that time period.

He put his hand on my shoulder, such a nice, clean hand for a mechanic. Then I realized that he had tucked his work gloves into his coveralls. "C'mon, I'll show you where they are. My name's Rob, by the way."

"I was hoping it was, since that's the name on your coveralls." I thought that that was smooth, very smooth.

He grinned and opened the door for me. "Ladies first."

I decided to hold back the response I normally used of how much of a lady I really was, fearing that that would make him lose a bit of respect for me. I thanked him and stepped through the door into …

A gorgeous atrium decorated in marble and crystal, with a multi-tiered chandelier about six-foot long hanging from the cathedral ceiling. On several insets and pedestals were monkeys and gorillas in various shapes and sizes and positions made of precious metals and stones. I turned to Rob, only to find a haughty butler standing behind me.

"Might I take your coat?" he asked, holding out his hand.

I was still wearing the blue jogging suit, and thought it would be unwise to walk around in my sports bra. "Oh, um … no thank you."

"Very well," he answered, "The others are in the music room, through those doors."

I glanced at the large, ornate wooden doors, engraved with a flying monkeys on it and heard an electric guitar warming up. "OK. Thank you."

I walked up to the doors and, spotting the large gold hinges, pulled the door open. My original companion was there, dressed in blood red jeans and an electric blue T-shirt with a monkey leaning out of the cab of a truck with the words Keep On Trucking on it. The boots matched the shirt and the scarf, the pants. The multi-colored bangles still decorated her forearms. Her crimson lips parted in a smile as she noticed me.

"I was wondering where you had wandered to!"

"So was I," I admitted, looking at the other teens in the room.

I hadn't met any of them before, and none were familiar faces from the football field. Instruments were arranged in the center of the room as if on a stage. A dark haired teen with similar features to my companion was strumming the guitar I had heard before, his fingers moving dexterously across the strings. He had hardly glanced up when I had walked in, and didn't seem any more interested in me now. His loss I thought, wondering when I had developed such an ego.

Next to him was an Asian girl, her long black hair braided down her back. She was wearing a purple and white cheerleader uniform, sans the pompoms, and she spoke with an annoying Valley Girl accent that made me tune her out very quickly. I noticed that she didn't acknowledge my presence either. Neither did the others in the room. The longhaired brunette with the sweet face continued her quiet conversation with the blonde working on the keyboards' wiring. The arrogant girl with the short, brown hair was rolling her green eyes (obviously contacts) and arguing with a pretty Latino girl who was expertly painting on the bass drum skin. When she turned away to respond, I noticed the words she had painted: The Left-Overs. I turned to my companion, who I realized had been watching me with a slight grin.

"Um ... can they not see me, or are they just rude?" The brunette linked arms with me, and that's when I noticed the electric blue earrings. "Well, they're rude as a rule, but in this case they just don't see you," she suddenly became upset, "I guess this means that your time here is almost up."

"Up?" now I was worried, "What do you mean 'up'?"

She didn't respond. That was starting to annoy me. "I had so wanted you to see ... I wonder if we can squeeze that in ... "

I had wandered away from her and was standing by the keyboards, watching the blonde work. I knew nothing about electronics, but it was obvious that she did. She looked up at her sweet-faced friend.

"Try it again," she said.

The brunette complied, running her fingers across the keys in a complicated melody. The guitarist responded to that with a scale of his own.

The Latino girl grabbed a tambourine and shook it to start a beat. The cheerleader picked up that rhythm on her drum set. Then I heard instruments, that I had not seen anywhere in the room, continue the beat … and that's when it started to sound familiar. I turned to my companion and, with more irritation than shock, realized the scene had changed once more.

I was in a restaurant decorated in the style of the 50s, with a chrome and vinyl décor, accentuated by red and white florescent signs and decorations. Five big booths lined the back wall, while white and red tables surrounded the dance floor. The place was crowded with teens, many of who were dancing to The Stray Cats' Rock This Town, the song I hadn't been able to identify a few moments before.

It didn't take me long to spot my companion, who was dressed in a yellow poodle skirt (except the poodle was a white capuchin monkey) and white button-down shirt, with saddle shoes to match. She was dancing with Denny, who didn't seem to have the same odd fashion sense as his dance partner. He was dressed in black jeans and a blue shirt, (and I won't go into how amazing he looked) and appeared very comfortable with the flamboyant brunette. Well, you didn't have to hit me over the head with a sledgehammer … those two were definitely a couple.

My companion smiled at me and gave a wave, her bracelets making their familiar music. Denny turned in my direction, obviously perplexed. "What are you waving at?" he asked, "The jukebox?"

That's when I noticed the music machine behind me, now silent.

"I'm waving to a friend," the brunette answered, walking towards the middle booth in the back of the room.

"But there was no one there … " his amazing blue eyes widened, "Oh, you didn't! Not again!"

"What?" she answered innocently.

"You brought another one to see us, didn't you?"

Another one? What did he mean another one? Why was I suddenly feeling jealous? What the heck was going on?

The brunette grabbed Denny's hands, her face earnest. "This one is different. She seems to accept us … to accept me! No screaming, no fear … she just accepted it."

"Maybe she's just in shock," Denny ran his hand through his hair, "Jeez, what are you trying to accomplish?"

My companion's expression changed once again. This time she was somber ... determined. She grabbed her boyfriend by the arms and stared deeply into his eyes. "Denny, I want people to remember us. To remember the good times, the strong friendships ... " she paused, and her voice cracked when she spoke next, "I want people to remember you, Dennis."

I don't know why, but I suddenly felt a chill go down my spine. I glanced at Denny, who was staring at the ground, his large hands now in his pockets. "What about the others?" he finally asked, "Rob and Whitney? Jeanie and Scott? Sharon, Tanya and Alice? Your brother Andy and his friends? What about the rest of the DeCostanza clan?"

I grinned at his wiliness. He didn't believe I was going to help them, but he made sure to mention everyone that was important in their lives. Shrewd ... very shrewd.

My companion smiled. She knew that she was winning him over. "She already met you, Scott and Rob. The others she saw, although they didn't actually meet her, while we were at rehearsal at Jeanie's house. She was already fading by then."

Fading. I certainly didn't like that term.

"Are you telling me that girl in the purple sports bra is the one you contacted? She could be no more than fifteen!"

And once again, that boy has won my heart.

My companion looked disgusted. I thought it was because the only thing her boyfriend remembered about me was my chest ... not that I could blame him ...

"You should know by now that that's not the way she really looks. Her soul is that of a teen. That's why she relates to us so well."

Well, that deflated my ego ... but I couldn't understand why my disappointment would make them get so blurry. I tried to get my companion's attention.

"Something's happening!" I called to her, hoping that she could still hear me.

She pushed Denny aside and ran over to me, pressing her hand against mine. I couldn't feel her. "Promise me," she said, "Promise me you won't forget us! Promise me you'll tell others about us!"

I was confused. Who were they? Why was she so desperate to have her story told? I glanced behind her at the restaurant. The images were fading. The chrome, the jukebox, the booths, the monkeys on the curtains, Denny ... Then I saw the look in his eyes: somber, despondent, grave. It was that awful look that helped me make my decision.

"I will, I promise," I told her. My voice sounded breathy, hollow. I wondered if she could even hear me. Her smile told me that she had. I couldn't hear her response, but I could read her lips: Thank you!

As she started to fade out of existence, I realized that she had never told me her name. I asked her for it, but it was too late. She was too far away ... I could barely make out her bright yellow skirt and the row of bangle bracelets on her arm as she waved her final farewell.

My eyes opened to the darkness of my living room. The rest of the house was silent. A quick glance at the clock on the VCR told me that my husband had already left for his overnight shift. I turned on the light to see the little surprise he had left for me: a cup of warm tea and honey was waiting patiently on a hot plate, next to a dishful of matzo bread and jelly. It wasn't filet mignon and a flagon of wine but when you're sick, you don't have many options ...

Next to the food were a ream of lined paper neatly clipped together and a handful of sharpened pencils. My husband knew me all too well. I grabbed the paper and pencils eagerly and began to write about everything I had just experienced: the marching band begrudgingly standing on the football field, the adolescent rock band practicing in haughty Jeanie's house. Pretty, sweet faced Whitney and Sharon, the electronics guru. Alice the Valley Girl cheerleader and Tanya the outspoken artist. Brazen Scott of the mirrored glasses. Andy DeCostanza, my companion's brother, strumming his electric guitar (I didn't guess his last name, Denny had mentioned it ... check back a couple of pages if you don't believe me). Auburn haired Rob, with the innocent face and the smiling eyes, and Denny, blonde, gorgeous and solemn, with a demeanor that alluded to a dark fate (just the thought of it gave me yet another chill).

Then there was her. Dark haired, dark eyed, and brightly dressed, with a bubbly attitude and a friendly smile, but with no name. I sat there on the couch, a list of names running through my mind. None of them fit with the images of her that flashed through my memory. The hot pink outfit with the yards of crinoline, the blue and red get-up at rehearsal, the poodle skirt and saddle shoes ... no names fit with those mental pictures.

I sighed and tapped the pencil against the paper in agitation. The visions of my companion continued to dance before my eyes. The long curly hair, the dimpled cheeks, the simple silver chain, the bright earrings and all of those noisy bracelets ...

I smiled as a name came into my head. And thus, with all of my notes laid out beside me on the couch, I started my first story about the trials and tribulations of these teens. This engaging group of high school students who called themselves The Left-Overs. I wrote about them and their unforgettable leader, Bangles DeCostanza.

But there was one thing I couldn't explain ... what the hell was with all of the monkeys?

Life is NOT a Cabaret, It's a Circus

"Where's Celeste?" Cher inquired. "I haven't seen her all night."

"I'm over here with the hairy college kid. Otto. He's a werewolf," a soft voice replied. "I am trying to avoid that little asshole Elvis and the rest of those elves."

"I didn't see Otto come in," Lucia said. "Cute kid. I have to spend sometime at the bar tonight," and she winked.

"Why are those elves obsessed with you?" Cher asked.

"It's Elvis, the group leader. The others just follow him. He wants me to bite him and make him immortal. Fat chance! And — he's a little pervert to boot. He's always sexting me on the phone now," said Celeste and she showed the girls some messages and a few pictures.

"Gross! He should be in a circus not this place."

"Yeah. I could see that.," Celeste replied. "While this genius is working on the great British novel, I have a little tale for you, oddly, about a circus and some people you may know of. I bet you never knew this …"

Circus Act

Robert Waters

BLUE and white smoke encircled Annie Oakley's head. She watched the tendrils closely, letting her eyes follow one strand then another as the Frenchman turned and twisted his hands while the spell dazzled the crowd. She kept her head still, as the smoke worked its way up and around the small, ripe apple that rested on her neatly fixed hair. The spot where the fruit lay began to heat, then heat some more, then more, until it grew hot. She resisted the urge to move, to shake it off, but the spell was working. It always worked, and she couldn't help but smile as the scent of freshly cooked apple soothed her senses. A great roar of approval erupted amidst the well-coifed men, finely-dressed ladies, and restless children under the big white tent.

Wizards!

Nikola Tesla did not say the word, but Annie could sense the rising frustration in her lover's actions. Well, used-to-be lover. Nowadays, as side-show acts for the Barnum & Bailey "Greatest Show on Earth," they retained a cordial and complimentary relationship, using one another in their performances to delight eager crowds. And the crowds were lively tonight, she observed, as the circus had come into Baltimore and set up in Patterson Park. Nikola, strapped in his steam-operated, twin-tank electrical oscillator and magnification emitter, was edgy and annoyed, the tips of his fingers popping with arch-light. The Frenchman was getting the best of him yet again.

"As you can see, my dear American friends," Maurice Larue said in his confident but slurred English, "one does not need modern mechanical vagaries to cook an apple. One simply needs concentration and the gift of the arcane."

Annie removed the steaming fruit from her head, and as was customary in the show, took a deep bite into the hot and juicy pulp created from the wizard's heat spell. She held it up and smiled as juice ran down her chin. The crowd clapped their approval. Maurice bowed as Nikola grit his teeth. Annie tossed the apple aside. She wanted to reach out and give Nikola a pat on the shoulder, or perhaps a light kiss on the cheek. But those days were over. 'Science is my love now, Phoebe,' he had said to her on their last night six months ago. He always used her real name when he was unhappy or unnerved. 'She's all I need. She's all I deserve.'

But science had let him down on more than one occasion, and it appeared that it was going to do so again tonight. His attempted apple-cooking had exploded the fruit right off her head, showering her, Maurice, and himself in Adam's Weakness. It excited the crowd to no end, but they were not laughing with him.

Nikola was nonplussed. "Not bad, my old friend," he said, turning from the crowd and moving to the center of the stage. "A clever trick that I'm sure looks impressive to the lay person."

Let it go, Nicky, Annie said to herself, looking into the crowd and seeing growing agitation with Tesla's condescension. They've come to see a show, not a fight.

"Now, I will stop playing and show you what science, what electricity, can really do." He put his hand out and waved Annie to the center of the stage. The wires that ran from the thimble-like cups on his fingers and thumbs grew blue with streaming light. The tanks on his back puffed like pipes on an organ with gears churning loudly. Annie wondered how Nikola didn't fry himself with all that electricity and steam. In truth, he considered the contraption on his back old and antiquated, but it was the best he could do for now. 'One day,' he had said on more than one occasion, 'man will be able to shrug off these shackles of wire and tubing and draw energy from any point in the universe.' Annie just smiled and nodded when he said silly things like that. It sounded like magic to her.

"Monsieur Larue," he said in his fake, mocking French accent, "will you give Miss Annie Oakley one of your cigarettes? One of your fine French Rochelle's?"

Larue, reluctant, produced a silver case from his cloak and pulled out a long, white stick. "Very well, old friend." He crossed the stage and handed it to Annie who accepted it with a smile. The wizard smiled back and gave her a short bow. Annie looked at his chest. Funny, she thought, but he isn't wearing his prized amulet.

"Miss Oakley, if you will place that cigarette in your mouth," Nikola said, "and please grab that mirror next to you on the stool."

Annie knew what he was driving at, but it was an old trick, one that he performed in the early days of their act, when electricity was new and unusual. Just lighting a cigarette was exciting. She could sense the impatience of the crowd as she took the mirror in her hand and angled it toward the tip of the smoke.

Nikola sensed the crowd's impatience as well. "Now, to the delight of all, I will arch my electricity across the stage and light Miss Oakley's cigarette." He paused, letting the crowd quiet. "The electricity will ricochet off her mirror, reach out and reignite all the gas-lamps, then finish by making Edgar dance on the head of a pin. How about that?"

Edgar, the clockwork ogre, sat slumped on the stage, his wooden limbs and iron joints limp and unresponsive.

At Tesla's words, Annie nearly dropped the cigarette. Was he mad? That certainly was the consensus in the scientific field, she knew, and why Tesla had been, more or less, delegated to "freak-show" status, running across the country under the big top. His employment with Thomas Edison and subsequent dismissal had drawn a lot of criticism and controversy over the years. He'd been accused of embezzling fifty-thousand dollars and taking unnecessary risks with the well-fare of his peers. The accusations were ridiculous, of course, at least the embezzlement part, though taking risks was a trademark of Tesla's act. But calculated risks and ones that were always planned and practiced beforehand. The little skit he now proposed had not been tried at all, at least not with Annie.

"Who wants to see Edgar dance?"

The crowd finally relented and gave the "mad" scientist rousing applause. Edgar had no opinion on the matter, because Edgar had no voice.

He was one of Tesla's "marvelous" inventions, filled with wires and gears and tiny light bulbs that sparked and flashed whenever electricity coursed through his frame. Tesla could even get him to dance without puppet strings or assistance of any kind. It was a jerky, silly movement that made children laugh. Edgar did not dance on the head of a pin, of course, but the slogan was reasonable given the nature of the act. Having this monstrosity, "Tesla's Frankenstein" as it was affectionately called, move at all, was sheer wonderment. It was the crown jewel of his act. But it had never been attempted in such a complex manner before, with so many untried pieces.

Annie glared at Tesla over the empty stage. She could not project her thoughts into his mind — although the crazy man was working on an invention to do just that — but she made sure he understood her dissatisfaction by rubbing the handle of her holstered Smith & Wesson. *If you electrocute me, Nicky, I swear I'll put a bullet between your eyes. They don't call me Little Sure Shot for nothing.*

"Nikola, my friend," Maurice said, offering his hand in friendship. "It isn't necessary to do this. Why, the crowd knows your skills. Don't let a simple off night spoil — "

"Lights!" Tesla barked, ignoring the Frenchman's gesture.

One by one, the gas lamps were doused and the tent darkened. Annie could barely see, save for the light emanating off Tesla's hands.

He was a brilliantly lit blue firefly, quite beautiful in fact, as the hair on his body stood on end. He slowly rubbed the tips of his fingers together to generate the spark that he needed. He rubbed and rubbed until a ball of light shown between his hands, wrapped with shifting blue and white currents of power. Then he swung his arms wildly into the air, in great circular motions as if conducting an orchestra. Despite her nervousness, Annie had to smile. Tesla had often spoken of being a musician. 'I'm a conductor of light,' he'd say, 'and the substance of the universe my instrument, my muse.' She could not deny how powerful, how beautiful he looked as the electricity swirled gaily about his thin body.

As the crowd reached a fever pitch, Tesla thrust his right arm forward. Lightning burst from his hand, arched across the stage, hit the mirror, and clipped the tip of Annie's cigarette. She took a drag and let a puff of smoke escape her twitching lips. The hair on her arms and head sprang to life. She had had many cigarettes lit this way, but it never ceased to amaze her how warm and energized she felt each time, as if God held her tightly in the hollow of His hand.

The lightning off the mirror split into two distinct lines. Exactly how Tesla was able to do this, she did not know, but it had something to do with the nodes and wires taped and hidden at the back of his neck. Somehow, his mind was able to shape the currents and split them off, energized and reinforced by the steam tanks churning on his back. The electricity sparkled above the crowd as children and their mothers screamed in delight. Their hair too stood on end, as one by one, the gas lamps along the posts of the tent lit as the currents touched each in turn. As light filled the room, the crowd saw the enormity of the trick … and they were enthralled.

Feeling his pride, Tesla thrust out his left arm and arched lightning into Edgar. The ogre's massive wood-and-iron frame glowed white hot, as if he were about to ignite. Then his smooth head straightened. His sapphire eyes opened, and the gears in his segmented face pulled back to reveal a line of teeth which had been polished to fine points. Annie took pride in those teeth, for they had been given to her by the Egyptian Consulate during PT Barnum's Mediterranean tour. A gift from the ancient Pharaohs, he claimed, and infused with the power of the gods. Annie accepted them freely and threaded them onto a cord of leather to wear around her neck. But they felt odd against her flesh and, quite honestly, she considered it morbid to wear human teeth. Tesla had accepted them happily, and now here they were, shining and grinning at the entranced crowd.

"Dance, Edgar!" Tesla said, snapping the lightning like a whip behind the ogre's back. "Dance!"

And Edgar danced, slowly at first, as his squeaky joints warmed to the energy flowing through them. His awkward frame lurched forward, as if he teetered on a wire, then his legs steadied and shifted under his weight. In a comical, wobbly motion, the ogre leaned over and grabbed a top hat lying on the stage. He placed it on his head and held it there with fingers grinding gears as Tesla moved his own hand to orchestrate the motions. The only thing Edgar lacked was a cane, but he did his best to strut across the stage. His heavy feet kicked forward. They were more like steel-toed boots, really, clumsy and uncoordinated, but when Tesla moved his fingers in short, staccato motions to give them life, they moved quickly and confidently, and children squealed.

Then Edgar began moving his free arm in a running motion, his mechanical fist thrusting forward and back as if punching a bag. Annie watched the act with fascination. She'd seen it a thousand times, but still it impressed her. The poetry of it, the danger too, the sheer power of the energy coursing through Edgar from simple steam tanks. The crowd loved it, and she could tell that Tesla was thrilled and reaffirmed by their reaction. Even the wizard Maurice, eyes wide and leering, fingers flayed and gripped against his chest, seemed to admire the raw display of science. For the first time in a long while, Annie was proud of her scientist.

But enough was enough. Her arm was tired from holding the mirror and she didn't like to smoke anyway. She let the cigarette fall to the stage, then said, "Okay, Nicky. That's enough."

Her words, however, were lost in the rumble of the crowd and the churn of the steam tanks. "Nicky, that's enough!" she said firmly, like a mother scolding a child. Tesla did not, or could not, hear her words. He stood like a statue, his hair tingling with light, his left hand moving rhythmically to keep Edgar dancing back and forth across the stage. His eyes had rolled up into his head and steam rose from his hot, red fingers. Annie's heart dropped as fear gripped her chest.

"Nikola! STOP!"

He was sweating, something she had never seen him do in their time with the circus. He had clearly over-done it. Steam rose from his head and hands, despite the protective caps over his fingers; they were not burnt, thankfully, but they were red and quite toasty. He shook his head and blinked his eyes. "I'm okay, I think." He breathed deeply. "I kind of blacked out there for a moment."

"What happened?" she asked.

Tesla shook his head. "I don't know. I ... I just — "

Someone screamed in the audience, and Maurice shouted, "He's still moving!"

Tesla was confused. "Who is moving?"

"Edgar!"

No cables or wires held up the ogre, nor was there any power supply making him move. But Edgar did indeed move ... and violently. His face was twisted angrily as if the gears and cogs behind his iron cheeks had been pulled into knife-like angles. He jumped into the crowd, and people scattered to flee the tent. Edgar seemed deranged, out of control. Of course he was. How silly of her to think otherwise. Annie pulled a pistol and moved to intercept the ogre. What she could do, she did not know. But she had to do something.

A brave man in the crowd tried to jump on Edgar's back, but the ogre swung its arm against the assault and drove his fist into the man's throat. The man fell to the ground in a lump. Another two men tried as well, but their efforts were thwarted when Edgar took up a chair and smashed it over the head of one of them. The other stumbled backward and crawled away.

"Edgar! Stop!"

Tesla's words were lost in the chaos of the crowd. Annie jumped off the stage and aimed her pistol toward Edgar, but Maurice got in her way. He was trying to be brave too, trying to divert Edgar's attention from smashing chairs and knocking people aside. The French wizard tried grabbing hold of the ogre's arm, tried casting some kind of halt spell by wiggling his fingers before Edgar's deranged expression, but the beast simply knocked him aside like the others. Annie held her gun firm and walked forward. *If I can get a shot at his head ...*

A little girl had lost her mother in the crowd. She sat on the ground, crying, holding her knees. Edgar saw her and swooped in. He grabbed her up and tucked her tightly underneath his left arm. *Holy hell*, Annie thought. How am I going to take a shot now?

But she had to. She had to do something. Edgar was not listening to Tesla's pleas, and Maurice lay on the ground nearby, nursing a bruised face.

Edgar tossed aside a woman and tore through the tent. By now, the circus at large was realizing that something was wrong, and people outside gathered to look. Annie waited until Edgar cleared the rip in the tent, then followed him outside. The girl in his arm was screaming, and her mother, now outside and realizing where her daughter was, screamed as well. Annie felt like crying. Her hands shook but she kept moving forward.

Tesla tried moving past her in the crowd, but Annie put out her arm and stopped him. "No!" she said. "You've done enough, Nicky."

She didn't know why she had said that. She didn't know what she meant really. Things were moving so fast, the chaos of the moment, the crying girl and her mother, all of it conspiring to cloud her mind, to confuse her and make her angry. This should not have happened. How it had happened, she did not know, but it shouldn't have. And now, once again, she was being forced to fix a "Tesla" act.

Security whistles were blaring somewhere in the park. Police were arriving, sirens on their paddy-wagons going off and making her ears hurt. This needed to end soon, or the little girl …

Annie pushed through the anxious crowd and found herself in front of Edgar. The ogre didn't seem to notice she was there. It kept moving forward; where it was trying to go, she didn't know, but nothing would stand in its way apparently. She looked down at the girl now lying limp under his arm. "Stop, Edgar!" She didn't know why she said it, as if the thing could understand. It had no brain, no heart. It couldn't respond to verbal queues, nor did it recognize voice at all. It was a machine, and somehow it had come alive, gone mad … just like its creator.

Annie raised her pistol and aimed it between Edgar's eyes. She counted down to five, like she had been taught: Take a breath, level the barrel, squeeze the trigger.

The shot rang out, and the bullet ripped through iron and wood. One of Edgar's sapphire eyes shattered. The ogre stopped dead in its tracks, raised a hand as if to feel the hole in its head. Annie cocked the hammer, aimed, and threw another round into its neck.

Edgar, Tesla's Frankenstein, dropped the girl, teetered in place, then toppled to the ground.

Tesla sat inside the ruined tent, handcuffed to a post. Annie faced him, her cheeks streaked with dried tears. What had happened was like a bad dream. Only an hour ago, she had stood on the stage, puffing a cigarette, admiring the power and vitality of her once-lover. Now here he was, wrecked and despondent, facing a battery of questions that he could not answer to the satisfaction of the Chief of Police and circus security.

"I've told you again and again," he said, shaking his head in anger. "I don't know what happened. This has never happened before. Edgar is a machine, a toy really. He functions only under direct power. And I cut off that power shortly after he began dancing. Tell them, Annie."

"Then how did he — it — keep going, huh?" The chief asked, leaning in close, holding his billy club forward as if he were going to pop the scientist on the head. "How did it find the power to kill?"

Luckily, the little girl was safe. She suffered bruises from Edgar's tight grip and a scuffed knee when he dropped her, but little else. The man who initially tried to stop the ogre, unfortunately, died. Edgar's strike broke the man's neck. Another male patron clung to life, his broken ribs piercing his lung. The circus was closed, and who knew if it would open again? Management had not made that decision yet. A portion of the grounds was now a crime scene.

"He's telling the truth," Annie said, rubbing Tesla's back in support. "He turned off the power. I swear."

The chief sighed. "Is that your assessment, Mr. Larue?"

The magician sat nearby, almost as distraught as Annie. Exhausted, Maurice rubbed his eyes and nodded. "That he did, sir. I swear it too. I've never seen anything like it, though. It was frightening."

The chief stood up and clipped his club to his belt, looked to his lieutenant and officers. He sighed deeply again. "Well, I don't know what to make of it either. But what I do know is that one person is dead, one clings to life, and several are wounded. Whether you meant it or not, Mr.

Tesla, your invention has caused a lot of trouble tonight."

"What are you going to do with me?" It was the most sheepish and defeated Tesla had ever sounded.

The chief paused, took out his timepiece, flicked it open, looked at it thoughtfully, then snapped it shut. "For the time being, sir, we're going to take you downtown. For your own safety, if anything else. There's a lot of angry folk out there, Mr. Tesla. A lot of them want to hang you and that ogre of yours. And frankly, I can't say I blame them."

"Where is Edgar?" Tesla asked.

"In your wagon, sir, and well-guarded. I trust it won't stand up and walk on its own this time?"

Tesla shook his head. "I guess not."

"Very well. Then if you will oblige me, Mr. Tesla, please stand."

Annie helped Tesla to his feet. She wanted to say something, anything, to soothe his worry. But what could she say? She didn't know what to say. She tried. "Don't worry, Nicky, it'll be all right."

"She's failed me, Phoebe," he said under his breath. "Science has failed me."

But that wasn't true. She knew it wasn't true. Something else had failed him. She didn't know what. Something else …

As the officers led him out of the tent, Tesla looked at her, his face grave but hopeful, the first time all night. He didn't say anything, but his probing eyes said enough. Save me, Phoebe. Save me.

Annie stood quietly in the muggy Baltimore night and watched as the police loaded Tesla into the paddy-wagon. Maurice was at her side. "Don't fear, sweetheart," he said, placing his hand on her shoulder. "It'll be all right. One way or another, it'll be all right."

She nodded and looked at him. She ruffled her brow. "Where's your amulet, Maurice?"

The Frenchman felt at his neck and chest, surprised at her question. "My amulet?"

"Yes. The one you always wear."

"Oh," he said, shuffling his feet and pulling his cloak tighter around him. "I must have left it in my dressing room."

Annie nodded at his answer and watched as the paddy-wagon

steamed away.

***

Two Baltimore police officers guarded the steps leading into Tesla's personal dressing room and "Wagon of Unparalleled Scientific Discovery & Wonder!" Luckily for Annie, Tesla had forgotten to seal shut the trap door in its floor. It was an artifact from the days when the wagon was a travelling magician's home. It had also been used on occasion by Annie to sneak in. The scientist had always meant to bolt it shut. Thank God for his absent-mindedness.

She didn't know what she might find to help her prove Tesla's innocence … prove that something else had made Edgar animate and attack the crowd. Despite their rocky relationship, she owed him that much. He might be crazy, but he was no murderer.

She opened the trap door carefully so that the guards could not hear. The door was well enough away so that they were unlikely to hear it open, but it never hurt to be cautious. She then slipped in quietly, taking a box of matches and a candle from her pocket. She sniffled at the musky smell in the wagon, a combination of sweat, dust, chemical fumes, and iron rust that permeated every corner of the dark place. Tesla was not good at cleaning up after himself, so there were bits of paper and old oily rags everywhere, not to mention coils, wires, and bulbs. Annie felt indelicate and nervous among such things, but she had been here before and could feel her way around readily enough.

She struck the match and lit the candle, then cupped it to shield its glow from the guards outside. She needed only a small flame, just enough to poke around the many inventions that covered the wagon's floor, counters, and walls. It was amazing that the place didn't explode with so many odd "things" lying about, so many peculiar gizmos and gadgets that Tesla was sure would revolutionize the world someday. She took a great risk just lighting a candle in the place. But that was the rub: Everything in this wagon was nothing but a piece of dead iron or cobalt or copper or glass; every tube or circuit, every robotic hand or articulated jaw bone, every so-called "x-ray" panel, needed power … and only Tesla could supply it. He had developed an alternate current device which used electricity more efficiently. He had designed a machine that would induce sleep; he had developed a thing called a "radio" which, according to him, would someday transmit, without wires, a person's voice from coast to coast. He had even sketched out a design for what he called a "ray gun," a direct-energy weapon that concentrated massive amounts of power that could literally destroy whole battalions if the delivery system were large enough. All of these machines and blueprints lay around her in silent, dead piles. Her puny flame was as powerless against these technological wonders as it would be in a rainstorm.

So what had happened? Tesla had cut power from Edgar; there was no lingering arc of light or current that she had seen. He had talked and talked about someday drawing power from the air, but he was not there yet, had not perfected that technique. He still relied on wires and steam tanks to generate the current. Certainly, he could arc the electricity across a short distance, just as he had two nights ago in the show. But nothing had powered Edgar itself. The ogre should have crumbled to the stage like a rag doll. But it hadn't. Why?

She crouched in front of Tesla's personal desk. Piles of blueprints and schematics were scattered across it. Annie held the candle up to see but far enough away so as not to set the dry papers alight. She scanned the desktop, peeking into all the little cubbies where Tesla packed his scribbled notes, inks, rubrics, and quills. Nothing.

She started to turn away when her eyes fell upon a small photograph tacked to the wall above the desk. The corners were old and dog-eared, the image faded. She smiled as she recognized the three friends standing in front of the Great Pyramids of Giza.

She was young and happy then, holding the necklace of teeth in her right hand while clinging to Tesla with her left. And he was dashing with his neatly trimmed mustachio, smooth witch-hazelled face, tan safari fatigues, and matching bola hat. Beside them stood Maurice, similarly dressed, and sporting the amulet given to him by an Akhenaton Priest as a token of his appreciation and fondness for the Frenchman's magical prowess. They were young, they were vital, they were happy. They were friends. That was many years ago.

It wasn't as if the gentlemen were not friends now, but over the years their rivalry had taken its toll: Tesla moving further and further away from Maurice, conceptually and, more importantly, spiritually. She did not really know where Tesla stood in terms of religion and faith, but his disdain for magic, for arcane knowledge of any kind, had caused a strain in their friendship. And Maurice was just as pig-headed, taking any opportunity to one-up the mad scientist. Men! Annie bit back her frustration. Why can't science and magic co-exist? What was wrong with a world where both thrived equally? But Tesla would not abide by it. The new century was closing fast, he always said to her, and science must prevail. Life on Earth depended upon it.

Annie sighed. There was nothing among these piles of papers and pictures that could help her. She was stalling. She knew where she had to look, but the thought of it made her heart sink. She was one of the bravest women, nay, one of the bravest people, around. She had built her whole career as a performer around that fact. She wasn't afraid of anything. But she was afraid of what lay nearby in an iron cage, trapped and covered in a burlap throw.

She cocked the hammer on her Smith & Wesson, fell to her knees, and slowly crawled over to the cage. Why am I so afraid? She asked herself the question to keep from dropping the candle. No reason to be alarmed. The cage was secure and bolted to the ground. She took a deep breath and pulled away the cover.

And there Edgar sat, a lifeless marionette of wood and iron, gears, glass, and copper wires. Almost comical in a way, now that shackles had been slapped around his thick wrists and ankles. That seemed kind of cruel to Annie now that she saw him, so innocent-looking, with his articulated mouth and eye lids shut like a grieving clown, the damage of her pistol shot displayed on his forehead and through the cavern of his eye. She smiled and found herself waving at him.

"Hi, Edgar," she whispered, her breath flicking the candle light. "I'm so sorry for you. Tell me what went wrong, big guy. Tell me what happened."

Edgar did not speak, nor did any of his joints or cogs spring to life at her voice. Nothing. Her heart went out to him. It was silly for her to feel this way, she knew. He was just a machine, a spiritless mannequin made to impress the crowds and to showcase the future of science. But he was family also. Edgar had been with her and Tesla and Maurice for years. He was part of their act. He was part of their life. He was family.

Family …

A thought gathered in Annie's mind as she reached in and caressed Edgar's cold face with soft fingers. His jaw was easily opened, the gears clicking as each sprocket found its groove. Annie locked the jaw open and reached into his mouth. She had to remind herself Edgar wasn't real, that this violation of his personal space would not hurt him in any way or cause him to gag or wretch. She slid her hand in as far as she could, as far as the internal cavity of his iron cranium would allow. Tesla had purposefully left the skull empty. "For future mechanization," he said.

But there was something in there, something fixed to the ceiling of the cranial mound. Annie put her hand over it. The object was smooth as glass. She closed her fingers over it and yanked. It gave way and she pulled it out, slowly. She had to soften her fist to get it through Edgar's mouth, but she pulled and freed her hand. She moved her arm back through the bars. She opened her hand and looked at a finely cut jewel that shone red and brilliant in the candlelight. And along its length was a coarse groove, a crease torn side to side by a passing bullet.

She opened her mouth to scream, but a shape formed behind her. She turned toward the motion, but before she could discern a face in the darkness, something fell across her head and knocked her cold.

Annie awoke to a headache and a blinding light. She squinted through the pain and tried to wipe her eyes. Something held her arms down. She was able to shake her head and she did so. Someone had removed the ivory hair pin from its perch at the back of her head. Now her long, brown hair hung around her face. Something was hard and caked on her forehead. She could only surmise that it was blood. Her blood, from the thing that had struck her in Tesla's wagon. She knew what — who — it was, despite the darkness. The object she pulled from Edgar's skull had confirmed it.

"Larue!" She said, her eyes now finding a dark shape in the haze before her. "You son of a bitch!"

The Frenchman, decked in black garments, black top hat, with black cape hanging about his sides, stood before her, smiling his nasty, petulant little smile, and hefting her holstered guns as if dangling a carrot before a mule. Around his neck rested the Egyptian amulet, red and sparkling, but chipped now, holding a dark, bitter substance at its heart, like a roiling smoke. As Annie's eyes grew clearer and stronger, they focused on the smoke, and she felt a burning in the pit of her stomach. She felt hot, angry.

"Now, now, now," the wizard said, wagging his finger at her like a scolding adult, "that's not proper language for a woman of your stature."

Annie tried to jump at him, but she was still held down. Then she realized where she was and why she couldn't move.

They were in one of the smaller tents, one where sideshow acts, clown troupes, and jugglers would ply their trade. Annie was tied, spread-eagle, to a wooden revolving disk, one marked with numbers and pegs around its edge. Annie knew the object well, for she had used it for gun play and target practice. Even knife-throwers used the circle to try their hand at hitting the red numbers as their scantily-clad assistants rotated around and around, squealing to the delight of the crowd when a blade nicked their clothing or cut through their blonde hair. She was tied to this disk. She looked down. She sighed. Thank God Larue had had the decency to keep her bloomers on.

"Why, Larue?" She asked, straining at her bonds. "He was your friend. I was your friend."

The wizard tossed the guns aside and walked forward. "It's a simple reason, really, and it should be obvious to you." He placed a hand on the circle and began rotating it slowly. "Without magic, without the arcane, what good am I? Tesla — science — is a mortal threat to my existence. A mortal threat to the world."

"What are you talking about? Nicky would never hurt you," Annie said, fighting the bonds while she spun. "He's not a threat to you or to anyone else."

"Oh, but he is. The world is changing, Annie, and wizards like me are quickly becoming redundant. Science grows strong while I fight to obtain whatever powers I can from sources that wane and wane as the seasons pass. Oh, I can cook an apple in a sideshow, but what good is that when electricity can do that and much, much more? And once the masses realize that science can do everything that I used to do, and better, what will become of me? What will become of my profession? My people?

"The priest we met in Egypt understood this well, Annie, and he gave me this amulet so I could help ensure the health of our profession. But what I didn't know was that he also challenged me to be the bearer of Anubis's gift, to bring death and desolation to all those who worship science. Men like Tesla must be destroyed. It begins with his discrediting, but it will not end there."

Annie tired to hold back the queasiness in her stomach as she turned and turned. "You won't get away with this."

Larue laughed. "Oh, but I will, Watanya Cicilla, my Little Sure Shot. In the morning, when they find you dead from a thousand cuts and the cause of your death at your feet, they will put it together, and Nikola Tesla will be finished."

Larue spun the wheel hard and clapped twice. As she whirled around, Annie tried to focus on a figure lurching across the stage, holding a large burlap sack. Edgar! There it was again, and like before, being manipulated by a mad wizard who now stood stolid at the center of the stage, holding the amulet in his hand and hissing some Egyptian spell that she could not understand. Edgar fell to its bolt-laden knees in front of its master, the sack crashing at its side. The wizard popped the red gem from his amulet and placed it again in Edgar's head. Then he backed away, and with a face contorted and twisted in rage, bid the ogre rise.

Annie blinked furiously to keep from losing consciousness. "Edgar, no!" she said, and suddenly her mouth felt dry and pasty. She looked at Larue. He stood there, his right hand thrust out toward her, tendrils of color snaking through the air from his sharp fingertips. He kept her from screaming while the spell that he uttered to the jewel in Edgar's head drove the ogre to rise and pull two sharp knives from the burlap bag.

Annie's screams grew to muffled shrieks as the first blade hit the wheel just below her left arm. She felt a sting as the steel tore through her skin. But it wasn't a terribly deep wound. She started to sigh as the second blade struck the wheel, this time near her right ear. It missed

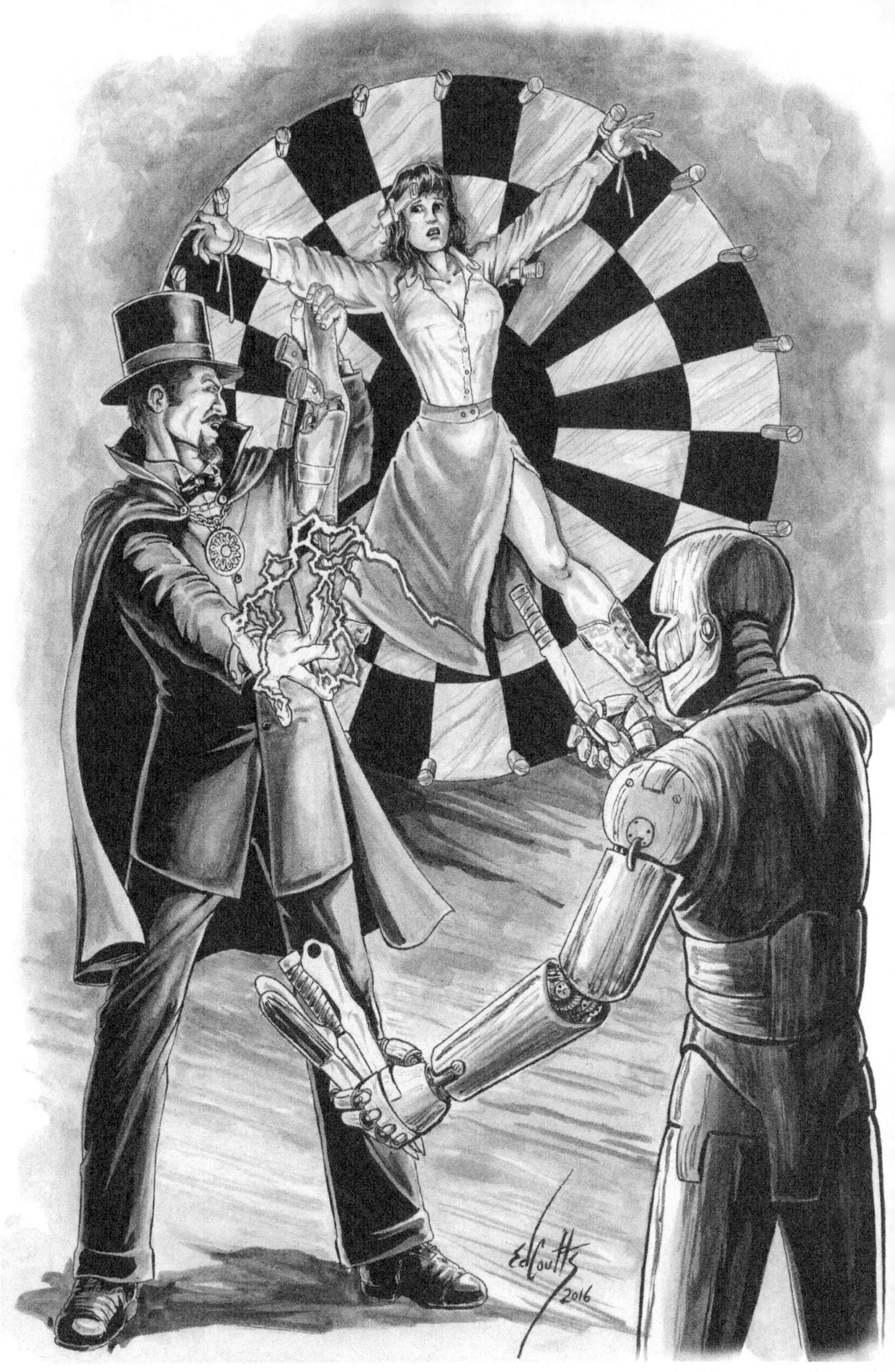
Ed Coutts
2016

flesh entirely. Round and round she went as blade after blade hit the wheel, some nicking her skin; nothing life-threatening, but very painful. It was clear that the power of the amulet was strong, but Larue could not keep her quiet and aid Edgar in the accuracy of his throws, especially with the gem damaged from her shot. The ogre was struggling to do what its master wanted. Annie saw an opportunity in this.

If I can get him to cut my binds ...

She started pushing her weight to the left as the wheel spun slowly. It was coming to a stop, but despite the nausea in her gut, she had to keep it turning for a little longer. She threw her weight into the turn, and Edgar flung another knife her way.

It hit the cord holding her right hand, just a small slice, but enough for her to pull hard and tear some of the fibers. Edgar threw another blade. This one hit the cord between her feet. She yanked her foot once, twice, three times. The rope pulled free. She pulled again at her hand as another blade came in, this one slicing her brassiere and bringing a drop of blood.

The wizard's eyes turned inside as the power of Anubis, the God of Death, consumed him. He tried shifting his focus on Annie, tried moving to seize her, but doing so made Edgar's next throw wobble end over end. With all her strength, Annie tugged at her left hand and finally pulled free. She grabbed a blade off the wheel and cut away the bindings at her feet. Then she cut the cords around her right wrist. She finished when another blade, the last one, sliced her leg and forced her to buck her hips backward. The force of her thrust turned the wheel up and over.

Annie crashed to the stage.

She was too weak and light-headed to spring to her feet, but she half crawled, half stumbled across the stage, toward the shadows where Larue had tossed her pistols.

Edgar was on her quickly, throwing his wood-and-iron arms at her like battering rams. But his motions were thick and inaccurate, much like his dagger throws, and Annie grabbed his arm and held it tightly, letting the gears wind and sputter as the wizard's spell, incapable of being held any longer due to his transformation, snapped and shattered the wires and iron joint at the elbow. She bent the arm back at the wrist and heard a loud snap. It was almost as if the ogre let out a scream as dark matter, as thin as mist, oozed out of the broken arm and dissolved in the muggy air. Edgar fell back, and Annie pulled away.

A hand reached into the darkness and tore at her hair. Annie screamed, her voice now full and active. She grabbed at the hand that held her tight, Larue's hand. The wizard was now ensorcelled in the ancient Egyptian spell, now a slave to it, his face contorted into the sharp, long muzzle of the jackal, teeth bared, cursed black tongue nipping out as if to pierce her skin and infect her with death. She had never hit a man in the face before, but Annie drove her fist into that demon snout. The shock, more than the power, knocked the wizard back, and Annie sprang for her guns.

Claws were on her ankle, raking at it, pulling her further and further into a black dust that now rose up from the boards of the stage. She reached out for her holster, touched it with a finger, but was pulled away. She tried again, her hands clawing the wood, scraping it as she forced her knees into the rough platform to give her leverage. It was enough. The holster was in hand, the gun, the hammer cocked. Annie turned and shot into the hideous black fog.

She shot again, and again, until all six bullets were spent. The fog persisted for a time, but then thinned, and thinned again, then disappeared. The faint light of the tent's gas lamps flooded her eyes. She stood up on a tender ankle, rubbed her wet face, holstered her smoking barrel, and pulled the other gun. Just to be safe. She learned long ago that sometimes, six bullets weren't enough.

Larue lay on the stage, his arm and chest bloody pulps. But he was alive. Edgar lay nearby, his lifeless, bloodless frame containing new holes in the chest and shoulder. His broken arm lay popping with residual power from the spell. With that much damage, however, he was incapable of further harm.

Annie walked to Larue's side. The Frenchman's face was normal again, though smeared with black soot, blood, and grime. His eyes were cloudy but Annie could see in their reflection the full, yet uncontrollable, power of a god. A god that had, for a time, prevailed in a small tent in Baltimore, but whose mortal vessel was incapable of maintaining that power. Anubis's magic had, indeed, been strong, but in a changing world, its strength grew weak. Annie was thankful for that.

Exhausted, she fell to the stage and wept as the distant siren of a paddy-wagon grew near.

***

Larue nearly bled to death before the authorities arrived. It was clear, however, that he and his ancient artifact were the cause of all the pain, suffering, and death of the last few days. He was hauled away, and all charges against Tesla and his "monster" were dropped.

The matter having been resolved, Barnum & Bailey began packing up. The circus had spent three more days in Patterson Park, and despite Larue's deadly schemes and the turmoil thereof, the circus had had a good run in Baltimore. Another successful show all in all.

Annie helped Nikola pack his steam tanks carefully away among his multitude of gizmos. He was disappointed that his performances of "Scientific Wonder!" had been cut short, but given the circumstances, he did not complain over-much. He never thanked Annie for what she had done for him, but that was not his style. A man of his intellect, his mental capacities, could not burden himself with undue emotion. He showed his appreciation in more subtle ways: a slight touch of her shoulder or an inordinate amount of chuckle at a weak joke; a carefree smile when no one was looking; a gentle wink at her useful assistance. She'd take it. Things were back to normal, and science was still his love. As it should be.

"Can you help me with Edgar?"

Annie nodded. The lifeless Ogre sat on the bare ground beside Tesla's wagon. The damage caused by Annie's pistol shots had been temporarily repaired. On their way to Richmond, she would help mold new pieces to fix his jaw and cranium, his chest and arm. Annie knelt down next to Edgar and was surprised at the tightness in her chest.

She wasn't afraid of him, really. She realized that Edgar's actions had been the cause of a wizard deranged and sick in the soul. Edgar was truly a gentle giant. But eventually, when that future that Nicky always talked about, the one with particle beam weapons and "jet" propulsion, radio transmission and robotic devices as intelligent as man; the future that would replace the steam and gears and clockwork and turbines of today. What then? How would a machine like Edgar play in a future like that? Would he be the master and humanity his slave? What would the world be like with a dozen, a hundred, a thousand Edgars, each imbued with powers ten-fold stronger than anything simple electricity could spark within him now? Annie did not know. One thing was certain: In a future like that, she would not have enough bullets to stop them all.

She reached her arms under Edgar's weight and started to lift. Then a sparkle caught her eye. She laid Edgar down and peered into the heart of his damaged chest. She squinted and, to her surprise, made out a smooth and handsomely-shaped gem that lay between his main stabilizing gears.

"Nicky!" She said. "What the hell is this? And how did you find it? I thought it was destroyed."

"Oh no," Tesla said, a sly smile on his thin face. "Just damaged."

Annie shook her head. "What do you intend to do with it? I thought you didn't approve of magic."

"I don't, but it would make an interesting part of the act, wouldn't you say?"

Annie relented and helped Tesla lift Edgar onto the back of the wagon. "But why? You don't know how to use it. What good would it do? It's dangerous, it's — "

"Phoebe," Tesla said, laying a soft hand on her shoulder, "there's an old adage in the business: Any sufficiently advanced science is indiscernible from magic. The crowds will never know the difference. And if I can make an ogre dance on the head of a pin, surely I can figure out how to use an old Egyptian trinket in the pursuit of scientific discovery. Trust me. Have I ever let you down before?"

By the time Annie was prepared to offer up a dozen answers to that question, Tesla had turned and walked to the front of the wagon. Annie shook her head.

Scientists!

She sighed, jumped into the wagon, and hugged Edgar tightly as the circus rolled out of Patterson Park and toward the future.

Romance, the Eternal Mystery

"Nothing like a happy ending," Cher said.

"Happy endings are very subjective," Druscilla answered. "One person's happy ending is another's nightmare, especially in less sophisticated times."

"How do you mean?"

"Well, I remember ages ago, Medieval times, in fact, when knights were bold, mysteries lurked around every corner, love was an elusive often dangerous thing and, if you were lucky, you survived it

"Do tell," Cher said as she popped the last of her petit fours into her mouth.

Love is in the Air

R. Allen Leider

It was a damp and uncomfortable night in the middle of the dreary autumn that saw the temporary end of the latest foreign wars and the false promise of better times. Sir Colin of Lockwood, knight errant, survivor of two Crusades and every inch the blue-eyed, well-muscled young hero, savored his first meal in his homeland in nearly five years. Sir Colin was sinking his teeth into a leg of roasted mutton when she came into his life. The bedraggled young girl entered the Inn terrified, bloodied and hysterical. She was a dirty thing, muddy and shivering. Her wet hair fell over one of her large doe eyes like the tangle of an old mop. All the dining hall patrons stared as she shook in the doorway, babbling incoherently, her eyes dilated and tear stained.

Beneath the outward signs of terror, Colin could perceive this mysterious intruder was a raven-haired beauty with the face of a French porcelain doll. She claimed to be fifteen, but her body beckoned to him, straining his Christian pledges and his courtly chivalry until the remembrance of his old sergeant-at-arms' words rang in his ears.

"Sire," he had said most seriously on the subject, "as I see it, if they be big enough, then they be old enough."

Such thoughts aside, however, Colin realized, the girl was clearly

An innocent damsel in distress. As she warmed her scratched, shivering limbs by the inn's monumental fireplace, wiping mud from her long,

Love is in the Air

slender legs with a rag, she told Sir Colin and Marcus the Innkeeper of her terrifying adventure and the dreadful curse that had befallen her.

"There's a fiendish monster from Hell after me," she cried. "It invaded my family's cottage not two days ago and ripped both my parents limb from limb. They could not defend themselves as they were both elderly and my father was crippled from service in the Crusades."

The patrons of the Inn, Sir Colin and Marcus gasped. As various of them comforted the waif, Colin commented to Marcus, "Damsels — it never fails. How do they get themselves into these situations? They start off as cute little girls; they grow up, get soft, supple breasts, a bit of fuzz here and there, start to smell fragrant like roses in May, generate heat, ripen like fruit ready to be picked and beg for us to enjoy them as apples in the orchards of Ferndale. Then, of course, some hairy, scaly, slimy, malformed creature from the netherworlds bent on ravishing the flowers of Christendom comes along and mucks things up."

"They do, do they?" asked Marcus.

"Oh, yes. It used to be dragons, but we vanquished all of them. At least I think we did.

"But, you know what I'm saying — it's always something! If it isn't dragons flying over your house, defecating on the roof, pissing in the well, carrying off your kinfolk and livestock, it's some other Hellish thing lurking in the night to do the same. Course, that's where we come in, the Knights of the Holy Order, sworn to rid the world of such abominations. It's a dirty job with little rewards, but someone has to do it."

Colin spit a bit of gristle into the fireplace. Marcus nodded sagely. Both raised their eye brows in self-congratulation, then went back to listening to the girl who tried to hold back her tears as she spoke ion a tense, quivering voice.

"The creature ripped my young brother Kevin's head clean off his shoulders when he went into the woods to hunt the beast. I pleaded with Kevin not to go, to gather a hunting party of strong men first, but he insisted on avenging our parents himself and now … "

The girl's voice trailed off as tears drizzled down her cheeks. Curious, Sir Colin asked;

"What manner of monster is this anyway? A demon or troll or some creature conjured by witches. I heard there are covens of those evil bitches about these parts."

"He's called Hundung," the girl replied. "Legends say he was once a handsome rogue knight who was transformed into a monster by a powerful witch who was his lover. He cheated on her and she punished him by twisting his flesh and soul into a hideous beast."

"Hell truly hath no fury like a magical woman scorned," commented Marcus. "Remember what Medea did to Jason?"

Colin nodded, acknowledging the reference and his education. The Innkeeper seemed quite concerned about the girl's situation, though a bit skeptical and sent one of his servants to bring Bishop Ignatus Pius, Mayor Glendower, and Sheriff MacDillon to the Inn. When the trio arrived, the girl showed them evidence of the truth of her tale. She reached into her pocket, she withdrew a folded handkerchief and slowly opened it as the men closed in to get a good look. The orange pallor of the fire flickered on their sweaty faces as they waited in great anticipation to see what was concealed in the small, tattered piece of stained linen.

"Here I have a hank of the monster's stinky hair and a claw. He lost them when he decapitated my brother."

She placed the items on the table. The men sniffed the hair, passed it around, and examined the claw. Marcus instructed his kitchen staff to feed the girl, whose name she told them was Maldonna.

While she ate porridge and beef scraps, the elders conferred near the great fireplace. They were sympathetic to her plight, but also frightened and somewhat resentful that she had led a Hell-thing from her hometown to their doorsteps. As Maldonna filled her belly, she stared into the huge fireplace, watching the orange-red fire dance wildly on the logs.

"We should send the knight to find out if this beast is truly real; and in the vicinity," Marcus suggested to the elders.

"Yes, and keep it very quiet," the Sheriff added. "The last thing we need is a panic in the town."

A deal was made. Sir Colin prepared to sally forth into the woods.

"I must go with you," Maldonna insisted. "The beast seeks only me. Legends say he tracks his victims with his nose. Go where you will, but if you go with me, then will you find Hundung. I am your bait."

"The forest past sundown with the threat of a blood-thirsty monster is no place for an tender young girl such as yourself," Bishop Pius admonished. "You would be better to stay this night at the priory with Mother Mary and the Good Sisters of St.Lennon ."

"Hundung will elude your knight." Maldonna said. "He hungers only for my flesh and blood and will only come out of the endless darkness for that wood for his intended prey," Maldonna wrapped her shawl about her bare shoulders. "I tell you that sooner or later he will get ravenously hungry and then, his hunger will bring him to me. No matter how dark your eternal forest is, I am only safe by Sir Colin's side."

The knight looked at the elders and shrugged.

"She may be right," he admitted. "But we will take one other with us, and several oil lamps to drive away any evil spirits who might stay us from our holy mission."

And so Ian, Marcus' boy servant from the Inn, was instructed to accompany the pair, and to carry a brace of both oil lamps for light and skins of wine for strength. Bishop Pius blessed the trio with holy water and prayers. An hour later, the three sallied forth into the great wood.

They soon found their evidence, more clumps of the beast's brownish hair caught on bushes, a pile of foul-smelling excrement unlike any Colin had ever found on hunting trips, and a series of huge footprints twice the size of a mortal man.

"Ian, go back to the town and fetch a stonemason," Colin instructed. "Bring him back with water and mortar to make a cast of this hideous footprint. The Bishop will want it for his occult studies library."

The boy was more than happy to leave the darkened woodland and made record time getting back to Landsdowne. When he returned with the stonemason and the job was done, there was no whistling on the trail while the expedition trekked back to town with their evidence.

Upon seeing the casting of the monster's huge footprint, placed before them along with a cup of its excrement and the additional clumps of hair, the Mayor, Bishop and Sheriff were both astounded and distressed. The casting was a full 20 inches long, and 10 inches wide — more monster than anyone had been prepared to imagine.

And, now that Hundung appeared to be a reality, it did not take long for the servants at the Inn to spread the word. Panic rippled throughout Landsdowne. In the middle of the night, all sweet dreams ceased and soon there was a mob of frightened townsfolk, from the nobility to the hog farmers at the front door of the Inn demanding immediate action be taken. Groups of armed men, women and older children rounded up livestock to guard it while huge bonfires were started around the perimeter of the town to ward off the impending attack of the beast Hundung. Bishop Pius left the Inn briefly, blessed the mob and returned with fifty gold crowns from the church coffers as a payment to Sir Colin to smite "The Creature of Satan."

The Sheriff and Mayor donated an additional fifty crowns from the town treasury to ensure that the beast was destroyed before it killed all the livestock and townsfolk. The blacksmith awoke to the loud clamor at his door to find Sheriff MacDillon commanding him to fire his forge and sharpen Colin's claymore, broadsword and daggers until they were razor sharp. The task completed, Marcus provided Sir Colin with skins of ale, chunks of bread and some cold sliced meat. Bishop Pius again blessed the knight and pleaded with Maldonna to stay with the nuns, to no avail: the girl had a will of iron.

Sir Colin found her strength of character refreshing. He also discovered that his interest in her was growing beyond either simple lust for the first tenderly-shaped English lass he had encountered since his return home, or his feelings of protective sympathy for any maiden in her situation. The view through the loosened top of her peasant blouse, revealing the roundness of her firm, young breasts churned his brain somewhat, for he had seen nothing but dark-eyed heathens in burnooses, and French camp followers for nearly half a decade. But the fact that this girl could see things so clearly, and conquer her fear, sat with him as a bit of solid English stuff, and he slapped his thigh and said that he would hear no more debate.

The pair set off on Rosebud, the knight's massive charger, he in his saddle, she seated behind, her arms wrapped tightly around his middle. They rode back to where the last traces of the beast had been found and set up camp. Sir Colin realized that Maldonna was a beauty in full bloom. While building their fire, he began to think that perhaps his triumph over Hundung would insure a closer, possibly intimate relationship with her. His ardor was inflamed by her scent, and as they sat by the crackling fire he explained his battle plan to her.

"You shall remain here, near the fire, in clear sight. This will lure Hundung to us. When he approaches, you will then fall back to safety as I spring from my place of concealment in the bushes. As he chases you, I should easily catch the beast by surprise and smite him swiftly."

Maldonna agreed and gave the knight a kiss of encouragement on his forehead. Her breast brushed against his hand and that evoked a hot flash in his groin and a surge of adrenaline in his blood. Colin was committed — Maldonna's family would be avenged that night; Landsdowne was to be protected; and Good would once more triumph over Evil.

As Sir Colin made to conceal himself, Maldonna snatched one of his daggers from its scabbard and pricked her finger, smeared the blood over herself, to heighten her scent. The knight grinned.

"With such teamwork," he thought, "how can we lose?"

In the distance, there came a great, bellowing roar, then a low growl that doubled in intensity with each passing second. The beast had caught the smell of Maldonna's blood and was moving toward them. Maldonna sat squat in the small clearing while Sir Colin waited, sword drawn, muscles tensed, ready to pounce. Sweat poured off both their brows as they waited. The horrible growling stopped for a moment, and then there was another, louder roar, followed by a terrible reverberating howl throughout the forest. The knight knew it was Hundung's challenge.

Suddenly, the monster appeared in the moonlit clearing, fully ten feet tall and crowned with small, curved horns. His twisted, massive body was covered with grey-green tinged brown hair, matted with blood and other dried bodily fluids — some his own, and some belonging to his victims. He bared his fangs and broken, blackened teeth and waved his huge bloody paws adorned with long, sharp claws. His breath was toxic like rotted flesh. His yellow eyes glared large and luminous like the eyes of the very Devil himself, and there was a stench about his body like excrement, urine and vomit. In short, he was extremely unpleasant.

Rosebud gave a whinny, emptied his bladder and large intestine in a single muscle spasm and was gone into the night leaving behind only a

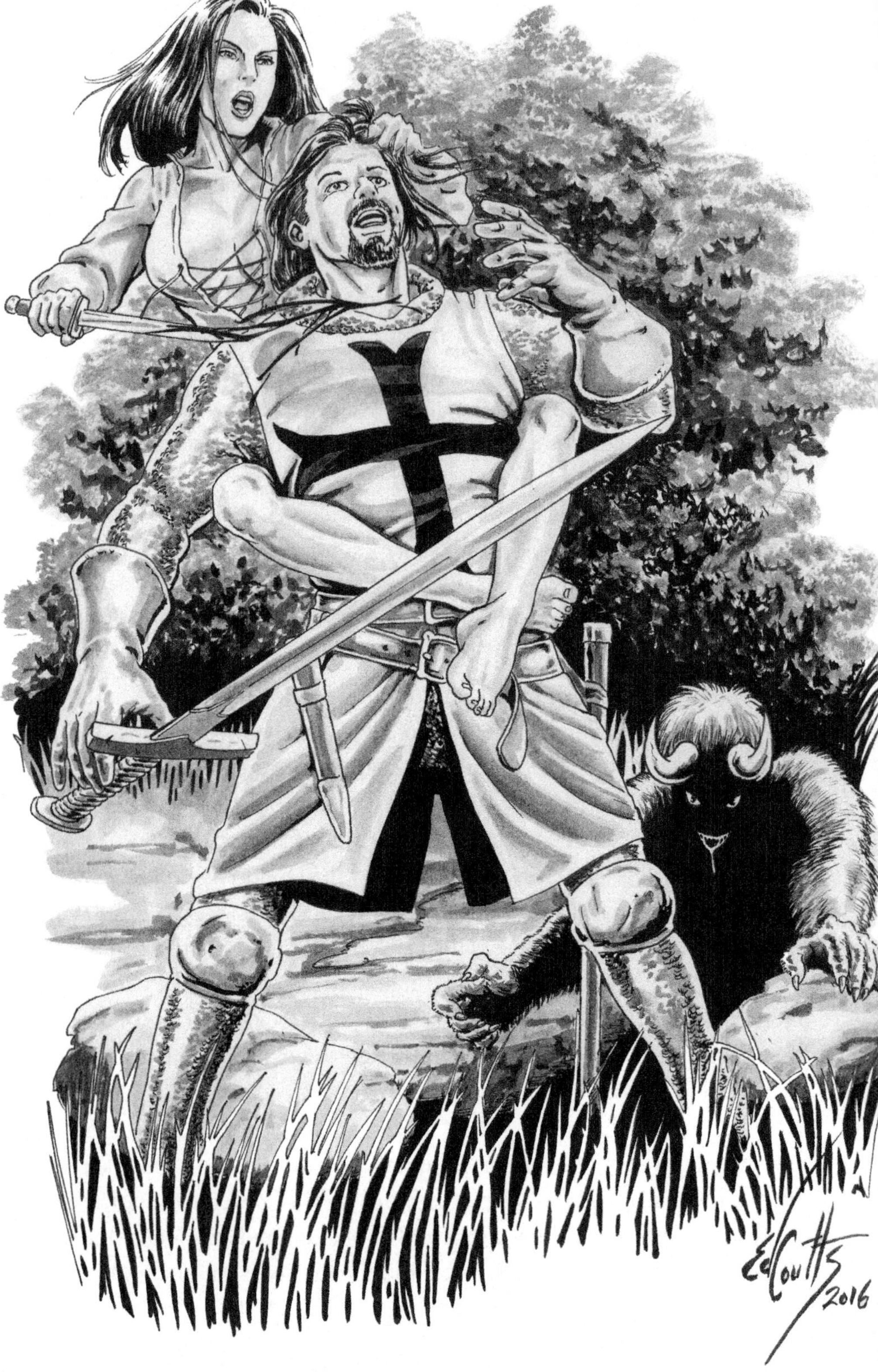
Ed Coutts
2016

Love is in the Air

large puddle and an even larger pile.

Hundung moved toward the defenseless girl. As he circled slowly around her, Maldonna scuttled away from him, eyes searching the thicket for her hero. The beast lowered himself to his haunches and sniffed as he approached the shivering girl. Sir Colin steeled himself — never before had he witnessed such a monstrosity — and leapt from the concealing bushes screaming a battle cry.

"Prepare to die, creature of Satan!" Sir Colin announced. "This is the holy sword of St. Eastwood, forged by the saint's own armorer in ancient times. It's the most powerful weapon in Christendom honed to razor sharpness and it can slice your head clean off! I command you to cease and desist. Return to whence you came or accept your fate at my hands. Pause and consider — dost thou feel lucky tonight?"

At that moment, clouds swallowed the moon whole, plunging the all three participants into seemingly limitless pitch blackness. There were cries, howls and the swishing sounds of Colin's claymore slicing the thick, inky black air. As suddenly as it disappeared, the moon was revealed again, regurgitated by the Heavens. Maldonna looked up to see a tableau of terror. Both her handsome knight and the devilish Hundung were disclosed lying on the ground in the clearing not ten feet apart. Bloody saliva dripped from the beast's maw.

Sir Colin staggered to his feet, trying to clear his dizziness. He grabbed up his claymore from the damp ground and prepared to behead the fiendish thing prone before him. Before he could lift up his claymore, something pounced on him from behind; arms circled his throat and chocked him, legs crushed his waist. Something stung his throat and warm liquid coursed down his chest. He tried to speak, but no words passed his lips. He could not breathe. His mind brimming with a thousand questions, he dropped his sword and both hands flew to his throat.

In his ear, a familiar voice called to Hundung:

"What are you waiting for … Christmas? Tear his head off!"

***

Days later, in a very comfortable cottage far to the north, Maldonna stood over a roaring hickory fire barbecuing her favorite dinner — BBQ knight's ribs. Nearby, a large cauldron of freshly-picked vegetables, hands, feet and stewed entrails bubbled in the fireplace. Above the fireplace was a display of heads, mounted and stuffed, of Europe's latest and greatest heroes. Sir Colin of Lockwood's head hung in the monthly place of honor, his new hand-blown blue glass eyes reflecting the fire's light, his features still twisted in an expression of bewilderment.

Hundung sat at a small table, whistling merry melodies as he sorted his booty — weapons he would trade locally for dry goods, jewels to be sold to the money lender, Moishe of York, later in the month. Then there were Colin's handcrafted leather knee boots that any cobbler would buy for a handsome sum. The knight's payment, one hundred golden crowns, was pitched, one coin at a time, into a large, hand-carved oak chest already brimming with gold coins from many lands.

Maldonna's eyes flashed red with the flames of her own massive stone fireplace as she sank her own razor sharp teeth into a large, meaty rib dripping with spicy tomato sauce of her own secret recipe of herbs and spices. She ripped flesh from the bone, swallowing it with scant chewing. The thick red sauce oozed from the meat and ran from her lips to her chin, trickled down her nubile bare breasts and formed droplets on her nipples that fell and disappeared into her loosened robe.

Maldonna motioned to Hundung and pointed to the rack of ribs, smiled and nodded. Hundung declined the char-grilled meat and pulled a few boiled turnips from the pot.

"That's just not good for you," Hundung admonished his paramour. "My great aunt Martha always said that it's forbidden flesh and full of grease and saturated fat. It makes me sick just to watch you stuff yourself with it. And the entrails in the stew, they must be full of foulness and disease. This is *not* good eating in the neighborhood."

Maldonna rolled her eyes at the poor beast, stuck out her tattooed tongue at him. She smiled and took another bite from the flesh dangling from the rib in her dainty, sauce-smeared hands.

My great aunt Fanny said that people who eat people are the hungriest people in the world," she replied with a chuckle.

"How much longer does this crap go on, my love?" asked the Beast.

Maldonna licked sauce from her chin and breats, then wiped her hands with Colin's blood-soaked, shredded shirt as she spoke.

"I'll go over this one more time. You will be restored to human form when we have five thousand golden crowns. We have only three hundred crowns to go. You also have to dispatch a few more of these horney, heroic, handsome knights. Your tally is now forty eight. You promised fifty — so go and do the mathematics. Finally, your last victim has to be that bitch Lady Lydia of Celton, with whom you cheated on me. You will eat her grilled flesh with or without the potyatoes, side salad, biscuits, dessert and refreshing beverage. Then — *and only then* — will I give your sorry, hairy arse a second chance to be human."

Hundung grumped, burped and accepted his fate with a loud turnip fart that made the flame in the oil lamp flare. Maldonna laughed a hearty laugh at the sight and turned down the lamp's flame for safety's sake, then dropped her loose robe. By the light of the fireplace, she led Hundung to a featherbed in the corner of the room covered with a thick, satin quilt spotted with many stains from wet spots past. She stared at him with 'that look' all fair damsels, and cannibal witches, excel at.

"Come here, Puppy," she cooed, patting the area on the feather bed beside her. "Who's my little snookie-wookie?"

Even in his cursed form, the lust in him was that which dwells in every man, and it came forth in full, unbridled passion. He looked down on the young, naked, forever-teenaged witch writhing on the bed in the throes of extreme heat and thought to himself;

"Well, if she doesn't care that I'm a ten foot tall, hairy, stinking monster with toxic B.O., killer flatulence and halitosis, what the Hell am I complaining for?"

Hundung picked up a cinnamon stick from the kitchen table and ran it over his bulbous lips and all eight-inches of his muscular tongue. He tied a thin, leather thong around the base of his bulging, twelve-inch erection and proceeded to the bed, to the side of his one and only true love, Maldonna, the teen-age witch. She giggled at the sight of him, and grabbed his rough fur as he bent in toward her, pulling him forward on top of her with squealing abandon.

And, in the thick of the damp, moonless night, in the mysterious cottage at the edge of the Cursed Forest of Stoneheim, love, sweet Love, was in the air once more.

About the Authors

CJ Henderson (1951-2014) created the Teddy London supernatural detective series and the Piers Knight occult investigator series. He authored 70 books and/or novels, including *The Encyclopedia of Science Fiction Movies*, *Black Sabbath: the Ozzy Osbourne Years*, and *Baby's First Mythos*. He wrote hundreds of short stories and comics, and thousands of non-fiction pieces. He also excelled in the mystery genre. His Jack Hagee, P.I. series is available from Bold Venture Press.

J. Brad Staal hails from Mt Pleasant, MI. After spending four years in the U. S. Air Force at Fairchild AFB near Spokane, WA. He attended Grand Valley State University, MI with a major in Advertising and Public Relations. Brad is a lifelong student and fan of cinema history and filmmaking. He works in the gRand Rapids area and is a contributing film critic for the online magazine *The Black Cat Review* and is a local Grand Rapids, MI cable TV personality on the horror hosting series *Dr. Mortose Commands*. His stories appear in other *Hellfire Lounge* volumes.

Jean Marie Ward writes fiction, nonfiction and everything in between. Her credits include a multi-award nominated novel, numerous short stories and two popular art books, and an eight-year stint as editor of CrescentBlues.com. Her video interviews and short subjects are regular features of BuzzyMag.com. Learn more at JeanMarieWard.com.

Film reviewer/screenwriter **R. Allen Leider** began his career in 1970 at CBS news as copy boy for *The CBS Evening News with Walter Cronkite*. In 1973, he became features writer for *The Monster Times* and went on to work at *Show*, *Celebrity* and *Glitter Magazines* and other international publications. His photojournalistic work has been syndicated worldwide. He lives in Manhattan with wife Barbara, a professional photographer. In 1984, created the original story and screenplay for *The Oracle* (1985), and hosted his own radio show *Cinemascene* on WWFM, for five years. Presently, he writes and edits the online *Black Cat Review* magazine. His newest projects are the *Wicca Girl Trilogy*, a magical fantasy action-adventure following 18 year old Maldonna Marie d'Lambert from her Medieval childhood thru her transformation to Witch Queen to her modern day assignments as a supernatural MI-6 agent ... and the *Hellfire Lounge* anthology series.

An amazing life so far, **KT Pinto** has been a teacher, an adult girl scout, a bartender, a funeral coordinator, a cocktail hour manager, a jelly-doughnut-filler, a children's party planner, mechanic and an adult boutique manager, but throughout all the changes, she has always been a writer. Find out more about her and her work at www.ktpinto.com Although KT Pinto has been writing since high school, the mythos of Celeste didn't occur until she created the vampyress as a one-shot for a LARP she had a hand in running. The rest, as they say, is history. KT's first short story was published in *Nth Degree Magazine* in 2004. Her stories have appeared in anthologies such as *Hear Them Roar* (2006) and *New Blood* (2010). She wrote three volumes in her *Books of Insanity* series, and her super-hero series *Sto's House Presents* is available from cPf Publishing. Recently, her hardboiled private eye Raphael Jones slugged his way through "The Emerald Eye," a genre-bending story in *Awesome Tales* #3 from Bold Venture Press. She is a regular contributor to the *Hellfire Lounge* anthology series.

April Grey and her family live in Hell's Kitchen, NYC in a building next to a bedeviled garden. Gremlins, sprites or pixies, something mischievous, lurks therein. Someday she'll find out. April has a background in theatre (BA, MFA, and Ph.D. ABD). She spent over twenty years as an actor, director, literary manager and producer. She also made her first short story sale over twenty-five years ago. When not writing, she teaches art and ESL, and does freelance editing. April Grey's short stories are collected in The Fairy Cake Bakeshop and in *I'll Love You Forever*. She edited *Hell's Garden: Mad, Bad and Ghostly Gardeners*. Caliburn Press will be publishing her dark fantasy novel, *Finding Perdita*, in 2016. Get the first two books of her Cernunnos Series at author.to/aprilgrey

Patrick Loveland is a screenwriter and author. He studied Experimental Filmmaking in San Francisco and worked as a projectionist and student small format film equipment instructor before moving back to his hometown in the early 2000s. Patrick lives San Diego, CA with his wife and talented young daughter. His first novel for April Moon Books *A Tear in the Veil* will be released later this year.

Award-winning author and editor **Danielle Ackley-McPhail** has worked both sides of the publishing industry for longer than she cares to admit. Currently, she is a project editor and promotions manager for Dark Quest Books. In 2014 she joined forces with husband Mike McPhail and friend Greg Schauer to form her own publishing imprint. Her published works include five urban fantasy novels, *Yesterday's Dreams, Tomorrow's Memories, Today's Promise, The Halfling's Court*: and *The Redcaps' Queen: A Bad-Ass Faerie Tale*, and a young adult Steampunk novel, *Baba Ali and the Clockwork Djinn*, written with Day Al-Mohamed. She is also the author of the solo collections *A Legacy of Stars, Consigned to the Sea, Flash in the Can*, and *Transcendence*, the non-fiction writers' guide, *The Literary Handyman*, and is the senior editor of the Bad-Ass Faeries anthology series, *Gaslight & Grimm, Dragon's Lure*, and *In an Iron Cage*. Her short stories are included in numerous other anthologies and collections. Danielle and Mike live in New Jersey with two extremely spoiled cats. She can be found on Facebook (Danielle Ackley-McPhail) and Twitter (DMcPhail, BadAssFaeries, eSpecBooks, and TheHornieLady). . .

John L. French has worked for over thirty years as a crime scene investigator and has seen more than his share of murders, shootings and serious assaults. As a break from the realities of his job, he writes science fiction, pulp, horror, fantasy, and, of course, crime fiction. In 1992 John began writing stories based on his training and experiences on the streets of Baltimore. His first story "Past Sins" was published in *Hardboiled Magazine* and was cited as one of the best Hardboiled stories of 1993. More crime fiction followed, appearing in *Alfred Hitchcock's Mystery Magazine*, the Fading Shadows magazines and in collections by Barnes and Noble. Association with writers like James Chambers and the late, great C.J. Henderson led him to try horror fiction and to a still growing fascination with zombies and other undead things. His first horror story "The Right Solution" appeared in Marietta Publishing's *Lin Carter's Anton Zarnak*. Other horror stories followed in anthologies such as *The Dead Walk* and *Dark Furies*, both published by Die Monster Die books. It was in *Dark Furies* that his character Bianca Jones made her literary debut in "21 Doors," a story based on an old Baltimore legend and a creepy game his daughter used to play with her friends. John's first book was *The Devil of Harbor City*, a novel done in the old pulp style. *Past Sins* and *Here There Be Monsters* followed. John was also consulting editor for Chelsea House's *Criminal Investigation* series. His other books include The Assassins' Ball (written with Patrick Thomas), *Paradise Denied, Blood Is the Life* and *The Nightmare Strikes*. John is the editor of *To Hell In a Fast Car, Mermaids* 13, C. J. Henderson's *Challenge of the Unknown*, and (with Greg Schauer) *With Great Power ...*

Patrick Thomas has had stories published in over three dozen magazines and more than fifty anthologies. He's written 30+ books including the fantasy humor series Murphy's Lore, urban fantasy spin offs *Fairy With A Gun, Fairy Rides The Lightning, Dead To Rites, Rites of Passage, Lore & Dysorder* and two more — *Statenders* and *Constellation Prize* — in the Startenders series. He co-writes the *Mystic Investigators* paranormal mystery series and *The Assassins' Ball*, a traditional mystery, co-authored with John L. French. His darkly humorous advice column *Dear Cthulhu* includes the collections *Have A Dark Day: Good Advice For Bad People*, and *Cthulhu Knows Best*. A number of his books are part of the props department of the *CSI* television show and one was even thrown at a suspect. *Fairy With A Gun* was optioned by Laurence Fishburne's Cinema Gypsy Productions. Drop by www.patthomas.net to learn more.

Since 1994, **Robert E. Waters** has worked in the computer and board gaming industry as technical writer, editor, designer, and producer. A member of the Science Fiction and Fantasy Writers of America, his first professional fiction sale came in 2003 with the story "The Assassin's Retirement Party," *Weird Tales*, Issue #332. Since then he has sold stories to Bold Venture Press, Nth Degree, Nth Zine, Black Library Publishing (Games Workshop), Dark Quest Books, Padwolf Publishing, Mundania Press, Pol-to-Pole Publishing, e-Spec Books, Marietta Publishing, Rogue Blades Entertainment, and Dragon Moon Press. Robert is also a frequent contributor to the Grantville Gazette, Baen Books' online magazine dedicated to stories set in their best-selling 1632/Ring of Fire Alternate History series. Between the years of 1998 — 2006, he also served as an assistant editor to *Weird Tales*. Robert's first novel, *The Wayward Eight: A Contract to Dir For*, was published in 2014 and is set in the tabletop gaming universe, *Wild West Exodus*. Robert currently lives in Baltimore, Maryland, with his wife Beth, their son Jason, and their cat Buzz.

About the Illustrators

Rich Harvey, Designer
Rich Harvey is a New Jersey-based writer and designer. His publishing company, Bold Venture Press, specializes in new and classic pulp fiction. Bold Venture is currently publishing *Zorro: The Complete Pulp Adventures*, collecting the original by Johnston McCulley for the first time. www.boldventurepress.com

Ben Fogletto, Cover Illustrator
Ben Fogletto has been active as a penciller, inker and cover artist in the comic and graphic novel industry since the 1990's. He is employed as a staff photographer for a daily newspaper in New Jersey. He lives with his wife, Cynthia, and two sons, Connor and Chase in Egg Harbor Township, New Jersey. (Cover art is pen and ink and watercolor)

Ed Coutts, Interior Illustrator
New York City based artist and illustrator Ed Coutts is a seasoned professional comic book illustrator, commercial artist and is available for commissions. He is known for his work in print and online at www.edcouttsart.com and the good girl art comics: www.Vavavavoomonline.com.

The swankiest nightclub this side of Purgatory!

Join us for the strangest happy hour with plenty of magical misfits and mystics! With authors such as C.J. Henderson, Paul Kupperburg, Daniell McPhail-Ackerly, and many more, *The Hellfire Lounge* series is loaded with artwork and stories that surprise and delight ... *and terrify!*

Belly up to the bar @ www.boldventurepress.com!

ZORRO IS ACTION!
ZORRO IS ROMANCE!

BOLD VENTURE — *The Complete* PULP ADVENTURES *by Johnston McCulley, Vol. 1*

ZORRO

The original swashbuckling hero in his original adventures by Johnston McCulley! Volume One is available now!

BOLD VENTURE
boldventuepress.com

Zorro ® & © 2016 Zorro Productions, Inc. All rights reserved.

Can two book hoarders make room in their collections for each other?

His passion was collecting old books, until she came along…

Pulp Noir
A cluttered romance

Audrey Parente

BOLD VENTURE
boldventurepress.com

Available in print and eBook editions.

WICCA GIRL
™

Meet the *ultimate* MILF — Druscilla Marie d'Lambert, a 900-year old witch whose century-spanning adventures lead her to become Her Majesty's most valuable MI-6 agent — codename Wicca Girl!

www.wiccagirlmovie.com

R. Allen Leider's
WICCA GIRL ™
Fighting Fire with Hellfire
Since 1091 A.D.

BOLD VENTURE

PULP FICTION

Over-Caffeinated! High-Octane!

AWESOME TALES™

BOLD VENTURE
boldventurepress.com

Classic characters, new thrillers!
Domino Lady, Fantomas, Dr. Mabuse, more!
Heart-stopping Super-Genre tales!